Whiskey Jack Family

By
Randall Probert

Whiskey Jack Family
by Randall Probert

www.randallprobertbooks.net
email: randentr@megalink.net

Art and Photography credits:

Front cover and chapter heading art
~ Robin Fraser, Newry, ME
Author's photo, page 276, by Patricia Gott

Disclaimer:
This book is a work of fiction, with some historical facts with a slight twist.

ISBN: 978-1721067398

Printed in the United States of America

Published by
Randall Enterprises
P.O. Box 862
Bethel, Maine 04217

Acknowledgements

I would like to thank Laura Ashton of Woodland, Georgia, for your help formatting this book for printing and Robin Fraser of Newry, Maine, for the art work on the cover. I would also like to thank Amy Henley of Newry, Maine for your help typing and for the many revisions and your suggestions.

More Books by Randall Probert

Whiskey Jack Family

Character List for the Reader's Perusal

Rascal and Emma Ambrose ~ Main characters

Rudy and Earl Hitchcock ~ Brothers, owners of Hitchcock Lumbering Company

Silvio and Anita Antony ~ Residents at the old village - when Silvio dies, Anita lives with Rascal and Emma at the lodge

Jarvis Page and his wife, Rita ~ Old game warden

Sam Grindle ~ Railroad Supervisor

Greg Oliver ~ Station master for the railroad

Kevin Cutlidge and his wife, Pearl ~ President of the U.S.A. in the 1920s

William Kingsley and his wife, Myrissa ~ Canada's Prime Minister

Raymond Butler ~ Head of President Cutlidge's Secret Service and bodyguard

Francois Dubois ~ Prime Minister Kingsley's bodyguard

Jeters Asbau ~ Friend of Rascal's

Herschel Page ~ Becomes a game warden when Warden Cyr leaves. Marries Perline Bowman

Fred Darling ~ Train engineer

Lt. Belle ~ An Army nurse in France during WWI who helped Rascal recover from surgery. Later marries Richard Cummings

Chapter 1

"If I could use your telephone, Emma, I would place a call to Annapolis now for an appointment in September," President Kingsley said.

"Sure you can," Emma replied.

"Would you by chance have a second telephone, Emma?" President Cutlidge asked.

"Yes, upstairs in the office. We had it installed two years ago."

While Kingsley was busy placing the call, Cutlidge went upstairs and was listening in with the office phone.

There were several minutes before Annapolis answered. "This is the switchboard at the Annapolis Naval Academy; how may I direct your call?" the switchboard operator asked.

"I would like to speak with Captain Bedford Ames in the admission's office."

"Who may I say is calling?"

"Presidents Kingsley and Cutlidge, Ma'am."

"Yes, Captain Ames in admissions."

"Hello, Captain, this is President Kingsley and President Cutlidge is on another telephone."

"Good day, Mr. Presidents. How may I assist you?"

"We have a young man that we would like to appoint to the Naval Academy," Kingsley said.

"I have only one slot still open."

"Good. President Cutlidge and myself would like it if you would reserve that slot for Archer Bellamy Ambrose."

"I must inform you that there are two other candidates

under consideration who applied earlier for admission."

"Captain Ames, this is President Cutlidge. Both myself and President Kingsley know this young man personally and this spring he graduated at the top of his class from the Beech Tree Academy. President Kingsley and myself would appreciate it if you would fast track Mr. Ambrose's acceptance as of today. You can send him the necessary forms to be filled out. Two former presidents are strongly recommending this appointment, Captain."

"You'll just have to take our word on his qualifications, Captain," Kingsley added. "You won't be disappointed."

"I must say this is a little unusual. But an appointment from two distinguished presidents must have merit. Consider it done.

"Now you said his name is Archer Bellamy Ambrose. What is his mailing address?" Capt. Ames asked.

"Whiskey Jack Lake, Captain."

"Oh yes, that is where you two first met to discuss Canada and the United States merger."

"Yes, Captain, we are here now and will be leaving tomorrow."

"I'll see that these forms are sent out this afternoon, Mr. Presidents."

"Thank you, Captain; you won't be disappointed."

"Yes, thank you, Captain," President Cutlidge added.

The telephone conversation took a half hour and they rejoined the others on the platform. "Archer, you have your appointment. In a few days you'll be receiving a bundle of forms to fill out," Kingsley said.

"And you must do so and return them posthaste," Cutlidge said.

"You mean just like that, I'm accepted into the Naval Academy?" Archer asked.

"With a strong recommendation from two presidents, you were, let's say, fast tracked."

"Thank you, thank both of you. I only ever dreamed

about attending the Academy. I never thought I would actually go."

"Captain Ames guaranteed it, Archer."

Emma hugged and kissed them both.

"We certainly never expected anything like this," Emma said.

Rascal had a difficult time to say anything except, "Yes, thank you both."

All afternoon Archer sat with Kingsley and Cutlidge talking about what he could expect at the Academy. "The first year will be your roughest. You'll train and study every day and it is purposely designed to sift out those who are weak and not used to working," President Cutlidge said.

"You'll be expected to participate in sports after your first year. You get to choose which sports," President Kingsley said.

"You know until I left here for the Academy in Beech Tree I had never played any sports. It was all new to me. But once I learned how, the games were fun. I particularly enjoyed baseball and running cross-country. I wasn't much at the fast sprints, but with the long distance runs, I broke the Academy's record and at the end of the runs I was hardly even breathing hard."

"At the Naval Academy you'll be up against more experienced opponents and teammates," President Cutlidge said.

Anita was sitting back taking all of this day in. She had been with Emma and Rascal for twenty years now and everyone here were like family to her. True enough, she missed Silvio, but her life here with Emma and Rascal were the happiest years of her life.

Rascal noticed tears in her eyes and he went over and sat beside her. "Are you alright, Anita?"

"Yes, of course I am. I'm just overwhelmed with happiness. I was thinking how happy my life has been with you and Emma, that's all. And watching Archer grow into a young man and now he'll soon be going to the Annapolis Naval Academy. And just think, Rascal, two of my best friends are two former presidents." She had to wipe the tears away now.

Rascal hugged her and kissed her cheek.

To change the subject, Anita said, "I think it's time us ladies started preparing supper."

That left the men on the platform; with a new pot of coffee.

President Cutlidge said, "When we were first here twenty years ago I thought the railroad was the C&A, but I hear you call it the S&A."

"The year after you two were here, the C&A extended another line from Lac St. Jean to the St. Laurent and changed the name to S&A, the St. Laurent and Atlantic Railroad."

"I'm glad that's cleared up. I thought I was losing my mind."

While they waited for supper, Herschel regaled them with stories about chasing poachers.

When he had finished, President Kingsley asked, "How bad did Bear work over Hans Hessel?"

"It could have been worse," Rascal said, "Bear hit him in the ribs and broke two and sent him into some bushes and had his face scratched by the bushes, and then Bear bit down on his foot and pulled him out of the bushes. Hessel was doing a lot of screaming. When I got there he was lying on his back and Bear was standing on his hind legs and straddling Hessel. When I spoke to Bear he backed off and that's when Herschel arrived. Bear left."

"That's remarkable——I mean Bear," President Cutlidge said.

"Yes, we all think Bear is quite remarkable," Rascal said.

Herschel said, "That experience with Bear had really frightened Hessel and he couldn't understand when Rascal spoke to Bear that he had stopped mauling him and left."

"Not knowing Bear as we all do, I think anyone of us would have been just as terrified," President Kingsley said.

"You know, with all the time I had spent with him, I was actually feeling sorry for him," Herschel said.

"As it was he was a real asset."

"Where is he now?" Herschel asked.

"I don't know. He was given immunity, a new identification and that's all I know about him," President Kingsley replied.

They were all quiet then, enjoying the comfort of shade on the platform and listening to calls of nature. President Cutlidge finally broke the silence. "You know, this is really a unique place. I only wish I could have seen it before the village left."

"It certainly is a unique place, Mr. President. Don't ever repeat this to my wife, but Whiskey Jack will always be my home away from home. Rita has learned to enjoy being here, but she would never agree to live here," Jarvis said.

Five years ago personal 35mm cameras had become very popular and Emma decided one day that she wanted one. "A 35 Kodak camera, Rascal," she had said. And since then she had become a camera bug. Taking pictures of everything that had to do with family, the lodge, their guests and the animals that grazed behind the lodge. And of course of Bear playing with Rascal and Whiskey Jack.

She excused herself from the kitchen and started taking photos of the women in the kitchen and the men still sitting in the shade on the platform.

After they had been seated around the table she took more pictures. "Before leaving, if everyone would leave me your addresses, I'll send you copies of these photos."

It was another smorgasbord, with plenty of frog legs and beaver meat. Later that evening as they all sat out on the platform watching the beautiful sunset, Emma and Paulette brought out platters of smoked trout, sharp cheese, brandy and wine.

There were pies, but everyone preferred the smoked

trout and cheese.

Raymond Butler said, "You Mr. President, when I first arrived here to set up for your arrival in November, I had no idea why you were wanting to come to this empty wilderness. But now looking back on everything I don't think you could have chosen a more secure place. When we left after that visit, I was glad to be leaving. But now there's an emptiness inside me, sadness that we will be leaving tomorrow. This place, and more especially you friends, have made me feel like this is home."

Francois Dubois said, "I couldn't have said it any better. I too feel the same and I want to thank you all."

The air was still warm even after the sun had set and they all continued sitting out on the platform talking and occasionally listening to the nightly sounds. Emma had brought out four kerosene lanterns so they would not have to sit in the dark.

Jarvis had a few stories to tell as did Herschel. He now had nineteen years and one week as a game warden. "How long are you planning to stay on, Herschel?" President Kingsley asked.

"I'd like to stay thirty years. And then maybe do some trapping."

It was getting late and the presidents and family would be on the morning northbound and the Page family later on the morning southbound. After everyone was in their rooms, Rascal turned the generator off and he and Jarvis continued sitting on the platform. The moon wasn't yet full but there was enough to see across the cove and the log cabin. The surface of the lake was covered with small ripples from the gentle westerly breeze. Sometimes the two only sat in silence watching the ripples on the water. If they did talk, it was more often than not about the old days of the village and the goings-on then.

They stayed out in the night air long after midnight before going to bed. As they were walking inside, Jarvis said, "You know Rascal, I'd like to come back and do it all over again."

****

Archer was so excited about his appointment to the Annapolis Naval Academy he didn't sleep much. When he had first left home for the Beech Tree Academy he found himself in a turmoil. Now that same feeling was coming back. Annapolis was a giant step from home at Whiskey Jack. He wasn't so worried about the academics as he was about fitting in. So just before daylight he rolled out of bed, dressed and went out on the platform to watch the sunrise.

Herschel and Perline's daughter, Emma Jean, was already out there. "What are you doing out here so early, Emma Jean?"

"I couldn't sleep. My dad snores something terrible. So I came out here where it is quiet.

"Why couldn't you sleep, Archer?"

"Too many thoughts going through my head."

"Worrying about Annapolis, huh?"

Emma Jean turned twelve in May and although she was still young there wasn't much that she missed.

"You want to go for a walk, Emma Jean?"

"Where to?"

"Out to the farm and back."

"Okay, do you think we'll see Bear?"

"Maybe, but with so much going on out there now I doubt it."

They left and Whiskey Jack was out in front of them. He was getting old and he soon dropped back behind them. "Maybe we'd better turn around, Emma Jean."

"Why?"

"Whiskey Jack is old and he is already tired. I don't think he'd make the trip out and back."

"How old is he, Archer?"

"He just turned sixteen and that's old for a black lab dog."

When they were back they sat out on the platform waiting

for everyone else to wake up. Whiskey Jack curled up next to the lodge wall and went to sleep.

"How long will you be gone, Archer?"

"Four years."

"Will you have any time off to come home?"

"I really don't know. But I would rather doubt if there would be a summer break.

"People are beginning to stir inside. I think I should start the generator," and he stood up to leave.

Emma Jean followed along behind him.

"You know something, Archer?"

"What?"

"I miss my dad an awful lot when he goes off for days at a time chasing poachers. I know he likes being a game warden, but when he comes home it's like he never left. He said when I get bigger he would take me with him. I think it would be a lot of fun spending a few days in the woods and watching someone."

The generator started and lights came on inside the lodge. Rascal met them as they were walking back. "I didn't hear you get up, son."

"No, we have been out here for a while now. Couldn't sleep," Archer said.

"Me neither. My daddy snores too much. We went for a walk too. Out towards the farm, but we had to come back because Whiskey Jack was tired." Emma Jean kept talking all the way back to the lodge.

There were already too many women helping in the kitchen, so she sat with the men in the living room.

"Archer, would you go to the hen house. We need a few more eggs."

"Sure." Whiskey Jack would usually go along, but today he stayed on the platform.

"I'll go with you, Archer."

****

When they had finished eating, President Cutlidge said, "Rascal, I don't know why you don't weight five hundred pounds. I mean, every meal is so delicious and so much."

When everyone had finished eating they slid their plates back and remained at the table talking and sipping coffee. They all knew the train would be coming soon and no one wanted to see the family break up.

Emma said, "We'll be having our Thanksgiving dinner on the twenty-ninth of November. As of the twenty-fifth there will be no guests here, so you can arrive any time after the twenty-fifth."

"Would you like us to bring anything, Emma?" Myrissa asked.

"Maybe some wine or brandy. And Mr. Butler and Mr. Dubois, don't forget your families."

"And bring your hunting clothes and rifle," Rascal added.

The half mile warning blew and they pulled away from the table and went upstairs for their luggage.

They carried their luggage out onto the platform to wait for the train. Pearl hugged Emma and said, "Thank you, Emma. I now can understand why Kevin likes the area so much. It's you people who live here that makes it so grand."

"Yes," Myrissa said, "Thank all of you and we'll see you in November."

William stepped over and hugged Anita and kissed her cheek.

Fred Darling pulled to a stop at the platform and said, "You can board, folks, when I pull ahead, but I have two freight cars that I need to take into the farm and hook up to the two loaded cars going to Lac St. Jean before continuing on."

Whiskey Jack was rested now and he walked down to the hen house with them.

Fred Darling had to switch trains with another engineer southbound from Lauzon, across the St. Laurent from Quebec City. And two hours later he returned to Whiskey Jack and dropped off two empty cars at the farm.

"Every time we leave here it feels more like we're leaving home," Jarvis said.

"Are you sure you don't want me to bring anything in November, Emma?" Rita asked.

"Well, maybe two pies."

"Okay, and we'll be here two days early so I can help you."

"Goodbye, Herschel and Perline, don't be strangers."

Chapter 2

Both presidents with wives and bodyguard left Whiskey Jack Friday morning and Tuesday the Naval Academy forms arrived with the morning mail.

Archer opened the large envelope and began reading and filling out the application and questionnaire about his personal history and family. At the very end he was asked to submit an essay on why he wanted to attend the Naval Academy.

Before writing the essay he went for a long walk up the tracks to Ledge Swamp. Once there, he sat down on the knoll beside the tracks to think. He had been deep in thought for several minutes when he saw Bear coming up the tracks towards him.

"Hello, Bear." Bear stopped and lifted his head smelling the air. "It's me, Bear, Archer," and then he raised his arm like he had seen his father do and then he made the same greeting noise. Bear replied.

Archer had never been allowed to play with Bear and he decided there would never be a more opportune time. He stood up and started running along the top of the bank. Bear didn't need any more coaching. Game on.

He chased after Archer just like he would Rascal and even butt-bunted him. Archer went sprawling and then he sat up and started laughing. Bear laid down to rest also. Archer wasn't accomplishing much by playing, so he stood up and started walking back. "Goodbye, Bear," and he outstretched his arm and Bear did also.

Walking back, he found what he wanted to write and

once he was back, he sat down and wrote a one page essay without stopping. Then he sealed everything in a large envelope and addressed it.

"Mom, Dad, I have finished my application and everything. I'd like to take the train in and see that this gets mailed. I'll walk over and stay the night with Herschel and Perline. I need to wash up and change my clothes."

"You'd better hurry; the train will be here shortly. And how'd you get so dirty?" Emma asked.

"Playing with Bear," he said as he shut the bathroom door.

"You were playing with Bear, Archer?" Rascal asked.

"Yes, he followed me up the tracks."

Rascal looked at Emma and shrugged his shoulders.

"He's getting old, Dad, and so is Whiskey Jack," Archer said.

"Yeah, I hear ya."

****

Archer boarded the 2 p.m. southbound for Beech Tree, and not wanting to be late, he ran to the post office. "You got here just in time son. The afternoon mail is almost ready to go out."

From there he walked over to Herschel and Perline's house. Emma Jean was sitting in the shade on the porch. When she saw Archer she jumped off the porch and ran to greet him. "Hello, Archer, what are you doing here?"

"Are your Mom and Dad home?"

"Mom is, Dad is off somewhere game wardening. Mom is in the kitchen."

"Hello, Archer. Are you alone?" Perline asked.

"Yes, I came in to mail my papers to the Naval Academy."

"That was fast."

"I was hoping I could stay here tonight."

"Sure you can. Herschel is off somewhere and I really don't expect him home in time for supper. Maybe later."

"Sit down, Archer. Would you like some coffee?"

"Yes, that would be good."

Emma Jean jumped up and said, "I'll get it, Mom."

"I think you have an admirer, Archer."

Archer just smiled and Emma Jean blushed.

****

Herschel didn't make it home that night. "Heaven knows what he is involved in now," Perline said.

Right after eating breakfast Archer excused himself and said, "I really must leave now so I won't miss the morning northbound. Thank you, Perline."

"It was my pleasure, anytime."

"My pleasure too, Archer," Emma Jean said.

"Goodbye," and he left. As he walked toward the train station, he couldn't help but think about Emma Jean. At twelve she was pretty. "Too bad she isn't older."

The train whistle blew signaling it was about to leave. Archer began running and just as he rounded the station house the train was moving. He began running behind it. The train kept gaining speed and he had to run faster. He ran a half mile before he caught up and jumped on. "Boy, I didn't know if you were going to make it or not," the new conductor Roscoe Whelling said.

"I didn't know there for a while if I could either. I didn't know I could run like that. Never had to before.

"How's your Dad now, Roscoe?"

"He's enjoying his retirement. You know Archer, if Canada and the United States had not come together and President Kingsley had not set in motion the retirement bill, my dad would have had to work probably until he died on the job."

This gave Archer something to think about on his ride home. Whiskey Jack was waiting for him on the platform and he stood up in anticipation when the train stopped.

"Did you have breakfast, son?" Emma asked.

"Yes. You know, Dad, while I'm still here, we probably should get to work on firewood."

A father and son had arrived from Boston the day before and had left the lodge early to fish up at the head of the lake. After lunch the son, Peter, asked, "Would you two like some more help with the firewood, Mr. Ambrose?"

"I'll never turn away help, sure."

Peter was the same age as Archer, but not as used to hard work. His father, Don, smiled and said, "You go along, son. I'm going to lay down for a nap."

They had brought in one wagon load of wood when they stopped for lunch. And now that was unloaded and Archer drove it back to the wood lot while Rascal and Peter walked.

Working up firewood was a new experience for Peter. Living in the city, he just assumed that people in the country heated their homes in the same way. He tired soon, but he wasn't willing to stop or complain. That afternoon they brought in three wagon loads.

"You hungry, Peter?" Anita asked.

"You betch-ya. . . ah, yes, Ma'am. I have never worked so hard in my life and my stomach has been growling all afternoon."

His father was smiling and so were Rascal and Emma.

After supper Rascal took Don out fishing. They had not had much luck in the morning. Peter preferred to stay at the lodge. He and Archer went for a walk out to the farm to see what the crews had been doing. Archer was hoping they would not run into Bear.

The brook trout were still not biting too well until the sun had settled below the tree tops. Like most eager fishermen, Don was about to cast his fly out as soon as they arrived. Rascal whispered, "Wait, Don. Sit quiet and don't make a sound. The fish left when we arrived and they won't come back if we make too much noise." Don nodded his head.

They sat quietly for two minutes and when Rascal saw

a trout break the surface of the water after a mosquito, Rascal whispered again, "Okay."

Don was being real careful now not to make too much noise, like he and Peter had done earlier. And instead of whipping his line back and forth to get out as much line as he could he whipped it only twice and eased the fly onto the water, not letting it slap the surface. Just as the fly touched down, a two pound brookie took it and went air bound.

Don wanted to shout out loud with excitement but if he did he was afraid Rascal would scold him. So he brought the brookie in and as Rascal netted it, he was smiling, but not a word was spoken.

Without having to be told he waited for a bit before casting again; to let the disturbance settle. He caught three more like the first one and then Rascal said, "Let's say we head back, and you might as well troll a warden's worry streamer on the way. I'll paddle, you tend your fly rod."

****

When Don and his son Peter went fishing the next morning they had much better luck by not making as much noise as the previous day. There was enough trout now for a good fish chowder and to smoke some for their trip home. While they were out fishing, Rascal and Archer worked on firewood. Instead of hauling the wood back to the lodge they split it and piled it up in the woods and would haul it in later.

As they were eating breakfast Saturday morning, Don said, "Peter and I have certainly enjoyed our stay here. Maybe next year my wife will come with us. And I want to thank you, Rascal, for showing me how to fish. I thought I knew all I would need to know to catch brook trout."

Saturday evening while there were no guests, Rascal and Emma had a long talk with Archer. Even though he had graduated from Beech Tree Academy he was only seventeen years old and they were concerned about him going off so young. He was young, but because of his life at Whiskey Jack he was more mature than boys older than he. Their real concern, they were apprehensive about letting him go. It would be for four years.

The next week Archer and his mother took the train to Beech Tree. She had to deposit money in the bank and had some shopping to do, and Archer wanted to make train reservations to Annapolis, Maryland. "When do you wish to leave, Archer?" Greg Oliver asked.

"I must be in Annapolis on September 1st."

"Okay, then you should allow five days. You'll probably make the trip in four, but just to be on the safe side, I'd recommend five days. That would mean you'd have to leave here on August 27th. The southbound from Beech Tree leaves promptly at 6 a.m."

"Okay, make the reservation please."

"From here to Portland, I'd suggest to ride in coach. From Portland to Annapolis I'd suggest a sleeper berth. That is more expensive, of course, but it'll include your meals. You would find it very uncomfortable trying to sleep in coach."

"Okay," Archer said.

Greg was several minutes before he had everything made out. "Now you'll have to switch trains in Boston and New York. To help you get on the right train, ask the conductor. I'm sure he'll help you."

Archer paid Mr. Oliver—his own money that he had been saving. Greg handed him his tickets and said, "Keep these in a safe place, Archer."

"Thank you, Mr. Oliver."

"Good luck to you in Annapolis, Archer." Everyone in Beech Tree already knew of the appointment from Presidents Kingsley and Cutlidge.

Archer left the train depot and went over to the grocery store. He knew his mother would still be there. "Is everything ready, son?"

"Yes."

When Emma had finished shopping she had to hire Mr. Stafford's son to take everything to the depot. As they were leaving the store they ran into Perline and Emma Jean just going in. "Hello, Emma, Archer," Perline said.

Emma Jean said, "Hi, Archer," and she smiled.

"Hi, Emma Jean. Did your father come home?"

"Not until supper time the next day."

Perline asked them to come up for coffee but Emma had to decline. "Thanks, Perline, but we have a load of groceries to get home and we don't want to miss the afternoon train."

When they were on-board and heading for Whiskey Jack, Emma said, "I think little Emma Jean likes you, Archer."

"Yeah, I know. I wish she was older. She is pretty, though, for only twelve years old."

"Just think how she'll look in four years when you graduate from the Academy."

"Hum, you have a point there, Mom. I do like her and enjoy being with her."

"Well, maybe a letter to her once in a while might be a good idea."

Archer chuckled and said, "Okay, Mom."

"What do you have to take for clothes?"

"Not much. As I understand the information that I received, I will be in Navy attire most of the time. I'll take a change of casual clothes and wear my sport coat and slacks on my trip down."

"This is an awful big step for you isn't it, son?"

"Yes, Mom, but I think your subconscious knew this day would come. I think that is the reason you made sure I was so well educated and why you suggested I go to the Beech Tree Academy. I think, Mom, that everything we do has a purpose. I don't believe in coincidences. I think that everything that happens to us, whether good or bad, happens for a reason."

"Hum, I have never heard you talk like this before, son."

Roscoe helped to unload their food stores onto the

23

platform and then the train went to the farm to hook onto two loaded freight cars.

They took the perishables downstairs to the cold storage room. Paulette and Anita had supper already.

"Did you get everything you needed from Mr. Oliver?" Rascal asked.

"Yes, he made it seem so simple. He said if I need help with switching trains a conductor will help me."

Chapter 3

For the rest of that summer before Archer was scheduled to leave, he would help his dad prepare the lodge for the coming winter. They had enough firewood worked up to last for two-and-a-half years. They went fishing and frogging to smoke and can. There were nuisance beaver at mile nine and mile twelve. And sadly, Whiskey Jack had to be left behind. The long hikes were too much for him now.

Rascal knew this would be the last time he would have time to spend with his son in the woods and doing what they both enjoyed.

Archer was a natural trapper and he was enjoying the outing with his dad as much as Rascal was enjoying the day. And Bear would make his presence at both mile nine and twelve and they both would play with him. And Bear's age was becoming obvious, but he still enjoyed playing. Then afterwards he would fill up with beaver carcasses.

Every other year Rascal would have to remove nuisance beaver from miles nine and twelve, and there was hardly ever a beaver colony on the lake. "Somewhere upstream from mile twelve there must be some very good beaver habitat. The beaver here I don't believe come up from below the dam, so there must be a swamp or something above here where these nuisance beaver are coming from."

"I'm surprised you never followed Jack Brook upstream to see."

"I think it would be a long walk."

Archer was almost as fast as Rascal skinning and fleshing

25

the beaver. "When I sell these, son, I'll put half of the money in your bank account."

They were a week cleaning out all of the beaver from both locations, and they had twenty-six beaver. Emma and Paulette were busy for two days canning all of the meat.

With the nuisance beaver and dams gone and enough firewood to last maybe three years, in his quiet times Archer and Whiskey Jack would go for walks. He would stop and rest often for Whiskey Jack's benefit. Sometimes the two would sit on the front steps of the log cabin all afternoon drinking in the quiet and serenity of Whiskey Jack, home. He wasn't regretting that he would be gone for four years but he knew he would miss his Mom, Dad, Anita and Paulette. He would miss his home.

Rascal noticed how quiet Archer had been and one evening at supper he asked, "Are you having second thoughts about the Naval Academy son? You have been so quiet lately and preferring to be off by yourself."

"No, no second thoughts. Only I haven't left yet and I'm already homesick."

"I guess I can understand that," Rascal answered.

"We just don't want you to think we'd be disappointed if you changed your mind," Emma said.

"No, no I'm not going to change my mind. I'm actually quite excited about it. It's just that for four years I'll be leaving everything behind that I love. And at the same time I know by leaving it also means my life will never be the same again."

"Archer," Paulette said, "maybe this is something that you were always meant to do."

****

Another two days passed before Archer was able to work through his feelings about leaving home. No matter where he was in this world, Whiskey Jack would always be his home.

A week before he had to leave he began packing. He didn't know why, other than to work off some nervous energy.

He was only taking one suitcase.

He had come full-term with being homesick. Whiskey Jack would always be home, but now he knew his destiny would be taking him into a different world. And once again this brought back his excitement.

"Before you leave, son, I'd like you to give me a hand mowing out back here and then the twitch road from the dam out back to the old log yard."

"Sure, now?"

It was promising to be a hot day, but Rascal wanted to get it mowed. Archer liked driving the old Model T tractor and Rascal rode the mower.

The ground was dry and the machinery was kicking up a lot of dust. Rascal tied a handkerchief around his head to cover his nose and mouth.

Whiskey Jack laid in the shade and watched.

As they were coming down the hill by the cabin Rascal hollered, "Stop."

"What's the problem, Dad?"

"Nothing, let's sit on the cabin porch for a bit and let this dust settle."

At first they just sat there drinking in the beauty, without saying a word. "Son, I just want you to know this is a big step you're taking. Your mother and I are so proud of you. We know you'll do good. You always have, no matter what you were doing."

"Thanks, Dad, that means a lot to me."

"Before you were born, son, your mother and I traveled to Washington, D.C., had dinner at the White House, we saw some of New York City and Boston, and your mother toured Washington with Lieutenant Belle. So you see, son, it's your turn now to travel and see what there is beyond Whiskey Jack Lake and Beech Tree."

"I know, Dad, and I'll make you and Mom proud of me. I think Paulette is hollering for us to come down for lunch."

****

August 26th, Archer's last day at home, arrived and Emma was very quiet, while Rascal went about his usual chores and Archer was excited. He had managed to overcome his home sickness after talking with his Dad on the porch of the log cabin.

"Paulette, will you be okay here with Anita? It'll be just the two of you and we'll be back tomorrow morning."

"We'll be just fine, Emma."

Emma made sure Archer had carefully packed his sport coat and good slacks so they would not wrinkle. Then she laid out on the bed, clothes for she and Rascal to wear. She really wanted to wear her evening gown that she had worn to the White House dinner. She settled on a nice flowery print and some presentable casual clothes for Rascal.

When it came time to dress, Rascal didn't balk. Emma thought she would have to wrangle with Rascal to get him to dress up a little. Archer had already changed and was waiting in the living room with Paulette and Anita.

The southbound had switched tracks to the farm. "Paulette, will you take a picture of us together?" They stood in front of the fireplace. "You too, Anita. You're part of this family."

Then Anita took a picture with Paulette with them.

"That was the last picture on the roll of film." She took the film out and loaded a new one and said, "Son, I want you to take this and take pictures at the Academy and you and your new friends."

A half hour later they could hear the train switching back to the main line and they all walked out onto the platform. Even Whiskey Jack. He knew his friend was leaving and he jumped up and put his paws on Archer's chest. "Goodbye, pal. You take care of the family."

Archer hugged Anita and kissed her cheek and said, "Goodbye, Grandma," and she hugged him again. Then he hugged Paulette and kissed her.

"All aboard, folks," Roscoe Whelling said.

When the train was out of sight, Paulette said, "If I was ten years younger I'd jump his bones."

Anita gasped with shock, hearing a nice young woman saying something like that. Then she began laughing and Paulette laughed with her and helped her back inside the lodge.

"You on your way to Annapolis, Archer?" Roscoe asked.

"Yes, but how did you know?"

"Heck, the whole town knows. You'll make everyone in Beech Tree proud, Archer. It isn't every day that some young fella has two former presidents appoint him to a Naval Academy." Roscoe left.

"Hum, I wasn't counting on any of this," Archer said.

When they left the train station they went directly to the hotel. The owner Harvey Long, met them at the registration desk and said, "We have all heard you would be coming today. You have the suite on the top floor. There are two large bedrooms and there is a television in the suite. And no charge, William," he said to the clerk. "The Ambrose family are guests of the hotel tonight."

"Mr. Long, what is all this about?" Rascal asked.

"It isn't every day, Rascal, that one of our own receives such an honorable appointment to the Annapolis Naval Academy. Archer, you have made everyone in Beech Tree proud. We are proud of you."

"Mr. Long, what is a television?" Emma asked.

"I will show you to your suite and I'll show you. Come, follow me," Harvey said.

They took the elevator to the fourth floor and there were two suites there. They were given the largest one for the night.

"This is the television. This is the on button." It took a half minute for the tubes to warm up before there was a picture. "We only have the one channel right now. At 6 p.m. and 6 a.m. there will be an hour news show. Local news and then national. I would ask that when you aren't watching the set to turn it off.

The set uses a lot of tubes.

"Will you be dining in the hotel restaurant this evening?"

"Yes."

"That you will have to pay for. The suite is yours for the night."

"Isn't this something," Rascal said.

They sat down looking at the television.

"I have never heard of anything like this," Emma said.

"Can't say I have either. What about you, son?"

"I have never seen one, but in the Academy I read about them."

"Where does the picture come from?"

"Something like radio, only this changes the radio waves into pictures. That's about all I know."

"Fascinating," Emma said. "Truly fascinating."

They watched the television for a while, but had little interest with the show, so they turned it off and decided to go down to the restaurant.

Herschel, Perline and Emma Jean were already there. They found a larger table, so they could all sit together. Emma Jean, of course, sat next to Archer. "Don't you look spiffy tonight, Archer."

"Thank you, Emma Jean, you do also."

"What's the occasion, Herschel?" Rascal asked.

"Well I've been gone for a few days and I promised to take them out to dinner when I got back."

"How long were you out there?" Rascal asked.

"Only three days."

"It must be rough on you sometimes, Perline," Emma said.

"There have been times. At first, but he is so good at what he does and he enjoys being a game warden so much, I would never want that to change. And when he does come home after being out for a couple of days, he always makes up for it."

While the adults were talking, Archer and Emma Jean were carrying on their own conversation.

"How long will you be gone, Archer?" Emma Jean asked.
"Four years."

"Oh wow, that's a long time. I'll be almost seventeen then."

When the waitress came for their orders, Rascal said, "This is on Em and me, so order anything you want."

They all settled on roast pork. "And a bottle of white chardonnay please."

Archer was used to having wine at home and Emma poured him a glass also. When she looked at Perline she nodded her head and said, "A half of a glass."

Rascal stood and said, "I would like to propose a toast." They all raised their glass and Rascal said, "To you, son."

The roast pork was delicious, "Almost as good as yours, Em."

When they had had all they wanted to eat, they remained seated happily talking. "Emma Jean," Archer asked, "have you ever heard of a television?"

"I have heard about it but I have never seen one."

"There is one in our room."

"I would like to see one sometime."

The restaurant was beginning to fill up, so Rascal paid the check and left a good tip.

"Thank you for supper, Rascal," Herschel said.

They walked with the Pages outside to the sidewalk. "Will you write to me, Archer?" Emma Jean asked.

"I'll write."

"Now, I'd better do this so I'll never live to regret it," Emma Jean said and she kissed Archer, not on the cheek but on his lips. And he responded.

"Goodnight, folks," Emma said.

On their way up to their suite Emma asked, "Are you going to write her?"

"Yes, I think I will. After all, when I graduate from the Academy she'll be my age."

"I think she really likes you, son."

"I think so, too."

Once in the suite, Archer turned the television on and sat back and waited for the picture to come on. When it came on a new program was starting. "What is it, son?" Rascal asked.

"Laurel and Hardy in the 'Flying Deuces'."

"We've heard them on the radio," Rascal said, "This should be good."

They sat back on the couch to watch and it wasn't long before all three of them were laughing so hard tears were streaming down their faces. Emma was particularly happy because she had never seen her husband and son do so much laughing. What an enjoyable way to lighten the atmosphere, as after this night they probably would not see their son for four years. For more than an hour the three sat and watched Stan and Ollie's comic and crazy antics and laughed almost continuously. It was good medicine for them all.

They all were still laughing when the movie ended. Emma got up to turn the set off and another movie was about to start, *Way Out West*. This was a shorter movie and they decided to stay up and watch it. Emma would just as soon have gone to bed, but she so enjoyed watching Rascal and Archer laugh so much and enjoy themselves. Her sides were aching from so much laughter.

****

They were up with the sun the next morning and after a quick breakfast they walked to the train depot. The southbound train was already there, but it would still be a few minutes before departure. Rascal handed Archer $100.00 and said, "Here, take this son. You'll never know when it might come in handy. And if you should ever need anything, let us know."

"Thank you, I will."

"I want you to write often, son," Emma said, "And take a lot of pictures."

People were starting to board and Emma hugged him and said, "We are so proud of you, son."

And then Rascal, instead of shaking his hand, hugged him and said, "We could not be more proud, son."

"I really want to do this, Mom and Dad."

"When you're doing something that you really enjoy then it never feels like a job. Do what is expected of you, son and then a little more. Do everything you have agreed to do. But most importantly, have fun."

"I will, Dad." And he picked up his luggage and boarded the train.

Rascal and Emma stayed on the platform until the train was out of sight.

Chapter 4

In April Herschel, Perline and Emma Jean went to the Willis Jeep dealer there in Beech Tree. Herschel's patrol district was getting larger each year and he needed some means to better cover it. The department wasn't yet providing vehicles for game wardens, but the agency would pay for the gas, tires and so much for each mile driven.

The family had decided on a Jeep station wagon; green with wood paneling on the sides.

Perline had even learned how to drive and sometimes she would drop Herschel off somewhere and after he had finished doing whatever, he'd work his way home.

Two days after Archer left on the morning train, Herschel put several sandwiches in his backpack, a thermos of coffee and a jug of water. He strapped on his gun belt with handcuffs; he always carried two sets of cuffs in his pack and there had been times when he had had to use them. He kissed Perline and Emma Jean and said, "I'm not sure when I'll be back."

Through the years Herschel had filled out some and his shoulders were broad. He was only an inch taller than his father but he was twenty pounds heavier. And not fat, but lean, tough muscles. He had earned a reputation in the area and those who knew him did not want to cross his path. His reputation now equaled that of his father's.

There was an abandoned woods road five miles south of town that went five miles west through some excellent wildlife habitat. And he had noticed all summer occasionally there would be tire tracks of a vehicle that had come out and turned south on the highway. He was determined to find out today what was going on. There were no lakes, ponds or streams accessible from the woods road, so the interest wasn't fishing.

"You be careful out there Herschel," Perline said.

"I always am, sweetheart." He looked at his daughter and said, "You like Archer, don't you, Emma Jean?"—more statement than question.

"Yes, Dad, I do."

"Good, he comes from good people. Goodbye."

He drove south of town, slowly, while thinking of his daughter and Archer. Then he grinned. Before he knew it, he was at the dirt road that went west, locally called the West Road. The area was good trapping and hunting, but there was no water for fishing. At the bottom of the hill there was a mud puddle and he stopped to look at the tracks. There were tire tracks coming into the water, but the water had washed away the tire tracks on the other side, meaning the vehicle was still in there. These tire tracks he figured were at least two days old.

After studying the tracks he drove on slowly looking for a hidey-hole where he could leave his vehicle. About a half mile in he was able to leave it on a nice twitch trail and behind a bank at the further end of a log yard. He locked the doors and shouldered his pack.

It was a hot day, but not humid. Before he had walked all the way back to the West Road, a doe and two spotted fawns walked across the road in front of him.

While walking along the road he would look at each mud puddle and mud flat checking for tracks. The tire tracks all were indicating that the vehicle had not come out yet. In the lower swampy areas he was seeing a lot of moose tracks.

In 1938, the state had stopped the legal moose hunting, due to a shortage of moose. About twice a year the S&A train would hit one and he would go out and salvage what meat he could. Usually he would give the meat to a needy family.

He was beginning to smell a slight scent of wood smoke

in the air. He hoped it would be a camp fire and not a forest fire. He had hiked a mile so far and the smell of smoke was stronger. The road surface was softer here, more dirt and not as much gravel, and he was finding many deer and moose tracks.

He stopped to listen for any sounds of human activity. All he could hear were blue jays and red squirrels scolding each other. He was beginning to question if he might be on a fool's errand. But at each mud puddle the tire tracks indicated that the vehicle was still in beyond. He had hiked about three miles now and he knew the road was only about five miles long.

He wasn't aware of any cabin in there, but he hadn't been in since the cutting crews had pulled out five years ago.

After four miles, he still had not seen or heard anything. Not being discouraged, though, he was determined to find the vehicle.

He was coming close to the old log yard and when the crews were working in here, the woods boss, Marvin Collins, had a cabin that set off to the right about one hundred feet back from the West Road. Up ahead he saw a flock of ravens take off. In the woods this always meant there was something dead they were feeding from. He stepped off the road into a fir thicket to listen.

There wasn't a sound. Then a gorbie landed on a tree branch not far from him with a piece of raw meat in its beak. Herschel was more than interested now. He began working his way through the trees, being as quiet as possible and staying out of sight.

It was several minutes before he was close enough to see smoke rising from the cabin, and parked in front was a gray panel truck and there were no windows on the sides.

The front door was closed, but what he could see of the windows, they were open. He checked his watch; 9:20. He was well hidden where he was, but he wanted a better view. So he moved to his right a little. The ground was dry and no dry leaves that would make noise. There were small fir trees that he could see over the tops at the edge of the clearing. For now this would have to be good enough. He was only fifty feet from the front door, close enough he hoped to overhear them talking if they should come outside.

There were voices inside now but he couldn't make out what was being said. Ravens were coming back now and flying over the cabin. He sat down to wait. He thought about eating a sandwich, but he only had three and he suspected he might be here for a while.

The ravens were making a lot of noise now. They probably were all back at whatever was dead.

An hour had passed and suddenly the door opened and three men stepped outside. Drinking a beer each. And they each were carrying a revolver in a shoulder holster. "Who in hell are these guys?"

The two younger and smaller men looked enough alike to be brothers. The third was much older, maybe fifty, stood about six feet and Herschel guessed he weighed probably two thirty. He was hoping it would be fat and not muscle.

"Hey, Pops, how much more are we going to can?" Tony asked.

"We must have a hundred and fifty quarts now, Pops," Armino said.

"We have three restaurants that need meat for our special sauce. I'd like to get that moose that we have seen."

"Four deer is a pretty good load for one trip, Pops," Tony said.

"It is, but if we can get that moose we'd be able to can another two hundred and maybe take some fresh meat home," Arnaldo said.

"I think we'd be pushing it, Pops, if we try to can a moose. We have been pretty lucky so far," Armino said.

As they were talking, Herschel wondered where they were shooting the deer. The panel truck had not moved. And where had they been seeing this moose?

Armino was talking now, "I don't think we have anything to worry about, being caught. We have never seen any law out here.

"Pops," Tony asked, "what if a game warden was to come snooping around?"

"How would we handle something like that in Boston?"

"We'd shoot him and take the body out to sea," Armino said.

Tony spoke up and said, "We could throw the body over the bank where we threw the deer carcasses. The animals would clean it up before anyone would miss him."

"I don't think we'll see any game warden in here. He's probably on some lake or pond harassing some fisherman," the old man said and laughed.

Herschel was now wishing his dad was here with him.

The three kept talking about killing the moose and how much meat there would be. And more about the three Romero Restaurants somewhere in Boston. They finished their beer and cigarettes and went back inside.

Herschel would have liked to have a look to see what was out back, but not in daylight. He would wait until it was dark. He knew the full moon was three or four days off, but there should be enough light for him to sneak out back.

As much as Herschel wanted to explore around the cabin and see what was out back, he didn't. He knew he would have all three of them for illegal hunting and possession and he didn't want to lose that by being careless. So he sat down and leaned up against a tree.

At a little before noon all three came back out carrying a beer and a plate of food. "Boy, does this fresh air feel good," Tony said. "It's so damned hot inside."

"This is the last of the deer meat, Pops. What if we don't see a moose?" Armino asked.

"Then we kill a few more deer," Arnaldo said.

"You know boys, since we have been using deer and

moose instead of ground up beef in our special sauces, our customer visits have increased, plus what we save on not having to buy the meat."

"How long do you think we can keep doing this, Pops?" Tony asked.

"If we were caught going out with this load, we'd still be ahead of the game. We have canned enough deer and moose meat so any fine they'd give us probably wouldn't cost us more than a nickel a pound."

Herschel grinned, thinking this conversation would be good to use in court.

They talked some more about their restaurants, but not where they were located in Boston. Herschel remained sitting on the ground and out of sight. He was really enjoying this as the three kept digging the hole deeper that they were in.

At 3 o'clock, by the sounds they had pulled the last batch of mason jars off the wood stove. Then the three men brought cardboard boxes filled with canned meat and put them inside the panel truck. When the side door was opened Herschel could see several more boxes, probably sealed mason jars filled with deer meat.

The three took another beer and smoke break. Herschel still couldn't figure out where they were shooting the deer. The panel truck hadn't been moved. He doubted if there were any apple trees around and even if there were, the apples would still be green. Maybe they had brought some apples with them.

After the break the three went back inside and they were quiet. No talking or stirring at all. He began to wonder if they might be sleeping.

Until he could look around unobserved there would be no answers for the many questions surrounding this operation. He was hoping he might find some of those answers tonight.

It was so quiet inside the cabin, Herschel began to wonder if they were asleep. Sleep in the afternoon and work all night canning deer meat. If he was sure, this would be a good time to have a look out back. But—he wasn't sure.

He poured himself a cup of coffee and sat back listening. After a while he poured another cup and ate a sandwich.

At 6 o'clock he could hear stirring inside and a column of smoke from the stove pipe rose above the cabin. Pops— Arnaldo— came outside and went to the outhouse. He had no sooner closed the outhouse door when there was a big caliber rifle shot from inside the cabin. Then the two brothers came out carrying the rifle and ran around to the back of the cabin and disappeared in the trees. But he could still hear them talking excitedly. The shooter had killed a moose. Tony was carrying the rifle when they came outside so he was probably the shooter.

Eventually Arnaldo walked out back to help his sons. They weren't long skinning the moose there on the ground and cutting off the four legs. Then the two boys went back to cut off the backstraps.

As they were walking back Herschel overheard the two talking about having the tenderloins with eggs for supper.

As Herschel sat there watching and listening he was wondering how long this has been going on. The cabin was far enough away from everything that no one would hear a rifle shot from inside the cabin. The cabin would have muffled the report.

After supper, the Romeros began cutting up the meat and filling mason jars. Herschel doubted if they would be able to can it all during the night. They had taken one hind quarter inside and were working on that.

Darkness came and no one had stepped outside. Herschel began working his way around the cabin to the rear. He could look through the window on his side of the cabin and saw that the three of them were busy. He stayed well back from the cabin and he found a wide, well used game trail leading towards the old log yard. In the moonlight he could see the many moose and deer tracks. He was careful about not leaving any of his tracks.

There was a much larger window in the rear of the cabin that opened inward from the top. He could smell moose remains and rotten apples. *That must be what they're using to lure the deer.* He followed beside the game trail out to the log yard and once there he was far enough away so he turned on his flashlight and looked over the far bank. There was a gut pile of new and old deer and moose remains—hide and bones.

He had seen enough and he went back where he had left his backpack. He wrapped his wool blanket around his shoulders and leaned back against the tree for the night. Whenever the front door would open he would instantly awaken.

He had no idea how long this stakeout would take. During the night he finished his lukewarm coffee and another sandwich.

Shortly after sunrise they brought out three more boxes and put them in the panel truck. Herschel was hoping they would finish up today and leave but he doubted if they would be able to can all of the moose meat.

As the day wore on, the Romeros were busy all day canning. As Herschel waited, he thought of something his dad had said to him when Jarvis came out of retirement to work a month with him, while they were on the border. He had said, "Sometimes, son, in your career, you'll find yourself in a tough position and if you can't get yourself out of it by using your mouth, then you don't deserve to wear the uniform." He was wondering now if this was going to be one of those tough positions. The Romeros had made it clear what they would do if a game warden showed up.

A hundred scenarios were playing through his thoughts on how this was going to play out.

The three men were busy all day canning the moose meat. *They just might finish up today,* Herschel was thinking. Hoping. At 6 p.m. they brought out several more boxes filled with mason jars full of moose meat, and put them in the panel truck. "Pops, I sure would like to get out of here tonight," Tony said.

"So would I son, but we're all tired and need sleep before we make that long drive."

Herschel had his answer. They were tired and sleepy. Now would be better than waiting until morning when they're refreshed after a night's sleep. He waited until they were all leaning against the picnic table and facing the other way.

He started inching his way through the trees trying to be quiet, his .45 drawn. He made it through the trees to the edge of the clearing and so far so good. He kept inching closer and closer. When he was finally in front of the cabin door he raised his .45 and said, "Game warden. Freeze. Don't make a frigging move."

"What the hell!" Tony exclaimed.

"What in hell is going on here?" Pops asked.

"Put your hands up. All of you." When they didn't move he said rather forcefully, "Now!"

"Okay, one at a time remove your gun from your shoulder holster and drop it in that bucket of water. Starting with you, Pops. Now. You make any sudden move and I'll blow your head off."

Arnaldo did as he was told. "Now you, Tony. Pops, you take one step back. Now Tony."

Tony had a weird expression on his face. When he pulled his gun out of his shoulder holster he said as he whirled around, "I'll kill you, you son of a bitch!"

Herschel was anticipating this and he brought his .45 down on Tony's gun wrist, as hard as he could. The wrist broke and Tony started screaming and dropped his gun.

Pops now charged at Herschel and Herschel had anticipated he would make the next move, and he broke his collarbone with his revolver and then hit him under the chin as hard as he could with the palm of his hand sending Pops over backwards. He was rolling on the ground, screaming.

Armino had his gun out and before he could level it at Herschel, Herschel hit him in an upward motion under his chin with his palm lifting him off his feet sending him backwards.

Tony wasn't done yet. He regained his feet screaming,

"I'll kill you, you son of a bitch and your whole family."

Herschel kicked his feet out from under him and he went down again.

Arnaldo was still on the ground, and he said, "You don't know who you are dealing with. When this is all over we'll be coming after you and your family. Nobody has ever done this to the Romeros and gotten away with it."

"Roll over on our stomach, Arnaldo." He did and Herschel handcuffed him with his hands behind him.

Then he cuffed the other two. "Oh, yeah, you three—Arnaldo, Armino and Tony—you are under arrest for shooting deer and moose in closed season. That's just for starters. There'll be more charges once I have finished my search of everything."

He opened the back door of the panel truck and there was just enough room for the three to lay on the floor while he drove over to the jail. They had the boxes tied securely to either side leaving enough room in the middle. There was some leftover rope on the floor.

He helped Pops to his feet and had him crawl in and lay on the floor on his stomach. Then he tied his ankles together so he would not be able to get up. Then he did the same to Armino and Tony. They were not happy and still threatening to kill Herschel.

He had the Romeros secured in the panel truck and he took their handguns out of the bucket and unloaded them (.38 stubnose) and put those in front of the truck. Then he went inside the cabin for a cursory search, only to see if there was a fourth man. He'd come back later for a more thorough look-see. He picked up his backpack and then climbed in the truck and said, "It'll only be a short ride to jail, boys."

The West Road was not rough and he made pretty good time. He was more worried about breaking some of the full mason jars than he was about jousting around the Romeros. He would have to come back after his Jeep.

He knew he'd have to take them to the hospital first to

get patched up. "Now you boys sit still, I'll be right back."

He went inside the jailhouse.

"Hello, Herschel, what can I do for you?" Sheriff Burlock asked.

"I have three prisoners in a panel truck outside and I could use some help taking them to the hospital before we lock 'em up."

The way they have been threatening to kill me and my family, I'm thinking they may be part of a crime ring in Boston."

"Sure, I'll help. What are their names?"

"Romeros."

"There are some Romero restaurants in South Boston, could those be them?"

"I think so, from what I have overheard them talking."

When Sheriff Burlock closed the passenger door he looked back at the Romeros and couldn't help from laughing. "Wow, Herschel, you have them hog-tied and piled like cordwood."

"This is the only way I felt safe."

At the emergency room entrance they untied the Romeros feet and pulled them out of the panel truck. They were hurting, smeared with their own blood and not happy. Tony said, "You wait, you fucking pig. When we get out of jail, we'll fix you."

"Kind of a rowdy bunch aren't they, Herschel," and Burlock grabbed Tony's arm in a vice-like grip and escorted him inside.

"Oh my, what do you have here, Sheriff?" the receptionist asked.

"Better talk with Herschel; they're his prisoners."

"I hope Dr. Hausman isn't busy, Ma'am; these three need immediate attention."

"Dr. Hausman retired. We have a new doctor now, a young woman, Doctor Valery Noonan."

"You know where to take them, Herschel."

Herschel and the sheriff escorted them down the hall to the emergency room. Dr. Noonan came in behind them.

"Hello, I'm Doctor Noonan."

"Hello, Ma'am, I'm Game Warden Hershel Page and this is Sheriff Burlock."

"Gentlemen. Who has the worst injuries?"

"Take your pick, Doctor."

"What happened?"

"They attacked me, Ma'am."

"But you don't have a scratch on you."

"No, Ma'am."

"You can take the cuffs off this one."

"This is Tony. Broken wrist and collarbone."

Doctor Noonan had to put his wrist in a cast and a cast to immobilize his collarbone. Arnaldo (Pops) had to have a cast for his collarbone also and his teeth wired together to hold his broken jaw secure. Armino had his teeth wired together also for a broken jaw.

With Sheriff Burlock to help him he didn't handcuff them for the short ride back to jail.

Burlock put all three in the largest cell and closed the door.

Arnaldo wasn't through making threats yet. Between his teeth he said, "Herschel Page, that's a name I won't forget. Sometime, mister, me and my boys will take care of you and your family."

"Now you listen to me, mister!" Sheriff Burlock said, "You're in a pretty poor position to be making threats. You shut your mouth!"

Burlock closed the door to the cell and asked, "What are you charging them with, Herschel?"

"For starters killing and illegal possession of deer and moose in closed season and criminal threatening and terrorizing with a deadly weapon. I'll have to go back tomorrow and look around some more."

"Where were they?"

"At the end of the West Road."

"What's in all these boxes?"

"Canned deer and moose meat. I'm also going to confiscate that panel truck. Do you have a secure place I can leave it?"

"Yes, out back. There's a fenced in vehicle security area. What about the canned meat?"

"That'll be okay tonight. When I come back from their cabin I'll remove the boxes and you and I will search the vehicle."

"I'll have to hold them over the weekend now. Ole Judge Hulcurt is going to like this one. I think I'll be there and watch." Herschel put the panel truck in the locked security area and took the three guns into the sheriff's office.

"Lee, can I lock these up here?"

"Sure you can."

Lee gave Herschel a receipt for the guns.

"And Lee, I don't want any bail set for these guys."

"I can guarantee it, Herschel."

"Thanks."

Herschel walked home. His supper was late. But Perline and Emma Jean were glad to see him. He told them about the Romeros, except for the threats they had made. Then he called his Dad.

"Dad, I need a ride in the morning to get my Jeep. Can you pick me up early?

"I'll tell you all about it then. Goodnight."

"You need a bath, Herschel, and a shave."

He started laughing.

****

Jarvis picked Herschel up at 6 a.m. Herschel had told him most of the story by the time they picked up his Jeep. They changed vehicles and used the Jeep to go all the way in. He drove right into the cabin. "This is a convenient spot to do some poaching. But I'm surprised no one ever reported hearing shots," Jarvis said.

They went inside and Herschel opened the back window. "Well I'll be damned," Jarvis said.

"Yeah, this is why no one heard any shots. They shoot from inside."

"What exactly are you looking for, son?"

"Anything that would tie them into organized crime."

They looked through everything. There were a few magazines and Herschel did get a mailing address from one of them. Jarvis found a .30-06 Winchester rifle, only one, under one of the mattresses and four empty shells on the floor under the bed.

They put the rifle in the jeep. "Let's look out back. There's something I want to show you."

Halfway out there, Jarvis said, "I can smell rotten apples." Then he saw them.

Much of the moose remains had already been eaten. The head and bones of the forelegs were still there.

"Where does this game trail go, son?"

"Out to the log yard and that's where they have been dumping the remains."

As they started out along the game trail a bear was running along it towards them. They stopped and Jarvis hollered, "Hey!" as loud as he could.

Without breaking stride the bear turned a right angle off the trail and disappeared. When he hollered, a flock of ravens took off. They walked over to the edge and looked over the bank. They could see four deer heads, a lot of hair, a few bones and the remains of the stomach material. "So four deer and a moose. How much did they can?"

"I haven't counted the boxes. We'll have to do that when we get back."

They walked back to the cabin. "I'd like to burn this," Herschel said.

"Maybe you should find out who it belongs to," Jarvis suggested.

As they were driving out the West Road, Jarvis asked, "What aren't you telling me son? There was a reason you were looking for evidence for connections to organized crime."

"The first day I was there the two sons were questioning the father—Arnaldo or Pops—what would they do if the law showed up. Pops said they would take care of them like they would in Boston. Shoot to kill and dump the body over the bank like the deer remains. Pops said in a couple of days the body would be eaten and the evidence gone. He said back home they would shoot the person and dump the body out in the ocean."

"And this has you worried, why?"

"They have threatened to do the same to me, several times. Even in the hospital in front of Doctor Noonan and Sheriff Burlock. And my family, Dad."

"I don't know what to say, son. I know sometimes in anger people you arrest will make empty threats. But you said you heard them talk about how they handle problems in Boston. If I were you I don't think I'd say anything to Perline or your daughter about these threats. Why don't you wait until after court."

Back at the jail, Herschel asked, "Lee, would you accompany Dad and me and search and inventory the panel truck? As a disinterested person."

"Let's go," he replied.

They unloaded the boxes of canned meat and there were thirty boxes and each box containing twelve quart mason jars. "These guys were busy." The boxes were even marked which were deer or moose meat.

A complete search of the truck didn't turn up anything. Only the vehicle registration papers.

"What are you going to do with all this meat, Herschel?" Burlock asked.

"After they have been to court, I'll give some to the senior citizen home, some to the school. Would you like a box, Lee?

"Yes, moose meat, if I could."

"No problem. Dad?"

"Moose."

"Okay, Monday after court."

"And Herschel, there's something I need to tell you about the Romeros."

"Yes."

"I've left the door open some so I could listen to what they were talking about."

"And."

"No specifics, but I believe there is something or someone they all are more afraid of than going to jail here. I distinctly heard Arnaldo say it would be best if they did some time in jail here rather than go home. As I said, I don't know what they were referring to."

"Ok, I think I'd better go inside and write some summonses and advise them what they are being charged with."

"Do you need me anymore, son?"

"Not unless you want to hang around until I'm done. Then maybe the three of us can go for coffee."

"Okay."

He sat down at an empty desk and started listing the charges: killing four deer and one moose in closed season, illegal possession of deer and moose meat for commercial use, assaulting a game warden. "Hey, Lee, I need some help on one charge. When I told them to one at a time remove their handguns from their shoulder holster, Arnaldo and Armino did. Tony leveled his at me and said he was going to kill me. That's when I hit his wrist with my .45 and broke his wrist. Would this act constitute assault with a deadly weapon?"

"Yes, no problem."

"Thanks."

There was another charge of criminal threatening for each of them. He was busy for the next several minutes writing summons to each of the Romeros for each charge. Then he went back with Burlock to talk with them. He handed the many summonses to Arnaldo. Then he told them what they were being charged with. There was no grumbling. Only Arnaldo said, "You'll get yours."

They went back out front. "I guess I'll be a good witness for you, Herschel, come Monday."

"What happened?" Jarvis asked.

Sheriff Burlock answered, "Arnaldo just threatened Herschel again."

Deputy Kendall arrived for his shift and they went for coffee.

****

During the weekend Herschel wrote a report about the Romero cases. Both for court, if it should go to superior court, and for his warden inspector. Inspector Pelletier had transferred to northern Maine.

Herschel told his family about the deer and moose charges against the Romeros, but nothing yet about the threats. When he had finished his report and typed it, it read like a novel. He was very thorough, beginning with the one-way tire tracks he had found at the beginning of the West Road.

Perline and Emma Jean were glad to have him home for the weekend.

Jarvis Page met Herschel and Sheriff Burlock at the jail at 8 a.m. Monday morning. "Have they been saying anything more, Lee?" Herschel asked.

"No specifics, like earlier. Only they seem to be terribly afraid of going home with these charges hanging over them. You know, it wouldn't surprise me any if these guys plead guilty to all charges this morning."

"That would be a surprise," Herschel said.

They had a cup of coffee before leaving for the courthouse. The three were put in handcuffs before leaving. As they walked to the courthouse people were stopping to watch them pass, wondering what they had done to end up in casts and in handcuffs.

Herschel escorted them down to the front row and he sat with them, and Jarvis and Burlock sat behind them for added security. When Judge Hulcurt entered, before taking his chair he stopped and looked at the men in casts and smiled.

There were only two other people there and he got rid of those two before proceeding with the Romeros. He had read Herschel's report before starting. "Now for the Romeros. You'll stand."

They did. "You three have been charged with several violations, ranging from killing deer and moose in closed season to assaulting a game warden with a dangerous weapon; to wit a .38 stubnose revolver. How do you plead?"

Arnaldo said, "I am their father and I plead guilty to all charges for all of us."

This certainly surprised everyone. Most of all Hulcurt. "Armino, do you agree with your father and wish to plead guilty?"

"Yes."

"Tony do you also wish to plead guilty to all charges?"

"Yes."

"I must inform you that because of the more serious charges against you, you would normally go to grand jury first for an indictment. Am I to understand that you wish to bypass the grand jury and still wish to plead guilty?"

There was a brief discussion among the Romeros before Arnaldo replied, "Yes, Your Honor."

"I have received your report, Herschel, but I do have some questions."

"Yes, Your Honor."

"First, were you alone when you apprehended the Romeros?"

"Yes, Your Honor."

"Let me see your hands."

51

Herschel knew what he was looking for and he held them both up showing his knuckles. "Your knuckles are not skun so I am assuming you must have hit them with the palm of your hand. Is this correct?"

"Yes, Your Honor."

"How many deer had they killed?"

"We found the remains of four deer."

"I thought you said earlier you were alone?"

"Yes, Your Honor. The next morning my father took me back so I could get my vehicle and we went to the cabin to look around."

"And the moose?"

"Only one, Your Honor."

"How much did you confiscate?"

"Thirty boxes containing twelve each of quart mason jars."

"And how will you dispose of this much illegal meat?"

"Most of it will go to the school and the senior citizen's home."

"How many days did you watch them?"

"Two days and Thursday night."

"All by yourself—hum—He is just like you Jarvis. You should be proud of him."

"I am, Your Honor."

"Before I pass sentence I'm going to say, this is my last day as judge. I'm retiring. And this is one hell of a case to retire on. Now to sentencing. I accept the pleas of guilty to all charges. For the illegal killing of four deer and one moose and for the illegal possession of meat for the intention of commercial use in your restaurant chain, I fine you each $1000.00 and five days in jail. Now to the more serious charges, I fine you each $5,000.00 and eighteen months in the state prison. And of the threats against Herschel Page's person and his family after you have served prison time, you will forever be banned from ever coming into the state of Maine. Is that clear?"

Arnaldo mumbled, "Yes, Your Honor."

"Court dismissed. Jarvis, it was good to see you again and looking so well."

"Thank you, Sir."

Out in the hall Herschel said, "Wait here a minute, would you? I'll be right back."

Herschel entered the clerk's office and asked "May I see Judge Hulcurt in his chambers?"

"Yes, go right in."

"Herschel, what can I do for you?"

"Will you be here all day, Your Honor?"

"Until twelve noon. Then I am officially retired."

"Okay, I'll be back here at noon and don't leave until I see you."

"Okay."

"You boys are going to have to spend three more days here then we'll have you shipped to Thomaston."

They still were not happy, but at least they were not making more threats.

"Lee, do you want moose or deer?"

"Moose."

"Dad?"

"Moose."

Herschel loaded his Jeep with boxes and went over to the school. They were more than happy to take the meat and the same with the senior citizen home. There was enough so each resident had a couple of mason jars. Then he took the last box of canned moose meat down to the courthouse.

"Your Honor, would you like a box of canned moose meat?"

"I certainly would and thank you, Herschel."

"You did a mighty fine job bringing those three in. It took a lot of nerve to stay, especially after hearing how they took care of their problems in Boston. From what they had said I wouldn't be a bit surprised to learn that they might be part of a crime syndicate."

"What are you going to do now, Your Honor, now that you're retired?"

"My wife and I are taking the train to Whiskey Jack for some fall fishing."

"Maybe I'll see you up there, Your Honor."

Chapter 5

Rascal and Emma were quiet on the ride home after seeing Archer off. Roscoe Whelling said good morning to them and they acknowledged him. But each were deep in thought.

When they arrived at Whiskey Jack, Roscoe gave them the mail pouch and said, "Archer will be okay, Mr. and Mrs. Ambrose."

"Thank you, Roscoe," Emma said.

"Did Archer get off okay?" Anita asked.

"Yes. I miss him already." They all were quiet for a while. It would take some getting used to. In the academy in Beech Tree he was at least close to home."

Whiskey Jack was looking for him, and then he settled down in the shade on the platform.

That afternoon after the dishes were done and the kitchen picked up, Anita lay down for a nap.

"Em, let's go for a walk."

"Where we going?"

"Oh, let's go up the tracks."

"Do you mind being alone here for a while, Paulette?"

"No, no problem. You two go on."

They had not gone very far when they could hear the afternoon southbound coming so they left the tracks and waited in the shade under a spruce tree at the edge of the right of way. Fred slowed and asked, "Do you folks want a ride back?"

"No thanks, Fred; we're just walking." He waved and continued on.

After the train had passed, they continued on. Rascal stopped and he said, "Can you hear that, Em?"

She was listening and wondering what he was hearing. "What do you hear? All I hear are the birds and squirrels."

"Listen again."

"The mill?"

"Yes. I have never stopped to listen for it before now. The sound reminds me of the days when the village and people were here. We have a good life now, Em, but you know I miss those times."

"I know what you mean; Anita and I often talk about them. Speaking of Anita, I can see her slipping, Rascal. I'll really miss her when she goes. She has been a mother to us both. We both lost our parents when we were so young. I almost cried when Archer called her Grandmother. I know she had tears in her eyes," Emma said.

They hiked all the way to Ledge Swamp and sat down on the grassy knoll. They were quiet for a long time enjoying the stillness and the sounds of nature. The mill noise was left behind.

"Rascal look," and she pointed up the tracks. "It's Bear. He's coming this way."

They remained silent watching as Bear came closer. When he was only fifty feet away, Rascal said, "Hello Bear." He stopped.

Emma also said, "Hi, Bear. Won't you sit for a while. It's too hot to play."

He lay down between the rails directly in front of them. "Relax, Bear; it's too hot to play today."

He stretched his front legs out in front of him and rested his head on his paws. "He has gray on his nose now, Rascal."

"Yes, I see."

They sat there in silence for a while longer, then Emma said, "I think we should be getting back."

"I have to try something, Em." She knew what he was going to do and she made no attempt to stop him. In fact she walked over to Bear with Rascal.

Bear lay still, but watching them. "Hello, old friend," Rascal said and then he reached out to pet his head. "That's a good boy. You have been a good friend, Bear, for most of your life."

Emma then reached out and she pet his head also. "Thank you, Bear, for saving my life." He seemed to understand this and he looked up at her—eye contact. And then he licked her hand a couple of times.

"Come on, Em," and as they were walking away, Bear stood up and then sat on his butt watching them leave. Rascal and Emma stopped, and at the same time, they turned to look at Bear and they raised their hand and made that peculiar greeting sound. Bear returned the greeting.

****

The next morning ten guests arrived for a week of fishing. There were two father and son teams. After lunch they all went out on the lake with canoes. Some were real serious about fishing and some just wanted to go canoeing and wait for evening fishing.

After the evening meal, Paulette decided to walk out to the farm. The evening air was a little cooler now and there was no humidity. She really enjoyed these walks out to the farm to see her Uncle Armand and Aunt Priscilla. Her father, Arnold, was a brother to Armand.

Armand was still in the yard inspecting things and Priscilla had just finished up the evening kitchen and dishes. "Hello, Aunt Priscilla."

"Hello, Paulette. Oh, I have never seen men who can eat so much."

They sat in the living room talking. "Why aren't you married yet, Paulette?"

"I have only met one young man that I would even consider marrying."

"What happened?"

"Archer Ambrose and he will be away for four years in the Naval Academy and I am too old or he is too young."

"The older you are, Paulette, the more difficult it is to find yourself a good man. Perhaps you have been too fussy."

"I have an idea, Paulette, if you play your cards right sometime this week a young man from Beech Tree is coming to work. He is a forester and he'll be taking over the woods operations for Armand. He isn't married."

"What's his name, Aunt Priscilla?"

"Henri, the French spelling. Henri Colton.

"He was up here last week talking with Armand. When he gets here I'll invite you for supper."

Paulette walked back to the lodge feeling a little less melancholy about Archer. Emma noted the change with her right off and asked, "Why are you suddenly so happy?"

"Aunt Priscilla told me a young forester will be arriving sometime this week and he isn't married."

Emma smiled and laughed to herself so she would not embarrass her.

****

Wednesday morning Henri Colton stepped off the train at the farm. He looked around and was impressed with the whole set up. He found Armand's office with little difficulty. "Good morning, Mr. Bowman," Henri said.

"Please, it's Armand, Henri."

"I really like how you have everything set up."

"I'm afraid I only supervised the construction. The entire layout was Earl Hitchcock's idea. He has since retired. But since this is a Hitchcock Company he does pay a visit once in a while.

"There is one point of interest that I would like to make clear. There is no hunting or guns allowed here. That is a rule set by Earl Hitchcock. It has always worked well, so I have kept it."

They spent the rest of the day looking over the large wall map of the area. Where they had already harvested and marked on the map for the year. The different types of forest growth was also noted on the map.

"Your living quarters will be in the farmhouse. You'll take your meals with my wife, Priscilla, and me or with the crew in the dining hall. The upstairs will be yours. There is more than one bedroom and occasionally a businessman will be staying over.

"For the rest of today get yourself acquainted with things and you start your forestry work in the morning."

Priscilla telephoned the lodge and Paulette answered, "Yes."

"Paulette, Mr. Colton is here. Plan on supper Saturday evening at 6 o'clock."

This week's guests were a nice lot. There were no complaints or grumbling even when there were two rainy days in a row. Emma and Paulette made cakes, pies, donuts and continuous coffee and tea.

With more fishing guests coming each year and more guests wanting to take home some smoked trout and togue Rascal had to build a new and bigger smoker. In this new smoker he could now smoke venison and make their own bacon.

"Rascal, if I were to get some rhubarb would you make some wine?"

"Sure, but we'll have to wait until next spring now. This winter I'll make fermenting kegs. You know, that might be fun."

Before that week's guests started arriving Sunday morning, Emma asked Paulette, "Well, are you going to tell us about this young forester?"

"I really like him, Emma. He's quiet around groups of people but after super we went for a walk and neither one of us could stop talking. And instead of talking only about himself, he wanted to know about me. He's a nice looking man too, with fine manners."

"I'm glad for you, Paulette."

Anita said, "You'd better marry this one."

On Sunday, Judge Horace Hulcurt and his wife, Marilyn, arrived at Whiskey Jack. When Rascal recognized him, he stopped and stared for a moment. "Welcome to Whiskey Jack, Lodge Judge."

"Thank you, Rascal, and it isn't judge anymore. I retired last Monday. Right after passing judgment on the Romeros."

"We saw the article in the newspaper but we haven't talked with Herschel or Jarvis."

"Well, for a cup of coffee I'll tell you the whole story. Oh, and this is my wife, Marilyn. This is Rascal and his wife, Emma."

They all sat down in the dining room with the other new guests, and Paulette brought out enough coffee and donuts for everyone. "Paulette, this is retired Judge Hulcurt and his wife, Marilyn. This is Paulette."

"I'd prefer it if you would just call me Horace. It has been a long time since I have seen either of you." Rascal was hoping he wouldn't mention the time Emma was in his court for shooting that July deer. Oh how he hoped he wouldn't.

"We have plenty of room in the lodge for you, but if you would prefer you can have the log cabin across the lake. You still would take your meals here, though," Emma said.

"We would like to see the cabin first."

"I'll walk over with you."

They stopped on the dam, looking up the lake. "My, this is such a beautiful place, Mr. Ambrose," Marilyn said.

"It is, and thank you and please call me Rascal."

"It's odd, Rascal. As much as I enjoy fishing I have never taken the time to take the train up here. I don't suppose you'd have any of that excellent rhubarb wine or brandy?"

Rascal laughed before answering. "No, we don't. We're planning on making some wine next spring when the rhubarb and raspberries are ready to pick."

Rascal and Archer had kept the bushes cut back and the grass trimmed and the weeds pulled around the cabin.

Once outside Marilyn said, "This is wonderful, Rascal. It isn't what I imagined."

"Before we started the lodge, Em and I lived here. There's force fed water and hot water coils in the stove and a root cellar outside. We always enjoyed living here. Now we keep it for couples who would prefer to be by themselves."

"We would like to stay here, Rascal," Marilyn said.

When they were back in the lodge Rascal said, "I'll take your bags up for you. I'll be right back."

While he was gone they were looking at the pictures and letters of commendation from Presidents Cutlidge and Kingsley.

"Emma," Marilyn asked, "Where was this picture taken of you and Rascal with all these dignitaries?"

"Rascal had his hip operated on at Walter Reed Hospital and we were invited for dinner at the White House." Emma explained who everyone was in the picture and why everyone was there.

"You mean you and Rascal played a part in the countries coming together?" Horace asked.

"President Cutlidge and Prime Minister Kingsley met here to discuss the possibility of the two countries merging."

"Unbelievable," Horace said, in a good way.

"What do you hear from Archer, Emma?"

"It has only been two weeks. He said he wasn't sure when he would be able to write."

"You have to have an appointment for the Naval Academy and I'm assuming friends like two former presidents were his appointment."

"Yes, they both were quite taken with Archer."

Some of the guests went fishing right after lunch, while some just wanted to walk around and stretch their muscles. After supper Rascal took Horace and Marilyn out and he wanted to fish up to dark. They both were having good success and releasing most of them. Horace did land one about five pounds that he wanted mounted.

Horace and his wife Marilyn probably enjoyed the week at Whiskey Jack more than the other guests. He was an avid fly fisherman. They had all they wanted to eat and were taking with them one brookie to have mounted.

"You are a different person, Horace, after this week here. You were always so uptight."

That Saturday evening, young Henri Colton, forester, came for supper at the lodge. Rascal, Emma and Anita were impressed with Henri. "Don't you lose this one, Paulette," Anita said.

One night as they were lying in bed, Emma said, "Rascal, have you noticed that most of our guests since the war ended are so much happier than our guests were before the outbreak of the war?"

"I never thought about it, but now that you have said something about it, most of our guests do seem to be merrier."

"I wonder if that might be because people are feeling more secure now and have more confidence in the government since the merger of the United States and Canada."

"I agree, Em. And maybe we should say something to Presidents Kingsley and Cutlidge when they come for Thanksgiving."

"You know, when history is rewritten, Presidents Kingsley and Cutlidge will be remembered as the fathers of this new nation."

****

Archer boarded the train at Beech Tree depot full of both excitement and sadness for leaving home. For the most of that first day he was beginning to question if this is what he wanted. To quit now and go home would disappoint a lot of people.

When he switched trains in Portland he met another young man, Ian McFarland from Dartmouth, Nova Scotia, who had received an appointment to the Annapolis Naval Academy from councilman John Drexel. He had someone to talk with now that took his mind off thoughts of home.

"I have been two days travel from home just to get here," Ian said.

"What did you do in Dartmouth, Ian? I mean your family."

"I come from a long line of fishermen. I told my dad that before I decided to make my life as a fisherman I wanted to see some of the world first and see what it had to offer. I like the ocean, but I want more than to be just a fisherman. What about you, Archer?"

"My mom and dad own a fishing and hunting lodge in the township called Whiskey Jack."

"How big is the township?"

"Thirty-six square miles. My family are the only permanent residents. And it is only accessible by the S&A Railroad. There is a lumber company not far from the lodge where men and women live and work. But when the trees are all harvested, the lumbering community will move on."

Ian's folks couldn't afford to pay for a private berth so Ian was riding in coach. But he and Archer would spend much of their time in Archer's berth.

They were a day early when they arrived in Annapolis. Ian had more experience with city life and transportation. He looked for a transit bus that would take them there.

They found the administration office and were shown to Capt. Ames' office.

"Captain, these are two new midshipman, sir."

"Thank you, Sergeant; that'll be all. Good afternoon. I am Captain Bedford Ames, Commander of the Annapolis Naval Academy and who might you be?"

"I'm Archer Ambrose, Sir, from Whiskey Jack, Maine."

"And I am Ian McFarland, Sir, from Dartmouth, Nova Scotia."

"You were not scheduled to arrive until tomorrow. But no harm done.

"Now I would like to speak with each of you privately. In the next two days I will be speaking privately with each new midshipman. So Mr. McFarland would you go out into the outer room until you are called."

When the door had closed the Capt. said, "You may sit down, Mr. Ambrose." Then, "You had received two appointments to this Academy from two former presidents; they obviously saw something in you. That must be quite an honor, Mr. Ambrose."

"I'm not sure how to comment, Captain Ames. Both presidents are friends of the family."

"How did this friendship come about?"

"Well, Sir, it began before I was born. They met at my family's fishing and hunting lodge to discuss the possibility of the two countries coming together to form a new nation. And they both have remained friends of my family ever since."

"This lodge wouldn't be Whiskey Jack would it, Mr. Ambrose?"

"Yes, Sir, it is." The Capt. was momentarily quiet and Archer continued. "At Whiskey Jack, our family consists of close friends and President Cutlidge and President Kingsley and their bodyguards Mr. Butler and Mr. Dubois, have become part of this family."

"Extraordinary, but your acquaintance—that is, friendship —with them both is not what impressed me most about you. You were asked to write an essay why you wanted to attend the Naval Academy and why you wish to become a Naval officer. You, Mr. Ambrose, wrote the shortest essay of any of them. Some essays were as long as four pages. Whereas yours was one page. Where others would use fifty words to say something you would use fifteen to say the exact same thing. You were very to the point and said, I think, exactly what you wanted to say."

They talked for a few more minutes before Archer was dismissed. "You can send Mr. McFarland in."

Twenty minutes later Ian came out of Capt. Ames' office. "He said to wait here and an upper midshipman will show us to our room. Here he comes now I believe."

"Mr. Ambrose, Mr. McFarland if you would follow me." They were taken to the dormitory on the fourth floor. "Tomorrow two more new midshipmen will be assigned to this room also. Dinner is at 1800 hours and since you do not yet have a uniform, you'll be expected to wear a tie and coat. Before entering the dining hall we line up outside in the hall. The lower midshipmen are at the end. After you have been excused from the dining hall you'll be free to walk about the grounds. And again, with coat and tie, since you have no uniform yet. Any questions?"

"No."

Archer chose a bed close to the window and Ian took the top bunk. "This is so different than the life I am used to," Archer said.

More new midshipmen started arriving at 8 a.m. By noon everyone was accounted for. Archer and Ian now had two more roommates, Harry Bibley, a farmer from Greeley, Nebraska, and Charles Andrews, a cattle rancher from Red Deer, Alberta. The four hit it off immediately. And Archer's homesickness was now a thought in the past.

****

The first two weeks were the worst. This traditionally was a testing period to see who could take it and who couldn't. By the middle of the second week, two young men from Florida had had enough. It certainly was a time of growing. Archer could now understand why President Kingsley had said he would be pushed beyond his limits. But neither Archer nor his roommates were about to quit.

They were up every morning at 4 a.m., running and calisthenics before breakfast, and then classroom studies until 4 p.m. minus a half-hour for lunch. At 1900 hours they had an hour of self-defense and then they studied for the next day.

During some free time on the third weekend, he managed to find time to write a letter home.

****

On Friday when Emma opened the pouch, she began screaming and shouting. Everyone ran to see what had happened.

"What is it, Em?" Rascal asked.

"Archer!" was all she was able to say at first. "Archer, we have a letter from Archer."

"Open it, Em, and read it out loud."

There were three pages. Emma was so excited she had a difficult time holding her hands steady enough so she could read it.

When she had finished she began to cry and she said in between sobs, "He did it. He arrived in Annapolis all on his own. Our son, Rascal, is going to be a Naval officer."

"He sure sounded like he got over his homesickness," Anita said.

Everyone wanted to read the letter silently to themselves. Even Paulette, who was now head over heels crazy about the new forester, Henri Colton. When she had finished reading she said, "Archer is going to *be* someone, someday." They all knew what she was saying.

The stress Emma had been feeling since Archer's departure was now lifted. She knew he had made it safely to Annapolis and his letter sounded happy. She took a deep breath and let it out. Rascal noticed her eyes were watery and asked, "Are you alright, Em?"

"Yes, it's just that now I know he is okay. I guess my emotions got the better of me." Rascal hugged her.

****

Three weeks after the Romeros had been sentenced and transported to the Thomaston State Prison, two men in dark suits entered the sheriff's office. Sheriff Burlock looked up from his desk and immediately recognized Special Agents Harris and Billadoc. "Good morning, gentlemen. What is the FBI doing back in Beech Tree?"

"We would like to talk to you about the Romero case," Billadoc said.

"Okay, but maybe you should hear the story from the arresting officer."

"And who is that?"

"Warden Herschel Page. You must remember him from the Hans Hessel case."

"Would you know if he is around?" Harris asked.

"He's off today so he probably is home. I'll telephone him."

"Hello, Perline, Sheriff Burlock. Is Herschel there?"

"Yes, he is right here."

"Hello."

"Herschel, Lee, can you come down to the office as soon as you can?"

"Sure, ten minutes."

"That'll be fine."

Ten minutes later in everyday clothes Herschel walked into the sheriff's office. He recognized the two men. "Agents Harris and Billadoc, what brings you back to Beech Tree?"

"You, actually, when you arrested the Romeros. When your sheriff transports them to prison, the warden always forwards the paperwork to the state police and then to our office in Boston.

"The family has a rough reputation. I'm surprised they didn't shoot you and leave you for the animals to clean up."

"They tried."

"We gathered that after reading their medical files. How long were they here, do you know?"

"Three days before I arrested them. I had seen tire tracks going in on the West Road. There are no streams, lakes or ponds accessible from the West Road, so when I returned two days later the vehicle had not come back out."

"How did you know this?"

"I would check the mud puddles. The only tire tracks visible had driven into the water and on the other side the water would wash the tracks away."

"Good observation," Billadoc said.

"I found a place to hide my vehicle and with my backpack I hiked in until I found the vehicle."

"What day was this?"

"September first."

"That explains a lot."

"Explains what?" Burlock asked.

"The old man, the one the boys called Pops, Arnaldo, had been released from prison four months earlier. He was sentenced to five years for nearly beating a police officer to death. He was sentenced to five years, did four years and paroled because of good conduct. We always figured the two sons were there at the time and Pops took the rap and we think he paid someone to give his sons an alibi.

"He was put on probation for five years and could not leave Massachusetts or be in possession of a firearm.

"What about the rifle and handguns?"

"I took the rifle to the headquarters in August and the handguns I left with Sheriff Burlock."

"They are still locked up in the evidence locker."

"We'll have to have those," Harris said.

"The grand jury in Boston had handed down warrants of arrest for the two boys; Armino and Tony. A year ago while Pops was in prison the two boys took a Mr. Sinclair out on a boat, about three miles off the coast and shot him, and after tying cement blocks to his ankles, they dropped him overboard.

"What the boys didn't know at the time was a new submarine was on a trial run from Groton, Connecticut. They had stopped and the periscope was up and the skipper just happened to be looking through it at the time and he snapped several pictures. He documented the exact coordinates. The skipper immediately contacted our office from the sub and if we liked he would get a diving team to recover the body.

"All this took time, and as the grand jury was sitting the Romeros disappeared. Now we know where they went, "Billadoc said.

"And that explains why they capitulated so readily. They would rather spend eighteen months in prison where they would feel somewhat safe, instead of facing murder charges at home," Sheriff Burlock said.

"That's what we were thinking, too, on our way up here," Billadoc said.

"While I was watching the cabin I overheard conversations that made me believe there was something back home that they were afraid of. And Pops said they would take care of any game warden who intruded just like they do police officers back home. So this is probably what they were afraid of.

"What kind of business where they in?" Herschel asked. "I know they had three restaurants. But they must have been involved with something more."

Harris said," We have suspected for a long time that they were using the restaurants to launder money for organized crime. We even offered Pops a deal if he would give us the information we needed."

"What will happen to them now, Agent Billadoc?" Burlock asked.

"We'll leave Pops in prison in Thomaston but the two boys we'll take back to Boston to stand trial for murder.

"When we're through with the Romeros none of them will ever be coming back to Maine."

"That *is* good news."

"Warden Page, why did you take it upon yourself to go after the Romeros?" Billadoc asked.

"Well, I had no idea who was in there or that they were doing anything illegal until I arrived at the cabin. There is no fishing in there and the lumbering operations had stopped. I guess I was just curious what was going on. Once I knew what they were doing I wasn't about to leave."

"Not even after you heard what they would do to you if you showed up?"

"I was concerned, but I had the advantage. They did not know I was there."

"That was pretty gutsy, just the same. I don't suppose we could talk you into coming over with us?" Harris asked.

Herschel grinned and said, "Not a chance. This is fun."

Sheriff Burlock smiled. He understood.

"Well, thank you very much, Herschel; you have certainly helped to put three bad-asses away for a very long time."

When Herschel returned home, his Mom and Dad had just arrived. "What was that meeting all about, son?" Jarvis asked.

"Those were the same two FBI agents from Boston who came after Hans Hessel." And he told the whole story of the Romeros.

"Well, I guess you won't ever have to worry about them again.

"Have you tried any of that canned moose meat?"

"Yes. They sure knew how to can. It's delicious," Jarvis said.

On their way home Jarvis said, "I'm so proud of our son, Rita."

"So am I. Just like I was always proud of you, Jarvis."

"He's busier than I was, though."

"There are more people from the outside now," Rita said.

"You know, except for missing you and the family, it was a great life."

Chapter 6

Every weekend Paulette and Henri would have dinner together and during the day on Saturday they would go for walks or an occasional canoe ride up to the head of the lake. They were falling in love and they both were aware of it.

They were always so happy when they were together, and Rascal and Emma were happy for them both. But maybe not quite as happy as Anita.

She still considered herself the grand matriarch. Although she would not ever tell anyone that this is how she felt.

Before the deer hunting season, they decided to get married, but not until spring breakup. "April will be a good time, Paulette. The woods will be shut down and there won't be any fishermen at the lodge until May."

One rainy day, Emma gave Paulette the day off and she and Henri took the train to Lac St. Jean and when they were back at the lodge, Paulette showed everyone her new diamond ring. This started Rascal thinking, but he didn't say anything.

By the end of September, and the end of fall fishing, and not having to work on firewood, Rascal prepared his traps. He had noticed the beaver were back in the flowage behind the log cabin and a new beaver house was at the mouth of the no name brook.

After all the fishermen had left for the year, occasionally they would see Bear lying in the sunshine on the hill by the cabin and once in front of the cabin. He was still watching over Whiskey Jack Lodge, making sure no unwanted intruders came near. After he had killed the wolf that was going to attack Emma, there was never again any wolf signs or howls around the lodge or lake. There were bobcats and lynx, but no mountain lions.

After supper one night in the light of the full moon, Rascal and Emma walked up to the log cabin and sat on the porch, reminiscing of the days when this was their home.

They were not as busy and the days were quiet, it seemed, even with the noise of the mill. The people who lived here were all good people. They were all friends. "It's been twenty years, Rascal, since the Hitchcock Lumber Company moved their operations and burnt the remaining homes. Where did the years go?"

"It has gone fast hasn't it, Em?"

"I wonder if Archer has time to remember his life here? I would hate to think that he would forget it."

"He won't forget, Em. The life he lived here is now part of him. It has helped to make him who he is."

They sat in silence then cuddling together watching the ripples on the lake in the moonlight.

"Is there any brandy here, Rascal? For some odd reason I would like a little right now."

"I think there is in the cabinet."

Rascal went inside and lit a kerosene lantern. There was half a bottle of ginger brandy. Emma came in and she put on a jacket and found one for Rascal, then they went back on the porch and put the lantern on the living room window sill. Rascal poured a half glass for each and then he sat back down with Emma.

The brandy was letting their blood circulate a bit faster and this made them feel warmer, even though the air was beginning to cool.

They stayed on the porch until they were too cold to stay any longer and with their arms around each other they walked back to the lodge.

****

At breakfast the next morning, Emma said, "The first three weeks of deer season we have almost a full house each week. Paulette and I need more help."

"What have you in mind, Em?"

"We hire another woman for the season."

"Okay, do you have any ideas?" Rascal asked.

Paulette spoke up first, "I do."

"Okay, let's hear it, Paulette," Emma said.

"I have a friend in Lac St. Jean who finished school this year and is looking for work."

"What's her name?"

"Amy Paquin. Her father is French and her mother is Indian, Abenaki. We keep in touch with letters and she said if you ever needed any more help to let her know."

"Can you telephone her and ask her if she is still interested?"

"I'll do it right now."

Fifteen minutes later Paulette came back to the table. "It's all set. She'll be on the afternoon southbound."

"I have an idea, Rascal. There isn't much left for goods in the old store. What if we cleared it all out and made another room, big enough for both Paulette and Amy. That would free up another room upstairs."

"It won't take much work, you'll need curtains, rugs for the floor and two more bureaus. I'll start making closets today."

"We'll need mirrors."

"Make a list of what you'll need and then you and Paulette can go to town after it."

What was left in the old general store, Rascal took out to the shed for now. Then on the wall which separated that room from Anita's, he began to build a long closet along the length of the wall.

Amy Paquin arrived at 2:30 p.m. on the southbound. Paulette was waiting for her on the platform. "Oh, Paulette, I'm so excited about working here. I was so wanting to be out from under

Mom and Dad. I really don't think they wanted me to come."

"Come in and I'll introduce you to everyone."

When Amy and Paulette entered the dining room, the others were quiet and stared at Amy. She was slim and taller than Paulette, her black hair long and in a ponytail, and a slight bronze tint to her skin color—a strikingly pretty young woman. "Amy, this is Anita Antony, Rascal and Emma Ambrose." Amy giggled at the name Rascal. Rascal was used to it, so it no longer bothered him.

Until Rascal had the new bedroom finished, Amy would use one of the upstairs rooms.

There wasn't much to do until deer season so Paulette showed her around. After Paulette and Amy went upstairs, Anita said, "How are you ever going to get your hunters out the door with such attractive help inside?"

"Maybe I'll teach her to guide," they all laughed.

****

The next day Emma, Paulette and Amy took the train to Beech Tree for two beds, bureaus, mirrors, rugs and anything else they would need for the new room, including wallpaper and curtains for the two windows. Emma made arrangements to have everything shipped to Whiskey Jack in four days.

Once that was done, they had lunch and then went grocery shopping for the upcoming season.

Amy was already feeling at home. Paulette was like a big sister to her and she liked Emma immediately. Rascal and Anita, well, maybe later.

That day as Rascal worked on the new bedroom, he began laughing. "What's so funny, Rascal?" Anita asked.

"So we can have this bedroom finished before our guests start arriving, I don't think I'll be doing too much trapping," but he was happy having to do it.

When Emma, Paulette and Amy arrived on the northbound, Rascal, with some of Anita's help, had supper all ready.

"This reminds me, Rascal, when you would have supper ready when I got home from work when the village was here."

There was enough flooring leftover from the spring addition, to do the new bedroom. Rascal had the room well under construction when the furnishings from town arrived four days later. "You women are going to have to do the wallpapering. I don't have the patience for that."

When the wallpaper was hung and dry, Rascal began sanding the floor and the next day he applied a coat of shellac. "Wow, this is the prettiest bedroom I have ever had," Amy exclaimed.

Rascal and Emma felt as if they had inherited a daughter and Anita a granddaughter. On Saturday, while Rascal was applying another coat of shellac to the floor, Paulette and Amy walked out to the farm. "I want you to meet Henri, Amy."

On the way out Paulette said, "Amy, there are a few secrets here that are just part of Whiskey Jack. And some of these I have not said anything about to my aunt and uncle or Henri. All I can say now, Amy, is that when the time is right, you'll be brought in."

"Okay, let's start with those pictures, plaques and letters of commendation in the dining room," Amy said.

Paulette explained all about Presidents Cutlidge and Kingsley. "Have you met them both, Paulette?"

"Yes, they both were here in July," she almost told her they would be returning for the family Thanksgiving , but she decided to let it be a surprise.

****

Working on the new bedroom long hours every day Rascal now had one week to set traps before guests started arriving. He loaded his canoe and headed for the head of the lake and up along Jack Brook. He would have liked very much to set traps around Ledge Swamp but he didn't want to offend Bear.

He set traps along the brook for two miles before

crossing over and setting a few on the north side of the brook as he worked his way back. By the time he was back at the lake, it was time to find a crossing. He had not seen any beaver wood along the brook and this surprised him.

The next day he set behind the log cabin. He made a set where his trap line trail met the road and another at the end of the log yard and then two sets on the beaver dam. He caught three extra-large beaver before moving on. He cut through the woods to his trap line trail and made a set and another near the old salt lick and another at the rock where the trail makes a hard left back to the lake.

The sun was just going down when he arrived home. "Will you tend your traps tomorrow, Rascal?" Emma asked.

"Yes."

"I'd like to go with you."

"Okay."

They made an early start and Emma helped to paddle. There wasn't a ripple on the water. They saw several does with lambs feeding along the shore. And two large bucks where they had their rocked fire pit near the mouth of Jack Brook.

At the first set was a covey set and a water set for otter. "You take the covey set, Em, and I'll take the water set."

"What do I do if there is something in the trap?"

"Use the axe handle and hit it on top of the head. You'll probably only knock it out, so put your foot on the ribcage and press down some. This will stop the heart."

Rascal heard a shrill scream and Emma hollered, "Rascal, it's a bobcat."

"Okay, I'll be right there." He had an otter. He shot the otter in the ear and then the bobcat.

He put them in his pack basket and reset both traps and they moved on. By the time they were at the end of the trap line on that side of the brook they had a male fisher, and three martins. "That's not bad for the first tend."

There were two spruce partridges sitting on the same

limb and with his .22 pistol he shot them both. While Emma was cooking lunch Rascal began skinning.

As they were eating Emma said, "I think I'd rather have beaver to eat, and this partridge tastes funny."

"It's a spruce partridge and they do taste different. Not as good. But it was either these two or nothing at all."

On the north side of the brook and going back towards the lake they picked up another bobcat, fisher and otter. They took the time to skin those while the bodies were still warm. Emma had made a small fire and made some hot tea.

When the skinning was done they sat on the bank next to the brook and in the sunshine, sipping hot tea.

They talked until their tea was gone and the sun was below the treetops. "We have just enough time to canoe back down the lake before dark."

There was a little breeze and it was to their back and it wasn't long before they were pulling up to the wharf. While supper was being made, Rascal put the pelts on stretchers.

Emma was tired and her head kept bobbing during supper. With the kitchen cleaned she excused herself and went to bed. Rascal stayed up until the others also went to bed and then he turned the generator off and joined Emma.

She woke up when Rascal crawled into bed and she said, "Being in the fresh air and doing all that hiking today made me tired. But a good tired, if you know what I mean."

Rascal stretched out on his back and put his arm around Emma and said, "This bed does feel pretty good, doesn't it."

****

At breakfast the next morning Rascal asked, "Do you want to go again today, Em? It'll be a shorter day."

To his surprise Emma said, "Sure, as long as we don't have to eat any more spruce partridge."

"No, no spruce birds. We'll have beaver to eat today."

"You go ahead, Emma, we'll clean up and take care of

things," Paulette said.

At the beginning of his trap line trail they had a nice big fisher that was angrier than hell. "Boy, is he mad," Emma said.

They had quite a surprise on the beaver dam. Both traps were gone and in one was a nice lynx. "Boy, this is a first," Rascal said.

"Do you suppose he was after a beaver and stepped into the trap?" Emma asked.

"That or he was after a drink of water." The other trap had another extra-large beaver and not wanting to carry the carcass all day, he took the time to skin it and cut off the meat for lunch later.

Before finishing the lynx, another trap snapped closed and there was a lot of splashing on the dam as the beaver struggled to swim to deeper water.

"That's five beaver from here. I think we should leave the rest. Will you pull the other trap and I'll skin this?"

It takes time to skin an animal while it is lying on the ground and by the time they reached the corner rock it was time for lunch. On the trap line they picked up two martin; at the rock they had a red fox.

Emma started a fire and put some beaver meat on to roast and water to boil for tea.

"Oh, this beaver is so much better than that spruce bird yesterday."

Rascal put more wood on the fire while they finished eating and their tea. Emma ate two hind legs before she had had enough.

They lay back watching the clouds overhead for a while. An hour later Rascal woke Emma up and said, "Come on, Em, or it'll be dark before we get back."

They had another fisher cat and two more martins. "I think I'll pull the traps tomorrow up along Jack Brook. Then on Saturday, before the guests arrive on Sunday, I'll pull everything on this line. We have done very well for a short time."

After supper they all sat in the living room talking and listening to the radio. Anita was the first to go to her bedroom, and then Paulette and Amy. Rascal shut off the generator and he and Emma went up to bed also.

Emma rolled over so she was resting on his chest and she said, "After eating that wild meat today, I'm horny."

****

The next morning Rascal was feeling like a new man. Emma noticed the difference; how he was happier and had more energy. "I can see last night did you some good, Rascal," Emma said.

Rascal grinned and said, "It sure did."

"Me, too."

Paulette, Anita and Amy looked at each other and smiled.

"Do you want to go with me again today, Em?"

"Yes, but I think I'd better stay. We working ladies need to do a lot of baking."

He kissed her goodbye and canoed up to Jack Brook. There was an otter in the first set which was a water set. And in the water set in the stream that comes out of the old beaver flowages by mile twelve along the tracks, he had a super large beaver. He was a while skinning it and cutting off the meat and castors.

Then he continued up the brook. By the time he reached the last trap on that side of the brook, he had one more fisher and two martins. Coming down the north side he picked up only two more martins.

He made a fire where he and Emma had two days ago, and began roasting beaver and boiling tea. He was hungry and put more meat than usual on to cook.

The tea was made before the meat was cooked and he sipped on a cup while he waited. It wasn't long and the smallest piece was done and he took it off the stick and replaced it with another to cook. That one piece of meat didn't last long. But by now the others were done and he had put more on to roast.

The air was permeated with the delicious aroma of roasting meat. He put on the front legs, whole, to roast, while he finished eating what was already cooked. Eventually he had had enough and he leaned back against a tree holding his cup of tea in both hands. His mind and thoughts were far away. Thinking about his son, Archer.

Being so still, he was aware of a very slight noise behind him. As he waited to see what it was, the noise was coming closer and closer. Rascal turned his head to the left, only a little. But enough to see Bear, now standing right by his left shoulder.

"Hello, Bear. Are you hungry?" Bear lay down beside Rascal and his head was touching Rascal's knee. Rascal pulled one of the legs off the fire and held it out for Bear. At first he just sniffed it and then very gently he took it from Rascal and began eating it.

Rascal finished cooking the other leg and took a bite and then gave it to Bear. Rascal was amazed at how gentle Bear was. Then Rascal got out the rest of the beaver meat from his pack basket to roast. He poured himself another cup of tea and leaned back against the tree waiting for the meat to cook and talking with Bear. He made no effort to pet him.

"You'll probably be hibernating soon fella—but maybe not until you cleaned up a few gut piles from deer my sports will shoot."

When the meat was done, Rascal ate one piece and gave the rest to Bear. When the meat was all gone he leaned back against the tree, again holding his cup of tea between his hands. Bear rested his head on his front paws and now he was touching Rascal's leg. All the while Rascal kept talking, to calm the gentle beast.

His tea gone he set the cup down and he just had to try it. He reached across Bear's back and gently laid his arm on him. This did not disturb Bear in the least. His eyes were closed and Rascal thought perhaps he was asleep.

Blue jays, gorbies and red squirrels had gathered in the trees and instead of scolding, they perched silently watching this rare moment of man and beast. Rascal was filled with emotions knowing that Bear must be about at the end of his life. And he smiled and said, "But you have had a good life, ole friend."

Twilight was beginning to creep toward the dark hours of night and Rascal knew he must leave. "I must leave now, Bear."

Bear reacted and stood and moved off to one side as Rascal picked up and put the fire out and shouldered his pack basket. Bear followed behind him as he crossed Jack Brook and down to his canoe.

Rascal seated in the canoe seat reached out with his arm and said, "Goodbye, Bear," and then he made that peculiar sound. Bear raised his paw and made the same sound.

It was almost completely dark when he tied off to the wharf. He left his pack basket out in the cool evening air and went inside to wash up.

Everyone was waiting for him in the dining room. "What took you so long, Rascal? Did you catch so many?"

"Bear. I'll tell you after I've washed up and changed my clothes."

Amy looked at Paulette and said, "Bear?"

"Yes, and I think you'll soon be included in one of Whiskey Jack's secrets." That's all Paulette would say.

Twenty minutes later they all sat down at the table. Emma said, "Okay, okay, what about Bear?"

"Do you remember where we stopped across the brook near the mouth and you built a fire and we had some tea?"

"Yeah."

"Well, I caught one whopper of a beaver in that stream, the beaver dam-up that causes problems for the railroad. I made a fire where you did and put a lot of beaver meat on to roast. I was hungry. Before it was cooked, Bear came in and laid down right beside me. I shared the meat with him until it was gone.

Then he put his head on his paws, so his head was touching my knee. After a while I put my arm across his back. He never flinched or moved. He laid right there until I had to leave."

"Did he look okay Rascal?"

"Yes, and he has put on a lot of winter fat. When I got up to leave he followed behind me down to the canoe."

"You have a pet bear?" Amy asked.

Emma said, "Not a pet. He is wild. But I think he has adopted us as his family. Now, Amy, we don't tell people about Bear. Only those whom we consider family."

"I haven't even told my aunt and uncle, Amy, nor Henri. There is much more to the story of Bear, but I'll—we'll tell you everything after supper."

"If you don't' stop talking," Anita said, "our supper is going to get cold."

"You have done real well haven't you, in so a short of time?" Emma asked.

"Yes, real good. I think it pays off not to trap every year. I'll pull the traps tomorrow behind the cabin and that'll be it for this year."

"Rascal, would you like me to put your hides on the stretchers tomorrow?" Amy asked. "I used to do all the stretching for my dad when he trapped."

"That would be helpful. Can you spare her tomorrow, Em? I know you said something about doing a lot of baking."

"We did some today, so you can help Rascal tomorrow if you like."

Later that night when Paulette and Amy were alone in their bedroom, Paulette told her all about Bear. "I hope I get to see him sometime."

"Remember not a word to anyone, Amy. Rascal does not let anyone hunt around Ledge Swamp because that is Bear's territory and he doesn't let anyone shoot bear. Not at all."

He had pulled the two traps off the dam two days ago so he was able to make the trip around and back home before the middle of the afternoon. "Well?" Emma asked.

"Two red foxes and two martin."

He looked at the hides Amy had put on stretchers and she had done a good job. Even the beaver pelt, and it was stretched oval and not round. "Where did you learn how to nail off beaver hides so nicely?"

"My dad was very fussy. He wouldn't let me flesh 'em, he said he didn't want me to be putting any holes in 'em. How did you flesh it? You didn't do it here."

"I flesh the hide as I skin 'em. It takes a little longer to skin but when I'm done it is also all fleshed."

Emma and Paulette baked all day, while in the afternoon Amy tidied up each room and made sure there were towels and washcloths in each room, and then dusted.

Whiskey Jack spent his day in the sunshine on the platform. When he saw Rascal walking across the dam he ran over to greet him.

Chapter 7

All of the week's guests arrived on the morning train. The women had coffee and fresh donuts ready for them. There were two rooms in the lodge not being used and neither was the log cabin. There were two fathers with a son each who was about Amy's age and they both were drawn to her like iron filings to a magnet.

That evening after supper Rascal explained the lodge rules and why no one was to hunt near or around Ledge Swamp. "We don't want you shooting any bear. This is a fishing and deer hunting lodge and that is what we want to be known as."

The next morning Fred Darling stopped the engine at the platform and Rascal asked, "What's up, Fred?"

"I hit a moose at mile nine. I think it'll only have a broken front leg."

"Thanks, Fred."

He went inside to change his clothes and to tell Emma. "Emma I'm going after an injured moose at mile nine. I think I'll take it out to the farm so I won't have to deal with it."

He strapped on his .45 in case he had to finish it off and put a chain and axe in the crawler bucket. The Jarvis Trail would take him close to mile nine. He drove out to the Jarvis Trail and met a few hunters going back to the lodge already after the morning hunt.

Where he intersected the tracks the right of way on the right was passable with the crawler. He had worried about this. Right at the mile nine sign post he found a mass of moose hair but no blood. The ground had been disturbed and he saw where the moose had struggled to its feet. Its trail was easy to follow. Now he wished he had brought his rifle.

To the right side where the beaver would flood the area there was an old road that went back about two hundred feet where the railroad had dug out gravel to use in the railroad bed. With one broken front leg the moose couldn't climb the steep bank. It was a large bull and when he saw Rascal he tried desperately to climb over. He fell back and Rascal placed a shot right behind the antlers.

He hooked a chain around the front shoulders and lifted the moose off the ground enough to make cleaning the innards out easier. He even removed the liver and would leave it with the paunch for Bear.

Not wanting to have to drag it all the way to the farm, he put the bucket under the mid-section of the moose and he chained the head and hind legs to the bucket support arms. "There that should hold it."

With the moose in the bucket it was a very slow trip. He was an hour getting to the lodge where he turned onto the old farm road. This road was easier going and he was only another half hour. Armand was happy to have the moose. "I want the antlers, Armand."

"Antlers—they are no good to eat. You can have them."

Rascal used the crawler to hang the moose up with block and tackle. "When we have the moose cut up, we will cut off the antlers for you," Armand said. "This moose the men and women here will enjoy and the women can make mincemeat from the meat in the neck. Thank you, Rascal."

Rascal walked the crawler back to the lodge. He had missed lunch and now he was hungry. Emma fixed him a bowl of soup and a sandwich. Paulette and Amy were upstairs making beds.

****

The next morning Rascal went out for the newspaper and

the mail pouch. There was a letter from Archer. He went back inside and gave it to Emma.

He had been at the academy now for six weeks and he was enjoying the physical training and he was learning things that went so far beyond what he could learn at the Beech Tree Academy, and he was just as happy with the academics and study as he was with the physical training.

He wrote about each of his roommates and how well they were getting along. Toward the end of his letter he said he would have liked to meet the new helper, Amy, before he left.

By the end of that first week, six nice bucks had been taken, two big does and a skipper. The nights were cold so the deer were freezing and the hunters wouldn't have any problem about them spoiling before they could get home.

The second week they had two more hunters than the first week, but this group were so much merrier. There were a few who didn't care if they shot a deer or not. They wanted the relaxation, camp life and good food. And there was always plenty of that.

Rascal was having to help Amy cleaning rooms and making beds. Anita was not able to do much now and Emma and Paulette were too busy in the kitchen to think about anything else.

One hunter from Pennsylvania shot a fourteen point buck Friday afternoon. And the weather had turned too warm for him to try to take the whole deer back. So he and Rascal skun it and boxed up the head and cape. "I really hate to leave this meat here but it would only spoil and I don't want the hide spoiled."

Rascal hung the skinned deer up in the cold storage room.

The next week two more large bucks were shot and they too took only the head and cape.

The next week Emma served deer meat for one meal. That week there was a little snow and the air was cold. Which made for good hunting.

By the time their season ended everyone at the lodge was tired and were ready for a rest. Except now the family was coming and would probably start arriving on Tuesday. So far no one had told Amy that Presidents Cutlidge and Kingsley were coming. Only that the Page families were coming. But Amy was wondering why so much food was being prepared ahead of their arrival.

Amy was aware of all the excitement of the upcoming family gathering and wondered why all the excitement. Who was coming? She really wanted to ask, but she didn't.

On Tuesday before their Thursday Thanksgiving, Jarvis, Rita, Perline, and her daughter, Emma Jean, arrived on the morning train. "Herschel said he will be here on the afternoon train," Perline said.

"Emma, if my daughter Emma Jean doesn't ask about Archer don't be too surprised. A new family had moved to Beech Tree during the summer and Emma Jean met their son, Jacob, who is only two years older, at school. And now she is head over heels for Jacob," Perline said.

There was plenty of kitchen help now and Perline, Amy and Emma Jean went off by themselves. After several cups of coffee, Jarvis said, "I'd like to take a walk to the farm."

"You men go ahead, we have enough to do here," Emma said.

"Did you do any trapping this year, Rascal?"

"Em helped me out some and we trapped for a week. Did quite well in fact, for only a week. Of course we had two long trap lines. It'll be interesting to see what they'll bring when I take 'em in."

"I've heard rumors that the price for beaver and otter have really increased."

"That's good news."

"How was the deer hunting?"

"The lodge shot more deer, but we had more guests each week than before. There was one fourteen pointer taken. A hunter from Pennsylvania. There were several six, eight and ten pointers and some does and two spike horns."

"Do you think the area is being over hunted?"

"There doesn't seem to be a lack of deer showing up. I think the lumbering draws deer in from other areas, because of the easy feed."

"That's good to hear." Then on a different note Jarvis said, "You and Emma have done well for yourselves with the lodge."

"Yes we have, and there have been times when we both think maybe we have bitten off more than we can chew. But those times seem to have a way of working out. We both still miss the activity of the mill and village and the people that used to live here.

"So do I, so do I. Everyone always made me feel welcome."

They were walking across the mill yard, Jarvis said, "Things surely don't look the same here, do they. This is set up much like Kidney Pond."

Armand saw them and walked over to greet them. "This is quite a set up, Armand," Jarvis said.

"Yes, it works real good. Most of the designs were Hitchcock. I've done a little to make operations easier."

"How long will you be in here, Armand?"

"The plan is for ten years. But that will depend if we have everything harvested by then."

Armand excused himself, "I really must get back to work. Walk around and help yourselves."

They walked through what was left of the old field and they could see deer in the old choppings. "I see what you were saying about the deer. They have no fear of us."

"Armand has been a good employee and supervisor for the Hitchcock brothers. I don't believe either one of them could have had this operation here run any more efficient," Jarvis said.

As they were walking back to the lodge, Jarvis said, "You

know, Rascal, someday there'll be roads into Whiskey Jack and the farm. I probably will never see it and you may or may not. But it will happen."

"I have thought along those same lines, Jarvis. If and when it happens, I hope I'm not around to see it. It would spoil the area.

"Do you want to go hunting this afternoon?" Rascal asked.

"Maybe tomorrow morning; I'd just like to visit today."

They were back in time for lunch and after the kitchen and dining room cleaned, they all sat in the living room talking with coffee.

Everyone wanted to know about Archer and how he was doing. Emma kept watching Emma Jean for her reactions. It was almost as if she wasn't even listening. Probably thinking about her new boyfriend, Jacob. Emma was thinking she was glad she didn't have to go through that puppy love stage again.

Even after supper they all stayed up late talking.

The next morning the rest of the Whiskey Jack family arrived on the morning southbound from Lac St. Jean. Everyone was on the platform to greet them. And still no one had told Amy who would be arriving. When the passenger car stopped, Mr. Butler and Mr. Dubois stepped off first and casually surveyed the area and then turned to look inside the car and they both nodded their heads. President Cutlidge and his wife Pearl and grandson, Jeffery, stepped off first. Then President Kingsley, his wife, Myrissa and their granddaughter, Susan. Then Mrs. Butler, Alice and their son, John, and his wife, Bonnie, and then Mr. Dubois, his wife Alice and daughter, Belle.

Amy looked shocked, "Oh my God! Presidents Cutlidge and Kingsley." She looked at Paulette and Paulette smiled and said, "Another secret."

They were shown to their rooms. The older adults were in the new addition rooms and the others were upstairs. Rascal looked at Emma and said, "This is quite a house full."

"Sure is. Fifteen plus Herschel when he gets here and five of us. That's twenty-one for Thanksgiving dinner. I'm glad we have been doing some baking already."

"Do we have enough food for everyone, Em?" Rascal asked jokingly.

"Well if we don't we can send them to the local restaurant."

Kingsley, Cutlidge, Butler and Dubois had brought hunting rifles with them. "We would like to go out this afternoon, Rascal."

"Okay. Do you feel up to it, Jarvis?"

"Certainly."

"Okay, you take President Cutlidge and Mr. Butler out to the glade and I'm sure you know how to hunt that, and I'll take President Kingsley and Mr. Dubois out behind the cabin.

Herschel arrived on the northbound before they left to go hunting and he decided to stay at the lodge and relax. He had had a busy deer season. With lost hunters and another hunting accident.

All of the new members of the family wanted to know all about game warden Herschel Page, and he kept them entertained until the hunters were back.

Jarvis had Cutlidge sit on the famous rock while he and Butler went up to the beechnut grove and then cut back down to the glade. He let Butler take the game trail while he stayed off to his right. "Don't walk fast. Take your time and stop often to listen. I'll be off to your right within hearing distance."

At the top of the hill, Rascal stopped to check for tracks at the trap line trail. There were three separate tracks made by large adult bucks. "The wind right now is coming towards us from the northwest. President Kingsley, if you'd sit back here on this rock, Francois and I will circle around and hunt back to you. Be prepared because I think we'll push a deer out of there."

Francois followed Rascal to the beaver flowage and stopped to listen. Francois whispered, "Why didn't you bring a rifle?"

"Several guests left their meat and took only the head and cape. We have plenty of meat."

Rascal pointed straight ahead. Two flags were just disappearing. "They're in here already. Come on."

Rascal and Francois followed the stream, so that the water would cover up some of their own noise. They went beyond the corner before starting back. "Stay on this game trail and keep watching to both sides and stop often to listen. I'll be on your right not too far away."

Jarvis watched Butler for a few minutes to make sure he was not going too fast. There were deer tracks and droppings everywhere. Ray spooked a pine martin that ran towards Jarvis and when it saw him the martin ran up a cedar tree and began screaming at him. And he wouldn't shut up, so Jarvis kicked the tree and the martin jumped to another and another and eventually it disappeared.

Ray was a little disturbed at first. He was not used to the woods or the creepy sounds. When the martin had stopped screaming he felt a little more at ease and started following the game train again.

Not long after Francois and Rascal started back towards Kingsley they heard a high powered rifle shot. They both stopped for several minutes listening before they continued on.

It had only been a few minutes when Francois saw a doe running towards him on the trail. When the doe saw and scented him, she veered off the trail towards the beaver flowage. Francois was so surprised he stood there and suddenly he could see movement directly ahead of him. Like a seasoned hunter he stepped off the trail, out of direct sight of whatever was coming towards him.

Francois was so nervous he was shaking all over. A nice buck stepped cautiously out from behind some bushes and stopped and lifted his head sniffing the air. He could smell Francois' scent and the scent of the doe he had followed.

Francois raised his rifle to his shoulder. He was still

shaking and had difficulty lining up the sights. In desperation he simply pointed the rifle at the brisket of the deer, about fifty feet away, and pulled the trigger. In the recoil he didn't see the deer drop and he thought he had missed.

After he composed himself he started moving slowly along the trail. When he saw the dead deer he began yelling, "I got him! I got him!"

Rascal came running over and looked at the buck. He had been hit at the base of his throat and dead center. "Eight points, Francois. Nice. Your first deer?"

"It sure is, wow."

"We'd better dress this off and drag it out to the road. I think we'll have another to dress."

Rascal was less than five minutes cleaning out the innards. "There, we can drag it back now."

When they reached the road Kingsley was still sitting on the rock and pointing towards the end of the road at the log yard. There twenty feet away was another eight point buck. It was shot in the throat like Francois' and it had an identical set of antlers.

"Both deer have the same build and identical rack. They were probably twins."

Rascal cleaned that one and said, "You two drag that one and I'll take this one."

Jarvis and Ray were within sight of the road when Cutlidge fired. They stopped and waited. All they could here was Cutlidge hollering. Laughing out aloud they both continued on to the road.

Cutlidge was laughing. No one asked why. "Nice deer Mr. President. I'd better get to work and dress it."

When he had finished, he and Ray began dragging and Cutlidge carried the rifles.

The two parties were back at the lodge at about the same time. Just as twilight was waning to darkness.

Darkness did come before they had the three deer hanging on the game pole. "The temperature is dropping. I think this will be a cold night and these deer will freeze up good." While hanging the deer both parties had agreed not to share their hunting stories until everyone was around.

"Hello, son," Jarvis said. "Are you all talked out now?"

"Well, everybody wanted to hear warden stories."

By the time the four hunters had washed up and changed their clothes supper was ready.

"Sit down please, wherever you want. We have baked beans with deer steak, coleslaw and hot biscuits."

"Boy Em, this deer meat is sure tender." Everyone, even those who had never eaten deer meat before were enjoying it. They all had eaten so much no one wanted dessert just yet.

Emma looked at the four hunters and said, "Okay, you all have been holding back your hunting stories. So let's hear 'em. Francois you first."

His face turned a deep red color and then he said, "I'm a little embarrassed, actually. But what the heck. I'm among family." Everyone was staring at him now wondering.

"Not long after I heard President Kingsley shoot I had stopped to listen and after a moment or two I saw movement up ahead. Only movement. I stepped off the game trail and behind a tree. Whatever it was was coming closer. I was beginning to shake some. I didn't know but what it might be Bear, and if it was would he want to play with me like he does you, Rascal, or would he be aggressive like bear are known to be. I waited and shaking more and more. Then I could see the buck. Antlers and all, about fifty feet ahead of me. I pulled my rifle to my shoulder but was shaking so much I couldn't line the sights up, so I pointed the rifle at his chest and pulled the trigger. I didn't see it go down and I thought I had missed, until I started walking again."

"Everyone laughed, even Francois."

"Now tell 'em Francois where you hit the deer," Rascal said.

"In the throat at the base of the neck. I was shocked," and he started laughing again and the others joined in.

"Okay, President Kingsley, your story," Emma said.

"Well, I was getting sleepy and my head was nodding. I snapped awake once and saw two bucks in the old log yard. One was a little behind the other and right next to the one in front. I sighted in at the base of the neck like Francois had done and I pulled the trigger." Now he was laughing almost uncontrollably. After he composed himself he continued, "The one on the right fell. I saw that and that other one ran off."

"That was some pretty good shooting, Mr. President," Francois said.

"Yes, it would have been," and he started laughing again. The others waited. They knew there was more to the story. "But the one I had sighted in on was the one that ran off." Now everyone joined him with some good natured laughing.

"Okay, President Cutlidge, you're on stage now," Jarvis said.

"Well, I, like William, soon fell asleep sitting on the rock. Then I heard this awful high pitch screaming and I didn't know if I was dreaming or not. By the time I woke up and became aware of things, the screaming had stopped. So now I figured I had only been dreaming. I was trying to stay awake, but I kept dozing off. I don't know how much time had passed after the screaming and I jerked awake and when my vision cleared I could see this buck standing in the middle of the road looking at me with the damnedest expression. I have no idea how long he had been standing there. And I did the same thing you did Francois. My eyes were too blurry to sight in the sights, so I pointed the rifle at it and pulled the trigger." Again everyone broke out in good natured laughter.

"Tell me one thing, Jarvis."

"I'll try."

"Was that screaming for real or was I only dreaming it?"

"It was real, Mr. President. It was a big pine martin. When they are frightened they'll scurry up a tree and begin a high pitch screaming."

"How big are they?"

"The body is a little bigger than a mink and the tail is much bigger and fluffier than a mink. A large one might weigh a pound-pound and a half. They are very vicious for as small as they are. If they weighed twenty pounds it wouldn't be safe for man to be in the woods," Jarvis said.

Now Rita and Herschel started laughing. "Go on, Jarvis, tell everyone how you got that scar on your cheek," Rita said while still laughing with Herschel.

"Sometimes I'd find illegal traps and if the animal was alive I'd try to release it unhurt. One spring I found a farmer's trap line in Beech Tree and one trap had a martin in it. As soon as he saw me he started the screaming. I knelt down and he wasn't as aggressive or fighting the chain trying to get at me. I slowly reached in and opened the trap jaws and as soon as I did that the martin pulled free and twisted around my arm like a coiled snake. He did it so fast, and all the time chewing on my fingers. I started hollering and he was still screaming. I couldn't peel him off with my other hand so I started shaking my arm. Well he jumped off onto my chest and run up over my head and left claw marks in my cheek. I'd rather release a wolf than I would one of those pine martins." Everyone was stunned and remained silent in awe.

Herschel started laughing again and said, "I became a game warden July 1st, 1927, and Dad came out of retirement for a month to work with me and show me some hot spots. We had hiked twenty miles up the border from Kidney Pond to the Lac St. Jean crossing and had arrested two men from Quebec trapping in closed season. After court the next week we returned to their trap line to pull all of their traps. There was a fisher caught in the first trap.

Dad grabbed the fisher by the lower jaw and laid down on it and then wrapped his free arm around it. That ole fisher was giving you a hell of a thrashing, Dad. The fisher rolled Dad on his back and after a while I was able to remove the trap, then

Dad rolled over again and released the fisher. The fisher ran off only a little and turned to face us. Its back was hunched over, hair standing on end and he was growling at us or at Dad. Well, Dad hollered, raised his arms and charged at the fisher. It ran off." Everyone was looking at Jarvis in awe. He just shrugged his shoulders.

Amy asked, "Who were the two trappers you caught?"

"Micheil and Maurice."

"Would their last names be Dufour and Condon?" Amy asked.

Now everyone was looking at Amy.

"Yeah, Micheil Dufour and Maurice Condon," Herschel said.

"They are my mother's second cousins. Her maiden name was Condon. They're old men now but they still talk about the garde-chasse Pages. As far as I know, or they say at least, they never illegally trapped again. And they are still afraid of you, Herschel. They never could understand how someone so much younger and smaller could lick them both. They tell all of their friends to stay away from the border."

"It's a small world sometimes," Jarvis said.

The Kingsleys and Cutlidges wanted to know all about Archer and how he was doing. "We receive a letter almost each week. He said for the first two weeks he was so busy there just wasn't time to write. He sounds excited about the academy in his letters and all his roommates get along real well. He says his studies are so much more in depth than what he was used to, but he said he enjoys what he is learning," Emma said.

All while Emma was talking about Archer, Perline would watch her daughter Emma Jean for any reactions. There were none.

About 9 o'clock Anita asked, "Would anyone be interested in some smoked trout and wine?"

While they sampled the smoked trout and wine they all wanted to hear more game warden poacher stories. So Jarvis and

Herschel regaled them for another two hours. "That's something I find difficult to understand," Mr. Butler said, "It seems that, except when you first became a game warden, Herschel, when your Dad worked a month with you, both of you have spent the most part of your careers working alone. You hardly ever see a police officer working alone except while on routine patrol. I mean you two have lived for the most part of your careers working alone. And look at the stories you have told us about this evening. You apparently think nothing at all about being out in the wilderness in the dark and alone. How many times has there been when you knew you'd be confronting two or three men and all armed with guns, and knowing there would be no help if things went wrong. How on earth do you work at a job where you put your life on the line every day, all alone?"

Jarvis spoke first, "There's one thing that I noticed through my career. Most people, maybe not afraid of the dark, but they do feel uncomfortable being in the dark. The people we deal with know we practically live and work in the dark and feel very comfortable doing it. And this is a big advantage for us."

Herschel said, "Besides it's fun."

"How did you adjust, Rita?" Pearl asked.

"It wasn't easy at first. But the more I came to know and understand my husband the more comfortable I became with his absence. I understood Jarvis could take care of himself."

"What about you, Perline?" Myrissa asked.

"I was like Mom for a long time. I always worried when he didn't come home. And like Mom, little by little I too adjusted. And when I walk in town or in the grocery store and hear other women talking about their husband or relative being caught by Herschel it makes me proud and I wouldn't want Herschel to do anything else."

What Rita and Perline had said made them all think. Even Jarvis and Herschel.

"I think it is time we go to bed," Emma said.

****

Rascal, Jarvis and Ray Butler were up early. Herschel had said the night before that he was going to sleep in. Emma was up also and while Rascal started the generator she made coffee.

"Where should we go this morning, Rascal?" Jarvis asked.

"I like the glade. As long as the ground isn't covered with snow the deer will still be feeding on beechnuts. Are you up for walking?"

"As long as you don't make it a ten mile hike, I should be okay."

"Okay, Ray, you sit on the rock where President Cutlidge was yesterday and Jarvis you go with Ray and you go to the further side of the glade and hike up along the edge maybe one hundred or a hundred and fifty yards until you come to a game trail that goes west. I have found that when I spook deer from the beechnut grove some always go out that trail also."

The ground had frozen during the night, but in the road, they were not making much noise. Again this morning, Rascal had only his .45 handgun. When they came to the cutoff to the grove not a word was said. Rascal didn't hurry. He wanted to give Jarvis plenty of time to get positioned.

When he reached the grove, he stopped to look around. The leaves were upside down and the ground had been pawed during the night. There were two raccoons at the base of the largest tree and they paid little attention to him as they feasted on nuts.

There was a fresh trail heading straight for the marshy glade, made by several deer. When he reached the edge he stopped again and waited twenty minutes before going out to the main game trail. The fresh deer tracks had turned south on the game trail heading for the road.

He noticed fresh scrapings on several cedar trees. A large

buck marking his territory. Before he was half way to the road he heard Jarvis fire. Only the one shot, and he knew he would have a deer down.

He continued on and five minutes later he heard Ray fire one shot. He was close to Jarvis so he walked over to help him drag the deer to the road. By the time he reached him, the deer was all cleaned and Jarvis had very little blood on his hands or deer hair on his pants.

"How many points, Jarvis?"

"Twelve."

"Wow, he has a large body."

They dragged it to the road and Ray was standing over his deer, and he was grinning like a Cheshire cat. "I'm going to need some help here, Rascal."

"No problem, nice deer. How many points?"

"I'm not sure. The ends of the brow times are webbed," Ray said.

Jarvis and Rascal looked at the antlers and said, "Holy cow. I've heard of antlers like this, but I have never seen one before."

Jarvis and Ray held the deer on its back while Rascal dressed it. "You know both deer are going to weigh over two hundred. I think I should hike back and bring the crawler and wagon out."

"I'll go for that," Jarvis said.

All while Rascal was gone Ray was so excited he kept up a nervous chatter. Jarvis grinned. Knowing this was Ray's first deer and such a nice one. An hour later Rascal was back with the crawler and wagon. It took all three of them working together to load each deer.

Jarvis and Ray rode in the wagon going back. Jarvis would never admit it but he was tired. Well, he had a right to feel tired. He and Rita both had turned eighty-five that year.

When the others heard the crawler they all came outside to see, even Anita. Jarvis' twelve point weighed 235 pounds and

Ray's 230 pounds. "I would have thought Ray's would have been the heaviest," Jarvis said.

"It probably was at the beginning of the rut. During the rut, bucks seldom feed much. I found where one of them, probably Ray's, had scrapped cedar trees during the night. Ray would you like to have the head mounted?"

"Yes."

"Jarvis?"

"No. That's okay. Although this is a nice buck."

After breakfast, they skun Ray's deer and left the cape attached to the head. "Now that's an impressive game pole," Emma said.

"It sure is."

"Where's Herschel? Did he have to leave early?" Jarvis asked.

Rita said, "No, he and Perline are still in bed."

Perline rolled off Herschel and said, "Come on you, get up. Everyone is outside looking at deer."

He pulled her to him again and said, "I hate to get up."

"I know, me too."

"It's been a long time since we played like that." They rolled out of bed, washed up, shaved, dressed, combed their hair and went downstairs.

"What time is it?" Herschel asked.

"Almost eleven," Rita said.

"Wow, we were more tired than I thought."

When Emma had finished making the first pot of coffee for the hunters, she put both turkeys in the oven. Now the air in the lodge was permeated with the delicious aroma of roasting turkey.

Dinner wouldn't be until 2 p.m. so the women set out some smoked fish and cheese to nibble on and of course coffee. Rascal made two wooden boxes to put Ray Butler's head and cape in and the other for the meat.

It took a little longer for both turkeys to cook. They

finally sat down to eat a little after 3 o'clock. There were twenty-one people there and more than enough food for everyone.

When they had finished eating, the men cleared the table and scraped the plates and bowls clean, while Paulette, Amy and Emma took care of leftovers. The other women washed and dried the dishes.

As they were sitting in the living room, President Kingsley said, "I surely must remark how well you do with your lodge, so far removed from everything. There are times when I actually think I envy you."

President Cutlidge agreed with Kingsley and added, "Pearl and I must leave tomorrow morning, but it will be with love in our hearts. And just a little bit of regret."

When their turkey dinner had settled no one wanted supper, but wine and brandy and glasses were set on the table. This was a special occasion and even Emma Jean and Cutlidge's grandson Jeffery had a little.

****

That night the cold had settled in and ice covered the lake by morning and all the deer were frozen stiff. Herschel helped Rascal drag the deer out onto the platform.

Presidents Cutlidge and Kingsley and parties would be leaving on the morning northbound for Lac St. Jean. Their deer were loaded into the baggage car and it was a tearful goodbye.

When the train was out of sight, Jarvis said, "They all are good people."

"Yes, they certainly are, "Emma said. "Look what they have done for this new nation."

They went back inside and had some more coffee. "How do you feel this morning, Jarvis?" Rascal asked.

"I'm not sore or lame or anything. I do feel like I have been doing a lot of hiking."

Two hours later the first southbound from Lac St. Jean stopped and the Page family said goodbye and boarded the train.

"Brr, it's cold out here," Emma said.

Rascal went down to feed the chickens and gather eggs and the women and Whiskey Jack went back inside.

"That's more people than I thought were coming from talking about it last summer," Anita said.

"Yeah, it was almost a full house."

****

Over the weekend Rascal prepared his fur to take to market in Beech Tree. Washing and restretching them and then combing out the snarls.

Both Paulette and Amy were not needed at the lodge, but if they wanted to stay, then what little work there was would be paid as room and board. Paulette had decided to work with her aunt Priscilla at the farm, in the kitchen. That way she could spend more time with Henri. And Amy was thrilled to think she could stay on at the lodge, though she would miss Paulette.

Tuesday afternoon Rascal and Emma, with the fur pelts and several rolls of camera film, boarded the southbound train for Beech Tree. "We'll be back on the second northbound, early afternoon," Emma said.

"How do you like your new camera, Em?"

"These will be the first photos. We'll see."

There was still time to get to Hoden's Furrier before he closed. So they hired a taxi to take them.

"Put them right up here, Rascal, so I can have a good look at 'em. These surely are beautiful fur pelts. You take good care of them.

"You have eighteen beaver; I'll give you $40.00 each." Even the twelve summer beaver were looking good. "In all Rascal I'll give you $1640.00.

"Call it $1650.00 and you have a deal."

"I can do that, since they all look so nice."

They decided to walk to the hotel. It wasn't that far. "I never expected to get as much for the summer beaver. We did good," Rascal said.

"How good?"

"$1650.00"

"I'd say that was good for one week."

"After paying the cost of the new bedroom we still have over $700.00 left. We need to go to the bank tomorrow, Rascal. I'm carrying around all the money we made from the deer hunters.

"Rascal, I'd like to do something special for Anita, Paulette and Amy for Christmas this year."

"Okay, what are you thinking of?" Rascal asked.

"I'm not sure yet. Maybe something special for their rooms. I'll work on it."

Chapter 8

The tree leaves and grass stayed green much longer in Annapolis, Maryland, than in Whiskey Jack, Maine. And in December the weather was still warm; compared to Whiskey Jack and this seemed so unnatural to Archer.

He was too busy to be homesick. And even though there were many nights when he and his roommates would only get two or four hours of sleep, this just made him work harder and he was enjoying every minute.

Two weeks after the families' traditional Thanksgiving, he received a small package from home with brownies, a letter and photos his mother had taken of the gathering.

"Hey, my Mom sent me some brownies. Would anyone like one?" They all ate brownies until there were no more.

"What have you there, Archer?" Ian asked.

"Pictures my Mom took at our traditional Thanksgiving dinner. We don't celebrate it on the nation holiday, because the lodge is full of hunters. Mom and Dad keep the last week of deer hunting open for family only."

As he looked at each picture he would hand them around to his friends. When they saw the group picture with both Presidents Cutlidge and Kingsley, he had some explaining to do.

"Who is this pretty dark haired girl?" Ian asked.

"I have never met her but she works for Mom in the lodge. Amy. She is a looker, isn't she?" Archer said.

"Wow!" Harry Bibley exclaimed. "Your mother took a picture of your father being attacked by a bear? Unbelievable."

Archer began laughing and then he finally said, "Bear

isn't attacking Dad, my Dad is his playmate."

"You'd better explain that Archer," Charles Andrews said.

"Well, it's difficult to believe, but Bear has been a friend of the family since 1919."

"That's some kind of pet," Ian said.

"Oh, Bear is no pet. Although he plays with Dad. He protected Mom from being attacked by a wolf behind the lodge. He killed a mountain lion that was stalking too close to the lodge full of fishing guests and he captured a German spy who had robbed a bank in Beech Tree and escaped from jail."

"Did you ever play with him?" Charles asked.

"Once, last summer. Our dog, Whiskey Jack, and I were out walking and Bear showed up, and we played until we all were tired."

Archer told them the entire story of Bear. "We have always kept him a secret because Mom and Dad didn't want crowds of people coming to see him."

"I sure would like to visit Whiskey Jack some time," Ian said.

"Maybe after we graduate we can set a date to meet there," Archer said.

All that night he had dreams about the dark haired Amy he had seen in the picture. He had forgotten about Emma Jean early on arriving at the Academy.

A week before Christmas it snowed during one night and come daylight the new midshipman had to run in two inches of snow. This made him think of home, and for the first time he was homesick.

The midshipmen had four days off for Christmas, but since most of the young men lived far away, only a very few went home. The others had no choice but to stay. Archer, like his roommates, received a large care package from home.

Archer and Ian spent much of their free time walking around Annapolis. Since arriving at the Academy, this was the first time either of them had been beyond the Academy's grounds.

When Archer wrote his next letter home, he wanted to know more about Amy, and was she now a year round employee.

****

The weather during the holiday in Annapolis was warm and the little snow had already melted. But at Whiskey Jack, they received twelve inches of snow Christmas Eve and during the day the temperature dropped below zero and even colder that night.

The lake made ice all night and sometimes the cracks were so strong they could feel the vibrations inside the lodge. After supper Rascal decided to start the kerosene heater in the hen house or the hens would die and the eggs freeze. To those inside the lodge the cracking and snapping of the ice as it froze and expanded was like music to them.

It was so cold the next morning, the train was two hours late, even though the boiler in the engine had to have a fire under the boiler all night so the water would not freeze. But the brakes on many of the cars had to be released manually. There was only the one train to Lac St. Jean and then a return to Beech Tree.

The sawmill at the farm never slowed. Although wood heaters were kept going all night inside the mill. The wood cutters also went to work that morning and before starting, each crew had to start a fire near where they were working.

Everyone was looking forward to the traditional January thaw. One advantage of the cold weather, the twitch trails froze solid each night making it easier for the draft horses.

When the cold weather broke, it began to snow and soon Armand asked Rascal, "Rascal, would you open up skid trails and twitch trails with your crawler?"

For six weeks he kept the trails open and made new openings and trails into the large pine and spruce so the men did not have to work in the deep snow so much.

Anita really began to slow down that winter and Emma had Amy go into town and buy a wheelchair for her, because her legs no longer had the strength in them for her to be mobile. With the chair and once she learned how to operate it, she became happier thinking she was not as much of a burden.

Armand's secret for getting the best work from the crews was to keep them happy and good food. The good food, which was plentiful, was his wife Priscilla's responsibility and Armand tried to make the work of getting the lumber to the mill, sawn and loaded on the freight cars as easy as he possibly could. Like hiring Rascal with his crawler to open the skid and twitch trails and keeping heat inside the mill. They were all appreciative and returned this appreciation with work.

On March 15th Rudy came for a visit. More to get away from the office than needing to inspect the farm. The day he arrived at Whiskey Jack he stayed there all day visiting and talking with Emma, Anita, Rascal and Amy. He boarded the train the next morning and rode into the farm. When he tried to pay Emma for his meals and lodging she said, "Certainly not, Mr. Hitchcock. You have done so much to help Rascal and me."

He stayed at the farm that night and took the morning train to Lac St. Jean. He wanted to talk with Mr. Colong at his office. Rudy had been very pleased with the operations at the farm. They were sawing more lumber each week now than Kidney Pond.

By April 1st Armand stopped the crews from cutting any more trees. The teamsters were another week cleaning everything up. On the first Saturday in April, the 6th, Paulette and Henri were married at Whiskey Jack Lodge. So many people came from the farm and what little family was now left in Lac St. Jean and Herschel, Perline and Emma Jean, there was only standing room left.

Henri and Paulette spent their wedding night in the log cabin. Rascal and Amy had spent two days cleaning the inside, turning the water on and filling the wood box.

The next day they took the train to Lac St. Jean and eventually ended up in Quebec City for the duration of their honeymoon.

Those who had to travel to Whiskey Jack stayed the night and for breakfast the next morning, with no charge.

As brutally cold as most of the winter had been April was beautiful spring weather. The snow was gone by April 6th, and the mud in the yard had dried. The birds were back and the tree buds had turned red, ready to leaf.

Emma and Amy took a trip to Beech Tree for groceries and then to Lac St. Jean, while Rascal stayed with Anita. For the most part of those two days Rascal sat with Anita on the platform in the warm sunshine, watching the ice melt.

Ten days after Paulette's wedding, Anita's body started declining. She had no appetite, and she would only pick at her food. And her speech was drawn out and slow and she had to mentally hunt for the correct words. "Anita, I think I should telephone the doctor and have him come in to examine you," Emma said.

"No need," and she left it at that for a few moments before continuing. Struggling for the right words she said, "No need, Emma—I'm dying and we both know it. No matter what the doctor would say, I am still going to die. No regrets, Emma. I have lived beyond my years. Oh, this warm sunshine feels so good. Emma, there is no way I can thank you enough for what you and Rascal have done for me. And don't be sorry. I have had a good life and have enjoyed every moment."

Whiskey Jack came over and put his head on Anita's leg and looked up at her. She petted his head and said, "And I love you too, Whiskey Jack."

Her words were coming with more difficulty now and she said, "Emma—would—like—some—water."

Emma went inside and came back out with a glass of cold water. She drank the whole glass and gave it back to Emma. "Emma, I want my headstone beside Silvio, but I want my ashes spread on the grass out back."

Emma noticed how Anita was talking now without any difficulty. Oh how she wished Rascal was here right now. Amy came out and sat down with them. "Amy," Anita said, "When I'm gone, there is a box on my dresser that I want you to have." Then she started laughing. Emma and Amy looked at each other.

In a clear and precise voice, she said, "Oh my word, Emma. Silvio is standing in front of me now. He's young, clean shaven and quite handsome. Oh my word, Emma! I'm in both worlds right now. Oh, this is so beautiful."

Anita stepped gingerly from her body and took Silvio's hand and she too was young again and they danced there on the platform.

Emma and Amy looked at each other again. There were tears in their eyes. Then suddenly a breeze started to blow and created a little whirlwind there on the platform and then it was gone.

When Rascal was back from the farm, Emma and Amy were still on the platform with Anita. Whiskey Jack was lying at her feet.

****

The funeral was in Beech Tree and besides Rascal, Emma, Amy, Paulette, Perline and the Pages, there were only a few others there. She had outlived everyone in her family. Dunn's Funeral Home took care of the cremation and the headstone. "When the ashes are ready, I'll send them to you on the train."

The Whiskey Jack family stayed behind in the church while the few others left. Talking about Anita and the life she had lived. Now that the family was all together, Emma told them about Anita's last few minutes and she and Amy seeing the small whirlwind on the platform. Everyone agreed she had lived a good life and that she would be missed.

Rascal, Emma, Amy and Paulette returned home the next morning. This was the first time when no one was left to sit the lodge. While Emma and Amy fixed lunch, Rascal took care of the chickens and gathered eggs. Whiskey Jack was glad to see them.

After supper that evening, Emma said, "Amy, I think it is time to see what Anita left you in the box."

The box was sitting on the bureau and Emma picked it up and she and Amy sat on the bed. "Here, Amy, she gave this to you."

Amy took the top off and there was a letter lying on top of hundreds of dollars. Amy read the letter out loud.

"Dear Amy. We have not known each other for long, but you are family now. I have always loved you as my granddaughter. You are such a nice person. The same as I feel towards Archer, and Rascal and Emma as my children. You can always trust them. They will help you in your endeavors.

"I give you this money and not to be used until you are married to the man who is meant only for you. In your heart I know you can understand this. This gift will help you and yours start your life together. Sometimes in your life you'll be faced with choices you'll have to make. If you always follow what your heart is saying you'll make the right choices. I would have loved to live long enough to see you at your wedding, but who knows. If there is a sudden little whirlwind at your wedding then you'll know I am there."

Goodbye, Granddaughter

Both Amy and Emma were in tears.

After lunch Rascal said, "How about a walk up the tracks. Do you want to come Amy? We might see Bear." At the mention of Bear, Whiskey Jack's ears perked up. He was ready for a walk too.

"You know, I have only known Anita for what, six

months. But she was more like my grandmother than my real grandmother."

"Did you tell her this, Amy?" Emma asked.

"I did, when Paulette and Henri were married."

"The train is coming; we'd better get off the tracks onto the knoll," Rascal said.

Fred waved when he went by.

They continued their walk between the rails all the way to Ledge Swamp. "This is Ledge Swamp, Amy, and this is where we do not allow anyone to hunt because I think Bear claims this as his territory. *I* don't even hunt or trap here, except along Jack Brook, which is that way," and he pointed across the tracks.

They sat in the sunshine on top of the bank and Whiskey Jack lay down with them. Rascal and Emma were talking and Amy was scratching Whiskey Jack's belly, when all of a sudden Bear started coming through the bushes behind them. Amy screamed and jumped up. "It's okay, Amy," Emma said, "It's only Bear."

Bear heard the scream and stopped. Rascal stood up and said, "Bear, it is only us.

"Speak to him, Em."

"Hi, Bear."

That's all Bear needed. But with real caution he made his way through the bushes and stopped at the edge of the cleared right of way. "Emma—I'm not liking this. He is so big. I wish now I'd stayed home."

Rascal and Whiskey Jack walked over to Bear. But he didn't touch him. "Come on over, Amy."

Amy didn't move until Emma took her hand and walked over with her. "Bear, this is our new friend, Amy."

Bear sat down on his butt and raised his paw and said, "Arrry."

"He speaks too!"

"Raise your arm, Amy, and mimic that greeting," Emma said.

She raised her arm and tried to mimic the same sound, but she couldn't do it without laughing.

"Standing here beside him, he looks even bigger," Amy said.

"I don't think he feels like playing today. Let's sit down on the bank and see what he does."

They did and Bear lay down beside Rascal and put his head on Rascal's leg and then Whiskey Jack lay down against Bear's back.

"How did all this get started?" Amy asked.

"The day Bear chased Elmo and me on the hand railcar. He chased us from mile nine to right here. That was in 1919."

"How old is Bear?"

"He chased us twenty-seven years ago. He was probably about three then."

"I understand now why you have kept Bear a secret. If the outside world knew about him, people wouldn't let him alone."

"That's how we feel," Emma said.

It was warm and sunny and Rascal and Emma lay back on the grass. Amy did also. Bear and Whiskey Jack were not stirring. They all had fallen asleep. And they were asleep for a couple of hours. Not aware of anything except the warm sunshine and the hike up had apparently been tiring for all of them.

Rascal was aware of the rumbling noise of the train. Bear heard it also and sprung to his feet, waking everyone. "Hum, train is coming, Bear," Rascal said.

Bear waited until the train was visible and then he disappeared in the bushes. Fred brought the train to a stop and asked, "Rascal, did I see a bear go off into the bushes?"

"A bear, Fred, nar, must have been the dog."

Fred knew what he had seen. He kicked the train into gear and proceeded to Lac St. Jean.

"What time is it, Rascal?" Emma asked.

"3 o'clock."

"Holy cow, we slept longer than I figured." They got up and headed back. As they were passing through a swampy area Emma said, "Isn't the air sweet. Take a deep breath and smell the sweetness."

They did and Amy said, "That's Balm of Gilead," and she left the tracks and picked a big bouquet of the sweet smelling branches. "Is it alright, Emma if I put these in a vase and on the dining table?"

"Sure."

Back in the lodge Emma gave Amy a vase to use for the Balm of Gilead branches. "I can smell the sweetness already."

"Emma, I'd like to ask something of you. Would it be alright if I write to Archer? I would like to tell him about his Mom and Dad."

Emma laughed, surprised.

"You, Rascal and Anita have made me feel so at home here. I would like to tell Archer about this. And how I will really miss Anita."

"I think he would enjoy hearing from you, Amy."

"You know he turned eighteen on April 1st."

"An April Fool's baby? Well, I'll wish him a happy birthday too. I turn nineteen next month. I assumed we were the same age."

****

The next week Archer received a letter from home, from Amy Paquin. He was on his lunch break and in ten minutes he had to be in the classroom.

Dear Archer,

I just wanted to write and tell you how great your Mom and Dad are. I came to work at Whiskey Jack last fall, just before the deer season. In that short time your Mom and Dad have accepted me as one of the family.

I was sorry to see Anita pass, but she was very lucid

and talking to Silvio. I loved her as much as I did my own grandmother. She will be missed.

Today your Mom and Dad and I and Whiskey Jack walked up to Ledge Swamp and I met Bear. At first I wasn't too sure. When he said hi, I started laughing. You have a talking bear. I'm sure your Mom has written you all about that so I won't go into anymore.

I hope you are doing well at the Academy and some day I hope to meet you.

Amy Paquin

He reread the letter again and smiled. It was time for class.

****

It had been an exceptionally cold winter and the ice in the lake was almost four feet thick, and Rascal was beginning to worry if the lake would be open enough to fish in May. Day after day the temperature would be between 65^0-70^0. Then one night towards the end of April it rained three inches during the night. The already softened snow melted like butter in a hot fry pan with the warm rain, and the sudden increase of water pushed the ice up and it broke up. There was so much water it was carrying chunks of ice over the spillway in the dam.

May 1st was on Wednesday and by the time guests started arriving Sunday morning the lake was practically free of ice.

Paulette was now back to work at the lodge and the three women made a trip to Beech Tree to grocery shop. Rascal spent the day cleaning up around the lodge and the log cabin. It was surprising how much debris would gather during the winter. Then he cleaned the smoker and made sure there was sufficient wood and chips.

The grass around the lodge was already green and the hardwood treetops were red with new buds ready to leaf out.

All the guests arrived on the first northbound Sunday

morning. After lunch many went fishing. By the end of that first week there were more togue caught than brook trout, but they smoked real nice. Two togue were just over ten pounds and the two guests wanted to have them mounted.

During the next week, although it was early, Rascal started planting the garden. When that was finished he picked dandelion greens and fiddleheads. It was Paulette and Amy's job to can them.

A few days before Memorial weekend Rascal went for a walk out along the Jarvis Trail to see what there was for hardwood he could cut for firewood. Halfway down the trail he stopped to look at an old hollow tree that he had used through the years to set traps in the base of the tree that was hollow. He noticed honeybees coming and going from the tree about seven feet up.

Some fresh honey would be a nice treat. He'd think on it as he cruised the hardwoods. He walked all the way down to the tracks and found just what he was looking for and there were also several dead and dry hardwoods still standing. "Good biscuit wood," he said.

He went back to the lodge and told Emma about the honey tree. "Would there be any honey, Rascal, this early in the season?"

"Not as much as later in the summer, but I'm guessing there might be enough for us."

"Have you ever done this before? I mean you could be stung many times," Emma said.

"I'll need some help," and he looked at Emma.

"Not me, I don't like bees."

"I'm allergic to bee stings," Paulette said.

"I'll go. It sounds like fun. When do we go?" Amy asked.

"We shall go real early tomorrow morning, about sunup."

Rascal washed out three, five-gallon pails. Laid out his two man crosscut saw and axe and two large spoons, two raincoats, gloves and knit hats they could pull down over their faces if they had to.

Emma and Paulette were up to see them off. "Good luck and I hope you two aren't stung too bad," Emma said.

Rascal and Amy hiked out to the Jarvis Trail and down to the honey tree. "What do we do first, Rascal?"

"We'll need plenty of birch bark and fir boughs for smoke."

They gathered wood also to keep a smudge going while they worked. They started the smudge first and when that was going good, Rascal put some birch bark in the hollow tree at the base and lit it then he put on some boughs for smoke.

"Smoke is coming out the top just like a chimney," Amy said.

Bees were beginning to buzz around their entrance hole. Rascal put on another fir bough for more smoke. "It's working pretty good. Let's cut it down now."

On their hands and knees they started sawing. So far the bees were not paying any attention to them. Halfway through they stopped for a rest and Rascal said, "When this hits the ground, that's when I expect the bees to be their worst."

They started sawing again and then Rascal said, "I think if we both push on the tree it'll go down."

Smoke was still coming out of the top when the tree started over. "Amy, we'd better back away some and make sure you are covered up." She did.

When the tree hit the ground, it split open exposing the honeycomb. Only now thousands of angry bees were flying around. Rascal moved into the fire and put more wood on it and more fir boughs. The smoke was keeping the bees away from them and the tree. After a few minutes they started scooping out the honeycomb into the pails. Once in a while Amy would holler "Ouch!" Rascal would just say, "Damn."

The smoke was clearing out because of a little breeze and the bees were coming back. They had three pails full. "I think we'd better go with what we have, Amy. It's hard to keep the smoke here with that breeze blowing."

"That's fine with me. I've been stung a lot."

"Me too."

"We'll leave the tools here and take the honey. I'll come back for everything else." The pails were heavy and they had to stop often.

When they reached the lodge the guests were just leaving the table and some were already climbing into canoes.

They left their raincoats, hats and gloves in the entryway and took the pails of honey to the kitchen. Emma looked at Rascal and screamed, "Rascal, what happened?"

"What do you mean?"

"Your hands and ears are all swollen. Take your shirt off and let me look at you."

Meanwhile, Paulette was checking Amy over. "A few stings on your arms and neck but not bad."

Amy sat down in a chair and screamed, "Ouch!" and jumped up.

"What's the matter Amy? Paulette asked.

"My butt. I must have been stung there. It didn't hurt until I sat down. Now my butt is really hurting."

"Turn around Amy and drop your pants."

She leaned over the island counter and slid her pants down and underwear. "Holy cow, Amy. You were stung six times and each one has swollen."

"Paulette, use some vinegar on the swells," Emma said.

Paulette did and Amy pulled her pants back up. "You may not want to sit down for a while."

Emma was putting vinegar on Rascal's stings also. "That feels better," he said. "I didn't realize I'd been stung so many times."

"I didn't know I was stung on my butt, either. But I sure do now."

"Was it worth it?" Emma asked.

"We got about fifteen gallons of honey. Yeah, it was worth it. We'll have to clean the wood pieces out of it. But it'll surely be good."

"After I have something to eat, I'll have to go back and get everything. We had to leave in a hurry."

"I might as well go to work, Emma, I can't sit down."

Rascal walked back out to the Jarvis Trail and the honey tree. Angry bees were still buzzing the honeycomb, what there was left. He picked up everything and returned to the lodge.

He and Amy spent the rest of the morning picking wood chips and bark out of the honey and occasionally sampling some. At lunch Emma set several bowls of fresh honey on the tables. Amy still wasn't able to sit down.

"Rascal, what about the honeycomb we have left? Isn't that still good?" Amy asked.

"I was tired of being stung and we already had plenty. Bear will probably find it and eat most of it. If not then other animals will."

Amy found she could sit down if she used a soft pillow, and even then it was only long enough to eat her meal. Rascal's hands and neck were still slightly swollen but the stings no longer hurt.

By the time she went to bed the swelling had reduced and she was able to lie on her back when she slept. Come morning both she and Rascal were fine. No swelling, no pain, only Amy's butt was still a little red, "But at least it doesn't hurt," she said.

****

The spring fishing that year was good, but unusual. There were no large brook trout caught, but many twelve to fourteen inches. And there were many togue caught and many over ten pounds. The fishermen would rather have one large togue caught on a fly rod than several smaller brook trout.

And for the first time since the beginning of the lodge, Rascal was finding small transparent smelts in both brook trout and togue. "This is good Em, it means there is an abundant food source for the trout and togue."

After the fishermen had left and during early July they

noticed Bear would lie down in the grass in front of the cabin for most of the day or as long as the warm sun was out. Then go back into the woods before night.

"I wonder if he is alright, Rascal?" Emma asked.

"I don't know. If he comes tomorrow I'll go over."

It rained during the night and cleared out by sun up. But the overcast didn't clear until after lunch. Around 2 o'clock, Amy said, "Bear is in front of the cabin now."

"Okay, I'm going to go over."

Emma and Amy sat on the platform in the shade and watched.

Bear saw him walking up from the dam and he didn't even lift his head. And he had lost a lot of weight since he had last seen him. Rascal sat down beside him and Bear licked his hand and then rested his head on Rascal's leg.

Trying not to holler and jump Bear, but so Emma could hear he said, "Bear isn't doing so good. He has lost a lot of weight."

"We're coming over."

"Would you bring a gallon of milk and something he can drink out of?"

Emma poured some cold milk in a small bucket and Amy grabbed a wide mouth mixing bowl.

Emma poured some milk in the bowl and put it down where Bear could drink from it. Bear lifted his head and licked Emma's hand. He was saying thank you in his own way. He drank half of the bowl and laid his head on Rascal's leg again. Paulette said, "I feel so bad for Bear."

Amy touched his nose, "It's warm." And then she felt of his ears, "They are warm also."

"I wish there was something we could do for him," Emma said.

"I think the only thing we can do is sit here with him. I think he is dying, Em," his eyes filled with tears.

"We knew it was going to happen someday, Rascal," Emma said.

They all sat in silence with Bear. His breathing was labored, but he was not moaning as if in pain.

They sat there with Bear all afternoon not saying anything. Each one with their own thoughts and memories of this unusual friend. As the sun was beginning to set, Rascal said, "You three don't have to stay any longer, I'm going to because I have been his playmate for the last twenty-seven years."

"And he saved my life," Emma said.

"And he is family. I'm staying too," Amy said.

Paulette said, "I'm staying too."

Darkness enveloped them and they remained there with Bear, each thinking thoughts of Bear not so different from the others. It was a long night and the only stirring Bear made was to move his head occasionally and to lick the drool from his lips.

Everyone was tired but neither would they leave their friend to pass alone. An hour after daylight Bear's body suddenly jerked and he raised one paw a little and very weakly made that laughing sound that he was now famous for and then he laid his head back on Rascal's leg and lay there still.

"Come on girls, it's time we made breakfast." Emma knew Rascal would want a few moments alone with his friend. Rascal still sat there with Bear's head resting on his leg and half hoping he would come back to life. Whiskey Jack curled up next to his body. He could still feel some of Bear's body warmth.

After a half-hour, Rascal stood up and started walking towards the lodge. Whiskey Jack stayed with Bear.

There wasn't much conversation until they had finished eating. "What do you suppose was wrong with him?" Amy asked.

"I don't know. Maybe just old age and it was his time. He was at least thirty-three years old," Rascal said.

"What are you going to do with him now, Rascal?" Emma asked.

"Bury him right there."

"I think he'd like that, Rascal. And maybe in his own way

he was saying that's where he wanted to be buried and that's the reason he chose to die right there. Where he could watch over the lodge as soul and be with his friends," Paulette said.

"He sure was a unique bear," Amy said.

Rascal got up and went outside and with a spade he walked back up. Whiskey Jack was still lying next to Bear.

The soil was sandy and Rascal found it easy digging. It was a hot day and he had to stop often and wipe the sweat from his face. It was more of a job than he had first thought. It required a large hole for Bear and deep enough so other animals would not be digging him up.

While he was digging Bear's grave, Emma said, "I think we should write a letter to each of the family and tell them about Bear."

"I think that would be a good idea," Paulette said.

"Would it be okay, Emma, if I write to Archer?" Amy asked.

"Sure, you go right ahead."

When Rascal finally had the hole deep enough he rolled Bear's body into it and with eyes red and tearful he filled in the hole. "Come on, Whiskey Jack, let's go home. Whiskey Jack hesitated at first and then he followed Rascal down with his head held low.

****

They were two days mourning the loss of Bear. Amy shared her grief by writing another letter to Archer. But not just his passing but about the amount of love that was shared with Bear and he was sharing with them.

Then in a more humorous tone she told him all about his Dad and her and the honey tree and bee stings.

Little by little things returned to normal and Rascal began working on firewood, frog legs and smoking togue and brook trout.

****

When Archer received Amy's letter he didn't have a chance to read it until after super, when all his roommates were in the room. Ian noticed how sorrowful Archer had become and he asked, "Bad news from home, Archer?"

"An old friend of the family passed away two weeks ago."

"How old was he?"

"At least thirty-three, maybe a year or two older."

"What was he sick or an accident?"

"No, everyone at home said it was old age." Archer saw the blank stares from his roommates and said, "Our friend was a bear, and we called him Bear." Then he had to tell them all about Bear.

He went on and finished his letter and began laughing when Amy began describing she and his Dad going after the honey and she being stung in the butt and being several hours before she could sit down.

He enjoyed getting letters from her and he began writing back to her.

In closing he said, "—sometimes it is difficult to believe that I have been here almost a year. We are kept so busy, one day is like the next."

****

One morning in the middle of August, Whiskey Jack started whining and looked up at the door . Rascal let him out.

After breakfast Rascal started mowing the weeds and bushes around the buildings with a hand scythe. Then he did along the shore in front of the lodge, around the dam and all he had left now was around the log cabin. As he walked up the hill he saw Whiskey Jack lying on Bear's grave.

He whistled and he didn't respond. "Come here, Whiskey Jack." He didn't move.

He walked over and afraid of what he might find. He sat down beside him and began petting his head. "You wanted to be with your friend, didn't you, boy."

After a few minutes he went back to the lodge and told the others. Again they all were in tears. Emma asked, "What are you going to do with him?"

"I'll bury him beside of Bear."

"I think they both would have wanted that."

Rascal got his spade and they all walked up to the cabin. Emma, Paulette and Amy all kneeled to pet Whiskey Jack and say goodbye.

****

The next week letters from the entire Whiskey Jack family arrived expressing their love and understanding of Bear's passing. They all agreed he was a very unique animal and would miss not seeing him on their visits.

Chapter 9

The new bandsaw in the farm mill was working so efficiently, the mill had processed its winter stockyard a month earlier than Armand had figured. It was dry dragging logs to the mill on the bare ground and the draft horses tired easily. So Armand and three of his best mechanics devised log trailers using the old wagons. By using smaller wheels and lowering the wagon bed to a foot above the ground.

This was working so well, they made up eight log trailers. Even though the mill was not operating at full capacity, Armand would only saw lumber three days a week. This kept everyone employed and the Hitchcock Company happy.

One evening Rascal walked out to the farm to look at these new log trailers. "This looks like a good idea, Armand. How do they work?"

"On dry ground—excellent. Not so good in soft soil or wet ground. But it is better than sending the men home."

"Armand, could I help myself to the dry slabs of wood?" Rascal asked.

"Surely, help yourself."

He thanked Armand and said, "I'll be in tomorrow with my crawler and wagon."

It was almost dark when he returned home. In bed that night, Emma said, "Tomorrow marks a year since we sent Archer off to the Academy. He'll be starting his second year next week."

The next day Rascal hauled three wagonloads of dry slab wood from the mill. After the first load Amy asked, "Would you like some help, Rascal?"

As they were loading the wagon Amy said, "I wish Archer had time off from the Academy, so he could come home. I write to him often, but I really would like to meet him." It wasn't any secret how attached Amy had become. And no one teased her or made fun of her.

****

As Archer and his roommates began their second year immediately their routine changed. The class had proven their desire to be Naval officers by not washing out because of the busy routine of 1st class midshipmen. They had been purposely pushed to extremes to see how they would bear up to demanding stress. Only two midshipmen washed out that first year. They had come from tobacco farms further to the south and could not adjust to such a busy routine and sleepless nights.

Archer and his roommates experienced a degree of superiority and self-confidence. They now had more time for sleep, but their academic studies were more advanced and more was being expected of them. For Archer and his roommates though, this was only another challenge.

Archer wrote home and said he had heard rumors that there may be changes coming in their curriculum. "But no one knows what these changes will be.

"I finished my first year at the top of the honor roll. I have to work hard, but I enjoy studying and learning. I feel so fortunate to be in such a famous academy."

"I wonder what the new changes will be?" Emma said.

"Rascal, I think we should get another dog. Without Bear or Whiskey Jack there is nothing to keep the predators away from here," Emma said.

"I think that would be a good idea. Maybe I could talk with Rita and see if she knows anyone in Beech Tree who would have any black labs."

"Okay, and I want two cats. There are too many mice and red squirrels around here."

"Okay, but no female cats. We don't want to be overrun with cats."

Rita knew the MacDonald's had had another litter of black labs and they always had cats to give away. "We women have to stay here Rascal, and cook and clean the rooms. You'll have to go to town alone."

He took the morning southbound out of Lac St. Jean and hired a taxi to take him to the MacDonald farm. The pups were six months old and only one male left. "We are getting $50.00 for these pups, Rascal," Mrs. MacDonald said. "The kittens are free."

She took him out to the barn and about twenty cats scattered that had been drinking fresh milk. In a nest of hay he saw the two he wanted. Two gray tiger toms from the same mother cat. "Do you have a grain bag I can put the kittens in?"

"Surely. How about some baling twine for a leash for the dog."

"That would be good."

From there he went to call on Jarvis and Rita. They were sitting on the porch. "What do you have in the grain sack Rascal?" Jarvis asked.

"Two kittens. Would you have a large box I could put them in while I wait for the northbound?"

Rita went out to the garage and brought back a large cereal box. "That's perfect."

"We were sorry to hear about Bear and Whiskey Jack."

"Thank you. It hit all of us pretty hard."

While Jarvis and Rascal talked Rita went inside and fixed coffee and sandwiches.

"What do you hear from Archer, Rascal?" Rita asked.

"He just started his second year and from his last letter he seems to be still as excited about the Academy as he was before he left."

"That's a nice looking pup. Do they have anymore?" Rita asked.

"Yes, but only females."

"Jarvis, I'd like a pup."

Much to her surprise he said, "Well, when Rascal leaves we'll take a drive out to MacDonald's."

She was speechless. She had assumed she'd have to do a lot of persuading and begging.

Rascal put the kittens back in the grain sack and was ready to leave. "We can take you down to the depot before we go out to the farm."

The new pup sat in Rascal's lap and the kittens meowed all the way down. "Thank you. When you get your pup come out to Whiskey Jack. We'll have room for you."

The two kittens meowed all the way to Whiskey Jack. Everyone in the passenger car turned to look at him.

Once on the platform at home Rascal turned the pup loose. He ran around smelling of everything and marking his territory with his pee. Emma, Paulette and Amy came out to greet him. They could hear the kittens meowing and wondered where they were until Rascal set the grain sack down. Paulette and Amy each picked up a kitten.

"Maybe these will help us heal," Emma said.

"What are we going to call him?" Emma asked.

"I have an idea for the two kittens," Rascal said.

"And?"

"Remember the TV movie we watched in the hotel with Archer?"

"The two comedians Laurel and Hardy?"

"Yes, how about Stan and Ollie."

"Sounds good to me, how about the dog?"

"I named the kittens, you three come up with a name for the dog."

The three women looked at each other and shrugged their shoulders. "We'll work on it."

"Probably the three are hungry." Paulette and Amy took the kittens into the kitchen. The dog followed Rascal outside and then ran down to the lake for a drink of water.

The two kittens were all upset or nervous when the lodge was full of guests. As they were eating supper, Stan and Ollie played in the living room. Chasing and wrestling with each other.

That night they slept on Paulette and Amy's bed. The pup was on the floor next to Rascal and Emma's bed.

****

In the middle of the last week in September Herschel had planned on spending a few days at home with his family. As he and Perline were eating breakfast the telephone rang. "Yes, just a minute, Lee. It's Sheriff Burlock, Herschel."

"Good morning, Lee, what's up?"

"I don't want to say too much over the telephone, (the operator just hung up with a click) but I need you to come to the office asap. I'll fill you in when you get here."

"I have to go sweetheart," he said. "He won't tell me what is happening until I'm in his office, but it sounds urgent."

He put on his uniform and strapped on his handgun and kissed his wife goodbye.

He hurried down to the sheriff's office. "What's up, Lee?"

"Billy Jenkins, he killed his wife sometime during the night. When their two kids got up this morning, Sally was lying on the living room floor—her head in a pool of blood. The kids went screaming down to the neighbors, Betty and Henry Jones. Billy wasn't around anywhere and his bed had not been slept in. Deputy Kendall is in court today, that's why I called you."

"So he has been on the run for several hours. Do they have a vehicle?"

"No. So he probably is on foot. Do you have any idea where he might head?"

"Well, I know of a hunting camp that he might go to."

"Where?"

"You cross Jack Brook down by the train depot and take the Howard Road. The camp is about three miles out on the right on the side of Antler Mountain."

"Would you go out with me, Herschel? I'm not as young as I used to be."

"Sure, when do you want to leave?"

"Right now. I'll leave a note for Kendall. Have you ever had any dealings with Billy?"

"Only once. He was up at the cabin we're heading to and he was trapping fox in closed season."

"Did he give you any trouble?"

"Not at all. He only said he needed the money for his family."

"Have you ever known him to carry a handgun?"

"Only when he was trapping."

"You might want to slow down, Lee. The cabin is just over that rise on the right about a hundred feet off the road."

Lee brought his car to a quiet stop on the road in front of the cabin. There was smoke coming out of the chimney.

"Looks like he's here."

They stepped out of the car and Lee said, "We'd better get behind the car, Herschel, until we know what he is going to do."

Lee cupped his hands around his mouth and hollered. "Billy—Billy Jenkins! This is Sheriff Burlock. I want to talk with you, Billy!"

A front window was opened and now they could see a rifle barrel protruding out the window.

"You ain't taking me in, Sheriff! Get out of here!" and he fired a shot over their heads.

"Billy, I only want to talk with you. Don't make this any worse than it already is!"

Billy fired another shot over their heads. "At least he isn't shooting at us," Herschel said.

"Not yet."

"Billy, come on down so we can talk." No answer. "Is there a back door to the cabin?"

"No."

"Let me try something, Lee." Herschel walked around the front of the car with his hands up and away from his handgun. "Billy, this is Herschel Page. You know who I am. Billy, I'm going to come up there and we can talk. I'll leave my handgun here," and he unbuckled his gun belt and held it up for Billy to see and then he laid it on the car hood.

"You be careful, Herschel. I'd hate to have to tell Perline you won't be coming home."

"I think I'll be okay, Lee. He hasn't shot at us yet. I think he is just scared."

"Billy, my gun is on the hood and my hands are up. I'm going to come up now, Billy."

Herschel walked slowly uphill to the cabin and talking with him to keep him calm. He could hear his father's words echoing in his head, 'Someday son you'll find yourself in a hard spot and if you can't use your mouth to get yourself out of it, you don't deserve to wear the uniform.'

Herschel had about decided this had to be the hard spot his dad was telling him about. *Use your mouth, son, and not your gun.*

Herschel was twenty feet away from the front door. "That's far enough, Herschel. I don't want to have to hurt you."

Lee Burlock watched as Herschel walked uphill to the cabin. He couldn't believe what he was doing.

"Billy, you and I are both men. I have come up here, Billy, to talk with you like a gentleman, not through an open window. I'm coming up Billy."

Herschel walked slowly up to the door and pushed it open, before stepping through.

One look at Billy and it was easy to see he was a bundle of nerves and probably had not slept any during the night. Herschel walked over and leaned against the counter. "Why don't you put the rifle down, Billy? I'm not going to do anything." He laid it on the couch.

"What happened last night, Billy?"

"Is she dead, Herschel? When I saw all the blood I was scared and I ran."

"Sheriff Burlock said she is Billy."

He started crying then. "I didn't mean to."

"Billy start at the beginning and tell me what happened. I know you didn't mean to hurt Sally."

He was still crying and trying to tell Hershel what happened. "Me and Sally—well we've been on hard times for a while and last night she just kept harping at me because we didn't have enough money. After the kids went to bed, Sally, she started in again and hitting me on the chest and arms. When I tried to walk away from her, she kept hitting me."

"Did you hit Sally, Billy?"

"No, I pushed her back and she fell. I don't know why she fell, but she did and hit her head on the brick hearth. That's when I saw all the blood. I didn't mean to hurt her Herschel—I swear I didn't." And he began crying again.

"I don't think you meant to hurt Sally, Billy. But now you need to go with me down to see Sheriff Burlock and tell him everything you have just told me. Your son and daughter, Billy, are going to need you."

"I'll go with you, Herschel, but don't put any handcuffs on me."

"Will this door lock, Billy?"

"Yes. I'll show you where I hide the key."

"Then we'll leave your rifle here."

Billy closed and locked the door and put the key under the flat rock to the left of the door.

"You okay now, Billy?"

"I guess so."

"Okay let's do this," and they walked down to Lee's car.

"Billy has agreed to talk with you, Lee, at the office."

Herschel put his gun belt in the front seat and climbed in back with Billy.

No one said anything on the ride down. Deputy Kendall was in the office when they walked in, and was surprised to see Billy, and not in handcuffs.

"Karl will you fix us some coffee and give Billy a donut. I don't think he has eaten for a while," Lee said.

"He'll tell you everything, Lee, just like he told me," Herschel said after Billy was in the bathroom.

Billy came back out and asked, "Where are my kids, Sheriff Burlock?"

"We took them over to your parents."

Karl came over with the coffee and donuts. Lee had always found that people are more likely to open up and talk while holding a cup of hot coffee in their hands.

"I didn't mean to kill her, Sheriff. It was an accident."

"Okay, Billy, why don't you tell us all about it. Take your time."

When he had finished Billy asked, "Where is Sally now, Sheriff?"

"She is at the coroner's office being examined."

"Are you going to lock me up, Sheriff?"

"For tonight, Billy. When I get the medical examiner's report I'll go talk with the district attorney. If the M.E.'s report comes back just as you have said Billy, the D.A. might release you. But I'm not making any promises."

Billy nodded his head and looked at Herschel and said, "Thank you, Herschel. I don't know what I would have done if you had not come up to talk with me."

Karl took Billy back to a cell and then closed the outer door. "That was fast work, Lee."

"Not me—Herschel talked him into coming quietly." Lee wasn't about to say anything to his deputy or the D.A. about Billy shooting over their heads.

"Can you give me a ride home, Lee?"

"Sure."

"Billy is a mixed up kid right now," Herschel said.

"You did a good job up there, Herschel," Burlock said.

"You know, Herschel, watching you walk up there facing that rifle not knowing what he was going to do took nerve, and in all honesty I think it's time for me to retire.

"Why did you do it anyhow, Herschel?"

"Something my dad told me when I was brand new."

"What was that?"

Herschel told him, "That was good advice. Thank you, Herschel," Lee said.

Herschel went inside and hugged his wife and daughter.

****

Four days later Herschel stopped in to see Sheriff Burlock. "Good morning, Herschel. Glad you stopped. I was going to ask you to stop by."

"What's up, Lee?"

"I have the M.E.'s report and he didn't find anything that would make me or the D.A. think that Billy didn't tell it just like it happened. The D.A. is not going to file charges. That was an awful accident that's all. But it could have been worse if you had not been there, Herschel.

"Oh yeah, I put in for my retirement. It'll be final the last day of October. Karl will fill in until the county elects another sheriff."

"I think the next moose or deer I get that's been hit by the train I'll give it to Billy to help him."

"I think he'll be getting a lot of help, Herschel."

****

Stories and rumors spread through Beech Tree and the county about Billy Jenkins killing his wife, Sally, and then when the D.A. had him released more stories and rumors circulated.

After Billy was safely in jail, Lee and Herschel drove back up to the cabin and went inside. "What are we looking for, Lee?"

"When you were here did you see anything of a note or letter?"

"No, but I really wasn't looking around."

"I'd like to know for sure if there is a note and what it might have to add to Billy's story and if he might have been thinking suicide."

They looked through everything and didn't find a note. Before leaving Lee picked up the .30-.30 rifle and worked the action. "Well I'll be to go to hell."

"What is it Lee?"

"The rifle is empty. Did you unload it?"

"No."

"I wonder if he even knew he had been threatening you with an empty rifle," Lee said.

"Do me a favor would you, Lee?"

"Sure, what is it?"

"I'd rather you not mention about me walking up here at the point of his rifle and talking him to come down with me."

"Okay, but it will have to go into my official report."

****

Good to his word, Lee Burlock retired on October 31st and Sunday evening on November 2nd the town had a retirement party for him. Jarvis had telephoned Whiskey Jack the weekend before and invited Rascal and Emma. "We will if we can get away, Jarvis. Maybe we can get someone from the farm to help out in the kitchen while we're gone."

Paulette said, "I think I know a couple of young women at the farm who would help out. I'll ask my husband if he would spend the night here with me. It might help to have a man here, with all these strange men."

"That probably would be a good idea, Paulette," Emma said.

When Paulette came back from the farm she said, "Debbie Harley said she would be glad to help out."

That first week of deer hunting only two bucks and one doe were taken, but everyone had seen deer and they left happy and some a little heavier than when they arrived, the food was so good.

Rascal and Emma left on the afternoon southbound for Lee Burlock's retirement party that wasn't until 6 p.m. so they got a hotel room for the night.

There wasn't a sit-down meal at the party, but there was a fancy array of appetizers, finger sandwiches, punch and coffee. "This reminds me of the get togethers we used to have before the village left, Rascal."

"It does, doesn't it? I always enjoyed those times."

"Maybe this year after the deer season and our family Thanksgiving we can do something like that at the lodge and invite the people from the farm," Emma said.

"That's okay with me."

Jarvis and Rita spent a lot of time talking with Lee and his wife Mable, while Rascal and Emma talked with Herschel and Perline. And of course everyone they talked with wanted to know about Archer.

Towards the end of the party Lee and Jarvis were alone and Lee said, "There's something I need to tell you Jarvis, but you must give me your word you'll never repeat it. 'Cause I gave my word."

"Okay."

"Do you remember ever telling Herschel that if he couldn't use his mouth to get himself out of a tight situation rather than using his gun, then he didn't deserve to wear the uniform?"

"Yes, that was the same advise I was given."

"Well, he surely stood by it the morning he and I went up after Billy Jenkins." Then of course he had to tell Jarvis the whole story. All the while Jarvis was smiling proudly.

"Why am I not to say anything, Lee?"

"Herschel doesn't want it known what he did. That he walked up to the cabin while facing the rifle."

"Okay, I won't say a word.

"What are you going to do now, Lee?"

"I'm not sure. I'm sixty-five and started my career in law enforcement when I was twenty, an MP in the army. That's all I have ever known. Maybe I'll take Mable on a vacation somewhere nice. She deserves that."

That evening after supper and while all the guests were still in the dining room, Paulette told them about the lodge rules. Henri was happy to see his wife step up and supervise.

During the train ride the next morning back to Whiskey Jack, both Rascal and Emma were feeling guilty for leaving just as new guests were arriving and handing over all of the responsibility to Paulette, Amy and Debbie Harley.

But when they were greeted inside by the three women, they soon put their concerns aside.

A week later Rascal had heard that Lee and Mable Burlock had closed up their house for the winter and had flown down to Myrtle Beach, South Carolina aboard a new DC-4. As the plane left the tarmac and began its elevation climb, both Lee and Mable were beginning to have second thoughts about this idea of flying. But once the pilot had leveled the plane at its cruising elevation of twenty thousand feet the flight became smoother and they stopped worrying.

Chapter 10

This had been a relatively good deer season. There were four fewer deer shot than the previous year but the guests were all happy. There was one incident where Rascal had to call Herschel and have him come up.

On the third week, a Mr. Alfredo Labonti from Rhode Island had decided to hunt by himself behind the log cabin. He had seen Rascal's trap line trail and he figured that would be good walking. He was hunting slow and listening, and every time a red squirrel would start scolding he would jump. Then about halfway to the salt lick he jumped a pine martin that was also using the trail and of course it ran up a nearby tree and started screaming. This really upset Mr. Labonti and he was several minutes before his heart stopped racing.

As he was approaching the salt lick he saw something brown moving in the distance behind the salt lick. But not enough to shoot at. Whatever it was had not yet heard him as it was only meandering through the bushes. Labonti kept watching and after ten minutes it turned broadside to him and he could see most of the body. He aimed where the heart would be and pulled the trigger.

When he got up the nerve to walk up to see what he had, a yearling cow moose lay dead. Never having seen a moose before he wasn't sure what was lying there. He didn't think it was a deer.

He didn't touch the animal but walked back to the lodge. Rascal was coming back from the hen house with a basket of eggs. "Mr. Labonti, was that you shooting a while ago?"

"I fired one shot, maybe an hour ago."

"Did you get anything?"

"Yes—but—but I don't know what."

"What do you mean you don't know?"

"Well, I don't think it is a deer; it is too big for a deer, I think."

Rascal's first thought was a moose. "Is it dead?"

"Yes."

"Did it have antlers?"

"No."

"How big are the hooves?"

Labonti showed Rascal using his hands. Yep, it was a moose. He was sure of it.

"I'll take these eggs inside and then you and I will go have a look."

On the way up, Labonti told him why he had shot at a moose. "I saw the brown body and white belly and I thought it was a deer. Although I couldn't see the head."

They rolled it onto her back, and Labonti steadied it while Rascal cleaned it. "How are we going to get this down to the lodge? You and I can't drag it."

"I'll have to come in with my crawler. But before I do that I'll have to call the game warden."

"I was figuring on that."

Rascal called Herschel's house and Perline answered. "Hello, Perline, this is Rascal. Is Herschel around Beech Tree today?"

"Yes he is in court until 11 a.m."

"Thank you."

"Operator, can you connect me with the courthouse?"

A few moments later the clerk of courts answered. "Is Herschel Page still in the courthouse? This is Rascal at Whiskey Jack Lodge."

"Yes, he is."

"Can you ask him to come to the phone this is very important."

Two minutes later, "What's up, Rascal?"

"Herschel, I have a hunter who shot a moose this morning. I've cleaned it, but I left it where he shot it."

"I'll be up on the afternoon train." Herschel had to hurry back into the courtroom. He had two more cases coming before the judge.

"The game warden is coming. He'll be here in about three hours. You might as well make yourself comfortable, Mr. Labonti."

Rascal went out and prepared the crawler and put his axe and chain in the bucket. Then he went in for lunch. Labonti ate his sandwich and a bowl of soup, but he was very quiet. He was more embarrassed than anything else.

The train was right on schedule and Rascal and Labonti went out to meet him.

"Hello, Herschel, this is Alfredo Labonti."

"Mr. Labonti."

"Herschel."

"Do you think you can get at it with your crawler?"

"We might have to work at it, but we should be able to."

"Let's do it, before we lose daylight."

Rascal walked the crawler across the dam and up the road. Herschel and Alfredo had walked ahead of him and stopped at the beginning of the trap line trail. "I think we'd have a better chance if we go to the end of the road and then down to the beaver flowage and then cut back to the trail. It's more open that way."

"We'll follow you."

As they followed Rascal, Alfredo told Herschel all about hunting that morning. So by the time they had located the moose Herschel knew the whole story. Through the years the beaver had felled enough trees to make the going relatively easy. The biggest problem was getting the crawler over the downed trees.

"How do you want to hook onto the moose, Rascal?"

"I'll use the bucket; that way I can lift much of the moose

off the ground. Make a short hitch and around the neck." There was not any time to waste and he started backing up through the maze of beaver downed trees. The sun had set by the time they were back on the road. And by the time it was hanging on the game pole it was pitch dark. "I hope you have room for me tonight, Rascal."

"That won't be a problem."

After supper, Alfredo Labonti asked Herschel, "What happens to me now, Herschel?"

"You'll be charged with the killing of a moose in closed season. The season has been a perpetual closed season because of over-hunting. And to ensure your appearance in court, I'll have to place you under arrest and take you to jail in Beech Tree. If we leave tomorrow morning, you'll have to spend tomorrow night in jail and court will be Wednesday morning."

****

Alfredo Labonti didn't sleep much that night. He had never been to jail before and he had no idea what to expect. He wasn't upset with Rascal for notifying Warden Page. It was his own fault, and he was so embarrassed. Nobody was berating him.

The next morning, Labonti even helped Rascal and Herschel bring the moose out onto the platform. "What will you do with this, Herschel?" Rascal asked.

"I'll give it to Billy Jenkins. You know he was the one that lost his wife and has two kids to bring up alone now. He could use a little help."

"That's good of you Herschel. Ah—Herschel, just one word about Labonti."

"Yes."

"When I asked him if he was the one I heard shooting, he didn't deny it and he could have said he missed. But he didn't. He knew he was wrong and he owned up to it. He's not a bad fella—perhaps a little nervous being in the woods alone."

"I'm not out to hang him. And thanks for the call, Rascal."

****

The last week of November turned off unusually warm and the family started arriving for their Thanksgiving on Tuesday, even Herschel, Perline and Emma Jean. "Let me help you with your luggage, President Cutlidge," Rascal said.

"I didn't see a rifle, Sir."

"No, I didn't bring one. I have shot two nice bucks and have the heads mounted. This year I want to visit and socialize."

President Kingsley had the same idea, as did Mr. Dubois and Mr. Butler. "That may prove to be a wise choice since the weather has turned so warm. The deer would spoil before we could get them home," Ray Butler said.

"On the train we were talking about Bear, and you, Emma, for letting us know. He was so special." Then President Kingsley started laughing. "I'll never forget the first time we saw Bear chasing Rascal at the farm. We all thought for sure Bear was going to maul you, Rascal."

"Where's Whiskey Jack?" President Cutlidge asked, "I haven't seen him around."

"He passed away also. Not long after Bear." Then he told them about finding Whiskey Jack on Bear's grave.

After lunch that day President Cutlidge asked, "How old are you, Jarvis?"

"Rita and I are both eighty-six."

"Same age as my wife, Pearl, and I. But how do you stay looking so fit and young?"

"Probably from all the miles I had to hike and, of course, good food. Rita and I still walk each day, weather permitting. But we both can feel that we're slowing down a little each year."

"What's the latest with Archer?" Pearl asked.

"He started his second year in September and he said they are not being pushed so hard now. Although some of their studies, he said, are certainly advanced. He did say there are rumors that the Academy is changing their curriculum, but he didn't know any more than that."

"Did he finish the first year at the top of his class?" President Kingsley asked.

"Yes he did. We're so proud of him."

"That change Archer mentioned, President Cutlidge and I had a little to do with that."

"Can you tell us?" Rascal asked.

"At the beginning of their fourth year, for the first six months all of the midshipmen that are in their fourth year will be assigned to an active ship with the rank of E-3, and for those six months they will receive E-3 wages. Then the last six months are back at the Academy to fine-tune their experience at sea. And after they have completed the six months at sea, each will have a ten-day furlough to go home and visit family. Remember these changes are being worked on; they are not definite yet, but are expected to be put into place to start with Archer's class fourth year."

"That seems like a good way to get some practical experience," Rascal said.

"That's what we thought also," President Kingsley said.

That night as Paulette and Amy were lying in bed talking, Amy said, "When you asked me to come here to work, Paulette, I never thought that I would become part of the family with two former presidents."

"A lot of good has come from the merger of the two countries and it all started right here, Amy."

"I miss Anita, Paulette. I never was around my own grandmothers much and Anita was more like a grandmother to me."

"I know what you mean and I feel the same. These are wonderful people, Amy. I mean everyone."

****

The next afternoon the entire Whiskey Jack family

decided to walk out to the farm. It was another of those unusually warm November days. "We'll pay later for this nice weather," Rascal said.

"Well, we'll just have to enjoy it while we have it and burn more wood this winter," Emma said.

"Wow, has this changed since we were here in 1926. This is quite the little village," President Cutlidge said.

This was just a regular work day and the mill was busy sawing out lumber. Several workers saw the group but paid no attention. Then Armand Bowman saw them and recognized many and walked over to greet them.

"Mr. Bowman," Rascal said, "everyone wanted to walk out to the farm and see the operations. We'll stay out of your way."

Armand recognized Kingsley and said, "Mr. President, I'm pleasantly surprised to see you out here." Then he recognized President Cutlidge.

"Oh, murdy, two presidents."

Paulette stepped up and said, "Presidents Cutlidge and Kingsley, this is my uncle Armand Bowman, supervisor for the Hitchcock Lumber Company."

"Please, Mr. Presidents, I would enjoy it if my wife Priscilla could meet you. Maybe a cup of coffee? We'll have to go to the main house."

Once inside Armand began hollering "Priscilla! Priscilla, come. Come here."

She came out of the kitchen with flour on her hands and face and she recognized President Kingsley first and then President Cutlidge. "Oh my, and I look so dreadful."

Everyone began laughing and Paulette introduced the two presidents. "Priscilla, do you have coffee already hot?"

Everyone had a cup and finished the big coffee maker. "I must get back to work. Walk around and look all you like. I am happy to have met you both, Mr. Presidents."

As they were walking back, President Cutlidge said,

"This whole area; the farm, the mill, the railroad and Whiskey Jack, is just so spectacular. Someday there'll be roads into all of this."

"I understand what you're saying, sir," Jarvis said, "and it will spoil this uniqueness."

"Every time I come here," Jarvis said, "it's like I'm coming home."

President Cutlidge began laughing and then said, "That's exactly how I feel. I even told Pearl the same thing."

"When you retired, Jarvis, why didn't you and Rita move here?"

"I would have liked to, but Rita doesn't have the same feelings about the wilderness as I do. And I owe her so much."

In the evening, after the Thanksgiving dinner, they all adjourned to the living room. Amy and Emma Jean were off by themselves talking while the others were savoring a glass of wine or brandy, strong cheese and smoked togue.

President Cutlidge said, "You know, Rascal, you and Emma have your own beautiful piece of the world right here at Whiskey Jack. It is always so relaxing when we come. But I'm afraid if we were to move here I'd be as plump as a fat pumpkin. But what a life you two have here. In a way I envy you and your lifestyle."

"Aye, aye to that," President Kingsley said.

"There, Rita, everyone thinks of Whiskey Jack as a tiny piece of heaven. Maybe we all should move here. You'd have family right here," Jarvis said with a smile.

The others laughed, even Rita. "I do understand how you all feel. I do also, but my home is Beech Tree."

****

Everyone left the next morning and once again it was quiet at Whiskey Jack Lodge. The only sound was when the wind would carry the sound of the band saw cutting through a log.

Paulette had moved back with her husband at the farm for the winter and Amy had more or less adopted Emma as her surrogate mother. The two were busy preparing for a Christmas celebration for everyone at the farm. There was plenty of food leftover from the hunting season that needed to be used up before it spoiled.

"Rascal, I'd like to invite the Hitchcock brothers and wives, and the Pages."

"Okay, you make the calls. You're better with the telephone than I am."

Jarvis and Rita said they would love to come and Rudy and Earl Hitchcock and wives also. They all wanted to bring desserts to help out. Some of the women from the farm were bringing desserts. Rudy brought a keg of hard cider which didn't last long at all. Emma and Amy had a glass and Emma didn't care for it, but Amy had a second glass.

Many of the guests were remarking how this felt like the get-togethers they would have twenty-five years ago, before the village was moved to Kidney Pond. Without a doubt everyone had a good time.

****

At the beginning of the new year, the weather turned warm too early for the usual January thaw. But no one complained.

Armand had taken on a new crew in November, three young fellas from Beech Tree. One morning during this warm spell, Andy was driving the team, twitching logs from the woods to the log yard. Billy and Jim were working on a tall big spruce tree. It was leaning slightly in the right direction and the notch was made proper, and just before they had cut through a strong gust of wind blew and forced the spruce tree backwards. Billy and Jim were able to jump out of the way while hollering to Andy. Andy saw the tree coming down towards him and there was nothing he could do. It all happened so quick. He was hit by branches, breaking his collarbone, and he fell to the ground.

The same branch broke his ribs. He started screaming with pain, but no one could hear him over the louder screams of one of the horses. The heavy top had landed on the outside horse breaking its back. It lay in a heap now screaming louder than Andy.

Billy and Jim came running as did others who were working close enough to hear. No one had thought that Andy was hurt also. The horse was making such a loud noise. As Billy stepped into the twitch trail he could see Andy lying there, "Jim! Jim! Over here—it's Andy." Between clenched teeth and pain Andy said, "Ribs—shoulder—broke."

Jeffery from the closest crew arrived, and Billy said, "Jeffery, go back to the farm and tell Armand we have an injured man and he hurts real bad. And we'll need a rifle to shoot the horse. Now hurry."

Jeffery ran, stumbled and fell all the way to Armand's office. "Mr. Bowman, Mr. Bowman," he was almost out of breath.

"Calm down, Jeffery, and tell me what the problem is."

"Mr. Bowman a tree fell on Andy and he's on the ground and hurt real bad. One horse is hurt real bad, too, sir and will have to be shot."

"Oh my word." He told his secretary Helen, "Helen, call Dr. Noonan and tell her we have an injured man and we need her out here as soon as possible."

"Yes, Mr. Bowman."

"Let's go, Jeffery," and he got his rifle from the closet.

Armand ran across the mill yard, down to the log yard and then the twitch trail. Jeffery had a hard time to keep up.

Armand gave Jeffery the rifle and said, "Shoot the horse.

"Jim, cut two poles we can use to make a stretcher.

"How are you, Andy?"

"I hurt a lot, boss." That's all he could manage to say.

When Jim had the two poles cut Armand took off his coat and Billy did the same and then Jim and they made a strong stretcher.

"Now, Andy, I need you to straighten your legs. Just relax and let me straighten them."

Andy did a lot of moaning. "Now I'm going to roll you on your good side so we can get the stretcher under you." This went easier than Armand thought it would.

The four of them each helped to lift the stretcher. It wasn't too bad with four of them. "Don't hurry, fellas. If one falls it will be bad for Andy."

It was slow progress to get him to the cafeteria and lying flat on his back on one of the tables.

Just by luck, Helen was able to reach Dr. Noonan and she immediately went down to the train depot. She told the S&A superintendent Sam Grindle what had happened at the farm and he and Dr. Noonan went over to one of the sheds, and he and Ralph got a special gasoline-powered small railcar onto the main line. "Get in, Dr. Noonan. This will be a fast trip to Whiskey Jack."

The new station master, Stanley Steamer, knew it would be a quick trip for the gasoline powered railcar. He telephoned Whiskey Jack Lodge. "Yes, Mr. Steamer, Rascal is right here."

"Hello."

"Rascal, there's been a bad accident at the farm and the Super is bringing Doctor Noonan up in the new railcar. It'll only take him a few minutes. I need you to stop the southbound from Lac St. Jean so the super can make the switch to the farm. Have the engineer or brake man help you to switch the rails, and the train is not to move until the engineer hears from the super, Sam Grindle. I'll stop the northbound from here. Do you have that, Rascal?"

"Yes."

"Okay, thanks, Rascal, and hurry."

"Is something the matter at the farm, Rascal?" Emma asked.

"There's been an accident and a special car is coming up the tracks. I have to stop the train," and he left and walked down to the tracks and then up above the switch. He could hear the train coming.

"What's the problem, Rascal?"

"From Stanley Steamer, the new station master, I'm to hold you here. Sam Grindle is bringing the doctor up in a special railcar to the farm. There's been an accident. And you are to remain here until you hear from Mr. Grindle. It may be a while, so you and your passengers are welcome to come inside and wait."

"Thanks. Do you need help with the switching?"

"Yes." The brakeman climbed down and just as the switch was made they could hear the railcar coming.

Sam Grindle slowed down through the switch and then opened the throttle again. On the way up they were traveling at 40mph.

Fred Darling and the brakeman secured the train, and then the crew and six passengers followed Rascal to the lodge.

Everyone had questions and no one had any answers. An hour later the lodge telephone rang. "Hello, this is Emma."

"Emma, this is Sam Grindle. Can you get a message to Fred Darling?"

"Just a moment Mr. Grindle, Fred is right here."

"Hello, Sam."

"Fred, bring the train into the farm. We have an accident patient that needs to go to the hospital."

The switches were made and the train backed up to the farm. By now they had managed to get Andy onto a soft mattress after giving him some morphine to deaden the pain.

"Will he be okay, Dr. Noonan?" Armand asked.

"In a few weeks. He had a broken collarbone and two broken ribs. Both are very painful. But he won't be doing anymore lumbering this winter. Maybe some light duty work."

"Thank you, Dr. Noonan."

Andy and the mattress were loaded into the baggage car where he could be laid flat on the floor. "A slow trip, Fred,"

Grindle said, "I'm going to stop at the lodge for a few minutes."

Dr. Noonan rode in the baggage car with Andy.

Grindle left the railcar on the tracks in front of the lodge and went inside. "Could I use your telephone, Rascal?"

"Sure."

"Stanley, this is Sam. Don't let the northbound go until I get back. Fred is bringing the train in slowly with the injured man."

"Okay Sam. Nothing leaves here until you're back."

When he had finished his call Rascal asked, "What was that smaller railcar you brought Dr. Noonan in?"

"That is a special gasoline powered car I had our chief mechanic build two years ago. In emergencies I can get somewhere much faster than the train."

"Can you tell us what happened, Mr. Grindle?" Emma asked.

He told them everything he could. "Dr. Noonan said he'll be just fine in a few weeks. They had to shoot the draft horse, though."

Just then the telephone rang. "Rascal, it's Armand and he wants to speak with you."

"Hello, Armand."

"Rascal, can you bring your crawler out tomorrow and haul the dead horse off and bury it?"

"Sure, I'll be up there in midmorning."

****

It was cold the next morning and Rascal had to build a fire under the crawler to warm it up. In twenty minutes he had it running and on his way to the farm. It was a cold ride out. By now the horse had frozen solid and he had to break it loose from the ground first with the bucket. Then he dragged it out to the mill yard and down to the corner of the field where there was a steep bank where he pushed the carcass over the edge with the crawler.

****

Andy was in the hospital for a week and after a month he returned to the farm and light duty, helping in the kitchen and dining room. He was only too happy to be back among friends and feeling useful.

In April, Emma received a long letter from Belle Cummings. She had been promoted to captain and head of the therapeutic division of Walter Reed Hospital and her husband was now the lead orthopedic surgeon at Walter Reed.

They wanted to come in July for a week to visit and wanted to know which week would be best. Emma wrote back immediately and suggested the first week in July. And she kept this a secret from Rascal. She wanted to surprise him. She was able to put the letter in the mail pouch and hang it out to be picked up by the train without Rascal knowing.

The spring fishing that year was once again excellent with more large togue being caught than brook trout.

When July arrived they were all happy for a break in guests. It had been a busy season so far and now they had two months to prepare for the fall and for themselves.

The first Sunday morning Rascal was trying to help in the lodge and Emma said, "Rascal, why don't you go sit on the platform. You are driving the three of us crazy."

"Come on, Harvey, come on boy, let's go sit on the platform." They both found some shade. It was early and promising to be a warm day, but no humidity yet. There was only a gentle breeze making a slight ripple on the water.

Fred blew the half mile warning and Harvey could already feel the vibrations. He came to his feet looking south and waiting for the train. Emma had taught him to go out and retrieve the mail pouch and bring it inside when one was dropped off. And he knew the half mile signal meant the train would be coming through soon.

This morning the train stopped and the mail pouch was

thrown off and that was Harvey's cue to retrieve it and take it into Emma. Rascal thought it was odd the train stopping this morning. As far as he knew they had no guests for the coming week.

Then he saw Belle smiling and looking at him, he rushed over to help them with their luggage. By now Emma, Amy and Paulette had come out. As soon as they were safely off, the train pulled ahead and the switch to the farm to hook onto loaded freight cars for Colong Lumber in Lac St. Jean.

Emma was smiling. Rascal took one look at her and said, "You knew they were coming?"

"I wanted to surprise you."

"Well, you sure did." Rascal shook hands with Richard and Belle hugged Emma and then Rascal.

"Amy," Emma said, "These are our good friends Richard and Belle Cummings. This is Amy Paquin and Paulette Colton."

"I thought she might be your daughter," Belle said.

"Amy lives here and works with us."

"Come inside, there's no need of us standing out here," Rascal and Amy took their luggage inside and to one of the new rooms off the living room.

Richard and Belle immediately noticed the photographs and awards. "This photo has to be at the White House dinner you were invited to attend. My, look at all of those influential people. We understand now what your secret was and why you couldn't say anything.

"These photos here, though, are taken here. Explain?" Belle asked.

"Presidents Cutlidge and Kingsley and their family and even the secret service agents assigned to protect them come here very November for our traditional Thanksgiving, after we have finished with the deer hunting season. It has become an annual get together. We all have become like family."

Richard said, "This is where the idea of the two countries merging. . .isn't it?"

"Yes, in 1926." Emma told them how surprised they were when the president and then the prime minister arrived, "We knew two important people were coming but not who until they stepped off the train."

"This must be Bear," Richard said, "Before my father died, he told us about Bear playing with Rascal. Is Bear still around?"

"No, he passed away a year ago. We miss him."

Amy said, "We had a dog, Whiskey Jack, and he left shortly after Bear. Rascal found him lying on Bear's grave."

"Whiskey Jack and Bear used to play together. Whiskey Jack was old, but I think he died of a broken heart," Rascal said.

"Would you two like to lie down for a while? You must be tired."

"That would be nice," Richard said.

"I'll make sure you're up before lunch," Emma said.

"This is quite a surprise, Em. Did you know anything about it, Amy?"

"No. But how do you know them?"

"You tell her, Em. I'm going outside."

"Come in the kitchen, Amy, so we don't disturb them." The coffee was still hot and Emma poured a cup for them both and then she sat down and began when Rascal was wounded in France.

Rascal worked in the garden pulling weeds and hulling the potatoes. Then he picked some lettuce, radishes, cucumbers and green peas.

"Thank you, Rascal, these will be good for supper."

"Amy, go knock on their door and tell them it's time to get up."

Amy left the kitchen and Richard and Belle were walking across the living room. "Did you get any sleep?" Amy asked.

"Some, but what is that strange sound? It sounds like it is a long ways off," Richard asked.

"Things have changed since you were here. Remember

the farm?"

"Yes."

"The farm is now a lumbering village and sawmill. It'll be the band saw that you heard. After lunch we can take a walk out if you'd like."

"We found two young cats under our bed."

"I'm sorry, I was wondering where they were," Amy said.

"No problem, they are both real nice and certainly playful. Every time Richard would move his feet under the blanket they both would pounce on it. What are their names?"

"Stan and Ollie."

"Oh, after Laurel and Hardy."

"Yes."

"You've seen them?" Belle asked.

"When we took Archer out to meet the train we stayed in the Beech Tree hotel, and there was a television in our room and we watched Laurel and Hardy. Rascal and Archer laughed all during the movie."

"Where is Archer?"

"He's at the Annapolis Naval Academy. This is his second year."

"How does he like it?"

"He does very much and he is doing well."

"I write to him at least once a month," Amy said.

"You have to have an appointment to attend, not just anyone can apply," Richard said.

"Richard," Belle said, "they are friends with two former presidents."

"Oh."

Over lunch and while they walked out to the farm they told Bell and Richard about Bear protecting them and about Hans Hessel.

"He really was extraordinary, wasn't' he?" Belle said.

"He sure was and no one can figure out why."

Richard said, "Well, God has many coworkers and maybe Bear was one of them. Watching over you like he did."

"Hum, we have never looked at it like that," Emma said.

They walked around the farm trying to stay out of the way. "This sure has changed," Richard said. "I think I liked it better when there was just the farm."

"Me, too," Rascal said.

"Rascal, I've noticed you're not even limping now," Belle said.

"If I try to do too much or hike all day, I'll begin to feel it. Doctor Henley sure did a good job."

"He's retired now, but he was one of the best," Richard said.

****

The next day Belle and Richard both wanted to have a fish fry outing at the head of the lake. "Like we did when we were here before."

Wednesday morning, Rascal and Richard readied two canoes, while the three women prepared lunch cooked over an open fire.

Richard and Belle were in one canoe and Rascal, Emma and Amy in another. "It is so beautiful out here this morning."

"Em, throw out a line and troll. Give Amy your paddle."

There was already a warden's worry streamer on her line and she worked out her line. Rascal guided the canoe closer to shore. About a hundred yards before the head of the lake, Emma hooked into a nice brookie that cleared the surface of the water by two feet.

Amy netted it for her and held it up. "Well, here's lunch," Emma said.

"You two go ahead and fish and we'll get a fire going and start cooking this fish and making some tea."

Richard guided the canoe up closer to the mouth of Jack Brook and Belle started to cast out her line and he whispered,

"Belle, remember were supposed to sit quiet for a few minutes before we start casting."

Their first cast out they both had one on at the same time. About a pound each. They waited for the water and noise to quiet and then cast again. And just like before they each caught one about a pound each. "Bring those in and we'll start roasting them."

"These will take a while to cook, so you can go back to fishing," They caught two more each and then just like snapping your fingers they stopped taking the fly.

"What happened?" Richard asked.

"The sun is higher in the sky and they have gone into the lily pads for shade."

"These trout are almost done; come on in," Emma said.

As they ate roasted brook trout and drank hot tea, Belle said, "I had forgotten how much fun this is."

"This fish is so much better than if we cooked it in the kitchen," Amy said.

"You know there is no way of telling you how much my folks enjoyed their trips up here. Even my mother, although she said she could never live in the wilderness on a permanent basis. But I think Dad would have enjoyed it."

After they had finished eating the three women started talking about Archer. Rascal and Richard paddled over to the lily pads. Amy would have liked to go also, but she would rather talk about Archer.

"Land your fly on a lily pad and when the ripples in the water have disappeared very gently pull the fly off the lily pad. When a trout hits it, it will try to dive and tangle the line in the lily pads. Don't let it."

Richard followed Rascal's instructions and as soon as the fly touched water, a huge orange-bellied brookie took it and tried to dive straight down. Richard kept a tight line and brought it in. Rascal held it up by the gills. "That is a beauty," Richard said.

Amy watched all this and said, "Emma, I want to fish."

The three women pushed off in the other canoe below Rascal some. Emma held the canoe steady while Belle and Amy fished.

Richard had two more large brookies and the two ladies, with their first cast, each caught one not quite as big as Richard's, but they were happy. Then they caught several more about a pound each

Emma said, "Let's go back and cook these."

"One more cast," Amy pleaded.

"Okay."

This time she landed the fly on the lily pad she had aimed at and waited. She started bringing the fly back and a trout larger than Richard's took the fly and went airborne three feet. She screamed and began stripping the line back as fast as she could. Belle already had the net ready. It was so heavy she had to use both arms to lift it. The fly fell out of the trout's mouth.

"You know, it's too bad to kill something as beautiful as that. Let it go, Belle."

"Are you sure? You may never catch another brook trout this big again in your life."

"I know, but let it go." Belle did and the fish swam off.

"Okay, we can go back now and cook these up," Amy said.

The fire was almost out and Rascal went after more wood and Richard cleaned the trout. Emma made more tea and Belle and Amy sat near the fire talking.

"Rascal, you know what would go good with the fish? Some frog legs."

Emma and Belle were busy cooking fish and Richard had taken a walk up to the railroad. "Come, Amy, it's you and me."

They went below where they had been fishing and found many frogs. Amy thought this was more fun than fishing. Many frogs were lying on top of the lily pads in the warm sunshine. They weren't long before they had plenty.

The slate rock Rascal had found years ago that he and Emma had used to cook frog legs on, she now had it sitting on the fire pit rocks and it was already hot. She used some of the fish oil from one of the trout to cook the frog legs, so they would not stick to the slate rock.

"Oh my, these are better than the fish," Belle said.

"You wouldn't find people we know back home that would eat frog legs or fish cooked over an open fire like this," Richard said.

They all ate in silence; everything was so good. Amy had even picked some teaberry leaves and put them in the tea while it was making. "I have never tasted better tea, Amy. Where did you learn about using teaberry leaves?" Emma asked.

"From my mother. We used to have teaberry tea all the time back home."

"Was your mother a naturalist, Amy?" Belle asked.

"I suppose in a way. She is from the Abenaki Indian tribe. She said her people always drank teaberry tea. They never had regular tea or coffee."

With their fish and frog legs eaten and the tea gone, they lay back in the grass and all was silent. Suddenly Richard sat up and said, "What is that noise?"

"That's the southbound train out of Lac St. Jean."

Belle asked in all seriousness, "I understand how beautiful Whiskey Jack is and you have a terrific business here, but don't you ever feel isolated and lonely?"

Rascal answered first, "Not really. When we were in Washington, we couldn't wait to get home. We produce our own electricity now, we have a telephone and a super railroad system and the train leaves twice daily for Beech Tree. And we have a small bulldozer and wagon for transportation. No car." Everyone broke out laughing, even Rascal.

"We have lived out here for thirty-two years. We have had a great life here and have met some really nice people. Like yourselves. We have a family get together for Thanksgiving, and last Christmas we invited everyone at the farm for a celebration dinner. There are quiet times, but not lonely," Emma said.

"When we first took over the hotel and turned it into a lodge, we stood on the platform and said goodbye to the last of the villagers. The moment was lonely and we both spoke of it and hoped we hadn't made a mistake," Rascal said.

"I think I speak for Rascal also. There is no other place we would rather be. And it was a great place to raise our son, Archer."

"What about you, Amy," Belle asked.

"I can't think of going any place but here. Rascal and Emma are like parents and Anita was like a grandmother to me. And Paulette, a big sister. I'm content to stay right here."

Richard said, "I think you three people are the luckiest and happiest people we know."

A wind suddenly came in from the north. "This isn't good. I think we'd better leave now."

Out in the middle of the lake the waves were too rough for canoes so they hugged the right hand shore. Just as they were turning the canoes over there was a flash of lightning. "We made it just in time."

****

It rained heavy all night, and the raindrops hitting the lodge roof was like music. Even for Richard and Belle. By morning the rain clouds had moved on and the sky was blue.

Even though the sky was clear and the sun was out, everything was wet. So they spent the morning on the platform talking and sipping coffee.

Without realizing it, both Richard and Belle were beginning to feel the Whiskey Jack relaxed atmosphere.

They spent the better part of that day sitting on the platform and simply enjoying each other's company. There were no schedules to keep and no push from the outside to get anything done. Yes, this was Whiskey Jack's atmosphere. And as Rascal thought about it he began to smile and Emma asked,

"What are you smiling about?"

"Ohh, I was just thinking about Whiskey Jack's atmosphere."

****

Richard and Belle were ready and waiting for the afternoon southbound to Beech Tree. The half mile warning signal blew. Rascal and Richard shook hands. Emma, Amy and Belle all hugged each other and then Richard hugged Emma and then Amy. Emma watched as Rascal and Belle hugged. Belle kissed his cheek and then put her lips gently to his ear and whispered something to him. Emma was interested and in a strange sort of way she was happy to let her husband, Rascal, have this secret. She did not feel threatened by Belle.

"Here's the train," Amy said.

Now everyone's eyes were red and full of tears. Even Amy was tearful. They stood at the entry to the passenger car as the train pulled away, watching as Whiskey Jack and their friends disappeared.

That night as Rascal and Emma lay on their backs in bed Rascal put his arm around her. "Rascal—every time you say goodbye to Belle she whispers something in your ear. What does she say?"

"The first time when they came here unexpectedly it was a compliment to you. She said, 'You did well, Rascal, I like her.'"

"When we left Washington she said, 'I still like her, Rascal.' And today she said, 'You are a lucky man, Rascal.'"

There was no way he was going to tell her about the goodbye kiss when they parted after his therapy in New York nor about dancing with Belle while Emma was having her hair done at the Walter Reed Hospital. He knew he had a special closeness for Belle and this would have to be his secret. Because he was not about to hurt Emma.

Emma had already fallen asleep.

Chapter 11

During the first two years at the Academy, Archer's studies were mostly minor courses. Certainly advanced from the Beech Tree Academy. At the beginning of his third year he would be overwhelmed with his major courses. He had decided on: general science, operation research, navigation and ship defense and armaments.

There wasn't much spare time to think of back home until he received a letter from his Mom or Amy. He found it so strange, the feelings he was aware that were beginning to be there towards Amy. A young woman he had never met, except through her monthly letters.

He wrote back after receiving her last letter and asked her to send a picture of herself.

He was never homesick until he would receive his letters from home. Even in his second year there was little time for homesickness. So he would bury himself in his studies. The last half of his second year he was studying chemistry, advanced physics and electrical engineering. These all were considered to be minor study courses, but he had to really apply himself.

So far none of the midshipman at the Academy had been told about what changes would be coming starting with the beginning of Archer's class fourth year. But Presidents Kingsley and Cutlidge had been working diligently to make it happen.

****

Presidents Cutlidge and Kingsley and wives were not able to make it to the family's Thanksgiving. Instead they were at the Annapolis Naval Academy making final arrangements for the 4th year midshipmen to go to sea for six months.

On Wednesday late afternoon a knock came on Archer's door and when he opened it a lower classman was there with a written order for Midshipman Ambrose to report to Capt. Bedford Ames' office. A written order from Capt. Ames could not be ignored. Archer ran down the hall and across the compound. When he knocked on the Capt.'s door he wasn't even breathing heavy.

"Yes, come in," Capt. Ames said.

Archer opened the door and entered and immediately came to attention. "At ease, Midshipman Ambrose. You have four visitors."

"Yes sir," and he turned around and immediately recognized them. He shook the presidents' hands and hugged Myrissa and Pearl. "It is so good to see you. But you should be at Whiskey Jack with the family."

"We're sorry we had to miss the family Thanksgiving this year, Archer, but there are changes here that require both of us to be here," President Cutlidge said.

"Yes sir, but it sure is good to see you."

"We were all so sorry to hear about Anita, Bear and then Whiskey Jack. All in the same year," President Kingsley said.

"We all felt the loss also, Archer," Myrissa said. "I mean we are all family. Bear was an unusual animal."

"And mark our words Archer, President Kingsley and I are not going to let his memory pass into oblivion. Not after capturing a German spy which truly shortened the war. We can't tell you yet what we have planned. It's to be a surprise for the family, so we would greatly appreciate it if you were to say nothing to your Mom and Dad."

"Excuse me, the dining room is open and we should start over now. Midshipman Ambrose, a place has been set with your friends at the head of the table."

While the others talked while walking over to the dining

room, Capt. Ames kept wondering about what had been said about an animal, a bear. *How had he shortened the war and how had he captured a spy?*

As they entered the dining room, all of the midshipman came to attention as the presidents and wives walked to their table—and midshipman Ambrose. Archer's roommates Ian, Harry and Charles were seated at one table and after everyone was seated Charles said, "He was telling us the truth all the time. Imagine being friends with the two most popular presidents in history."

Later after supper, Archer said goodnight to the presidents and their wives and returned to his studies. Myrissa and Pearl were escorted by an upper midshipman to their quarters, while their husbands talked business with Capt. Ames.

Before the business talks, President Cutlidge asked, "How is Mr. Ambrose doing, Captain?"

"In all honesty, I have never seen a midshipman who is so eager to learn. And he seems to grasp everything with a higher level of understanding than any other midshipman. He has a heavier course study than any midshipman. There doesn't seem to be anything he cannot learn or do. He is simply amazing."

"Captain, some day you and your wife should take a trip to Whiskey Jack, Maine. Meet his parents and friends and see where he grew up."

President Kingsley added, "Incognito, though. Go in July or August when there won't be any fishing guests."

"That would be cutting it too close to assigning his class of midshipman to active navy vessels. I could make the trip in May next year. I'll work on it."

"I expect that Midshipman Ambrose will work up through the ranks rapidly."

****

When the two presidents left Annapolis, the new changes in the 4th year curriculum were final. They had agreed not to say anything to Rascal and Emma about how well Archer had acclimated into the academic life. And they didn't want any leaks to occur just yet about the curriculum changes.

When Archer wrote home he told his folks about the presidents' visit to the Academy and how he had been invited to sit at the head of the table with them. Then he wrote another letter to Amy. He sure did enjoying getting her letters. Emma Jean was long gone in his memory.

****

That fall of 1948, another first time hunter, this time from lower Maine, shot a moose on the tracks above the lodge. He was hunting alone and had been sitting on a knoll in the warm sunshine, where he could see in both directions along the tracks. He had fallen asleep and when he awoke a yearling bull came out of the bushes only about thirty feet away from him. The moose had surprised him and he was intimidated with its sudden appearance and he shot it in the ribs without aiming. He didn't move for a long time; finally he stood up and started walking back to the lodge. The train came through and when Fred Darling saw the dead moose he stopped at the lodge and told Rascal. "Train didn't hit it, Rascal. There's a hunter walking down the tracks towards the lodge."

"Thanks, Fred."

Rascal knew who it was. He went inside and telephoned Herschel. "He isn't here right now, Rascal. He went up to see Mom and Dad," Perline said.

"Perline, would you tell him a hunter shot a moose on the tracks above the lodge."

"I'll tell him, Rascal."

Rascal had decided not to approach Mr. Rhyston. He would wait and see how honest he was. Rascal was tending the smoker when Rhyston walked into the lodge yard. He tried not to stare at Rhyston, so he busied himself around the smoker. At first, Rhyston started straight for the lodge back door, then he turned and walked over to Rascal.

"Hello, Jim. Did you see anything?"

"I shot a moose, Rascal."

"Where were you?"

"Just below the mile eleven sign."

"Where's the moose now? Is it dead or did it run off?"

"It's lying to the side of the tracks. I didn't mean to shoot it, Rascal. I had fallen asleep and when I woke up this moose came crashing out of the bushes and it startled me. I just leveled my rifle and fired. I didn't even aim."

It was obvious to Rascal that Rhyston was shaken up and telling the truth. "Go take care of your rifle then we'll have to go up and take care of it."

Rascal told Amy, "Amy, Mr. Rhyston has shot a moose up the tracks. Would you tell Em I'm taking the crawler up to bring it back. If Herschel should get here on the northbound, tell him what's happened."

Rhyston followed Rascal on the crawler and while he held the moose on its back while Rascal cleaned it, he never spoke a word until Rascal had his chain hooked through both gambrels in the hind quarters. "Why did you hook the chain there and not around the neck?"

"If we pulled the moose head first the antlers would dig into the ground and hang-up on everything. Like this the antlers will be dragged along, you'll see."

"What's going to happen to me now, Rascal?"

"Warden Herschel Page will be coming up on the train and he'll decide what to do."

While the southbound train was dropping off two empty cars at the farm, the northbound stopped at the lodge and Herschel stepped off. They met the northbound halfway back to the lodge.

Herschel was inside drinking coffee when they arrived back. The sun had set and all of the hunters were back.

****

Herschel and Mr. Rhyston and the moose left on the first southbound the next morning. "He looked really worried, Rascal," Emma said.

"I know he's embarrassed."

The Cutlidges, Kingsleys, Butlers and the Dubois family didn't come for Thanksgiving that year because both presidents were in Annapolis, Maryland. But both Page families were there and again this year no one wanted to go hunting. It was more important to relax and socialize with family. Paulette and her husband Henri also were there. The next week, Paulette would move back to the farm with Henri and work in the kitchen until spring.

This was the third year that Whiskey Jack hosted the Christmas celebration and to save Emma and Amy from doing most of the cooking, each woman brought a pot luck dish. It was a very happy time and Armand handed out to the workers a Christmas bonus.

Two feet of snow fell Christmas Eve and by daylight the temperature fell to -5° and the wind blew all day. At times it was impossible to see the log cabin across the cove.

But again this New Year's Day, the weather was unusually warm. But after a week of chilling cold and wind, no one objected to the warmer weather.

In March of 1949, the third year midshipman were finally told what the new changes would be and everyone was excited about going to sea for six months and using what they had been preparing for, for the last two-and-a-half years. Archer was excited about the changes and he immediately sent a letter home telling his Mom and Dad.

The days at the Academy began to drag on now. Now that everyone in the upper class knew that in a few short months they would be receiving orders to deploy on their first ship. No one knew yet which ship each would be assigned to. That would not come until the first of August.

****

During the winter of 1948, for an experiment Armand hired Rascal and his crawler to haul a train of loaded sleds with pine and spruce logs from the log yard in the woods to the mill. He had had two men rebuilding five sleds so that they would hitch to one another and the sled in front to Rascal's crawler.

In the early 1920s Earl Hitchcock had purchased a steam driven log hauler that worked well. But when the company moved to Kidney Pond the log hauler also went. And it was plagued with problems. In extreme cold the cast iron tracks would break and it might have to sit out in the woods for a couple of days before repairs could be made. And the fire would have to be kept going so the water would not freeze and the boiler tubes expand and split.

Five sleds were a little too much for Rascal's small crawler. Four was doable but he ran into problems when crossing a gulley or up a steep grade. So he had to settle on three sleds.

Armand worked up some figures over the viability of purchasing a crawler and travelled to Kidney Pond to talk with Rudy. Armand had all his facts and cost savings and in twenty minutes he had convinced Rudy, and three days later a new D-4 Caterpillar dozer was delivered to the farm. The first thing Armand did was to expand the log yard and had three more sleds rebuilt.

Eight loaded sleds were not enough to slow the dozer down, but anymore would have been difficult to maneuver around some of the corners. In the future Armand would see that the haul road would be made straighter. Once Armand was satisfied he had Henri Colton operate the dozer, until he could find someone to replace him.

On the weekends Henri continued the haul road deeper in the woods and made another log yard. With the dozer to haul the logs to the mill during the dry, snowless months Armand wanted shorter hauls, so not to wear out the lags and final drives. Then in the snow months they could go back to the back end of the wood lot. The haul road was also made straighter and the gullies were filled in. "What we need, Henri, is a fleet of smaller crawlers like Rascal's to twitch the logs to the yards and do away with the draft horses, their feed and care. Come spring breakup, I'll talk with Rudy again."

For the rest of the winter Armand paid Rascal for the use of his crawler, with one of his own men to operate it. In equal lumbering conditions he wanted to see if the crew using Rascal's crawler would outproduce the horse crews. He kept a daily log of the crawler. And one advantage he found, that in deep snow the crawler produced more than twice as much wood and the crew were not as tired at the end of each day. He had the mill mechanic build an arch on the back of the crawler so to lift the log ends off the ground making it easier to twitch them to the yard. He also ordered a cable winch that would bolt on the back and driven by the pto drive.

Armand wasn't long seeing the advantages of this. The work horse was being slowly replaced by mechanical tractors, now only if someone would invent something to make cutting the trees down easier.

One day Rascal, Emma and Amy walked out to the farm to watch the D-4 crawler hauling the train of loaded sleds. Henri had straightened the original haul road and now the crawler was hauling twelve loaded sleds without any difficulty.

In the summer the D-4 crawler would be used to upgrade the haul road and make new ones and grade the mill yard, once it had dried out. With more lumber being hauled to the mill now, even in the summer the mill was operating six days a week.

By spring breakup Armand had compiled his figures on using Rascal's crawler versus any of horse crews and it nearly doubled the output. He took all of his paperwork to Kidney Pond and had a long talk with Rudy.

"How many do you want, Armand? I mean you have certainly proven your case with Rascal's crawler."

"Well, I have twelve crews now and the crew using the

crawler almost doubled the output each week against each of the horse crews. I think it would be beneficial to get rid of all the work horses and replace them with six crawler crews. Here's the savings Mr. Hitchcock."

"I'm surprised. I knew horses were expensive with their feed and care, but cutting the number of men is a real bonus," Rudy said.

"I would like one more crawler, Mr. Hitchcock, for the mill with fork tines and not a blade, to load the sawyer deck and move pallets of sawn lumber. I have seen what they can do at Colong's Lumber in Lac St. Jean."

"You have me convinced, Armand. There is a Caterpillar equipment dealer in Lac St. Jean. Go get what you need and have them send me the bill."

"I'll see what they have, but I would prefer diesels over gasoline engines."

"Why?"

"They run cooler, more power and use less fuel. I'll need a fuel tank and I'll have to make arrangements with S&A to deliver fuel.

****

Three weeks later, at the end of April, the afternoon southbound from Lac St. Jean made the switch for the farm and Rascal saw seven new Caterpillar crawlers loaded on three rail cars. The following week all of the work horses were shipped out to Lac St. Jean, to a work horse auction.

"Did you see that, Em?" Rascal asked.

"See what?"

"Looks like all of the work horses from the farm are being shipped to Lac St. Jean. Armand must be replacing them with the new crawlers we saw on the train last week."

Before going to sleep that night, Rascal said, "I've been doing some thinking, Em."

"What about?"

"I would like to get a rubber tired farm tractor."

"You thinking about doing some farming?"

"No, nothing like that. That wagon I use behind the crawler isn't safe to use anymore. It is falling apart. I'd like to get a good rubber tired trailer with it also. That way we would have transportation to the farm and back and we could use it to haul guests around."

"Wouldn't it be uncomfortable sitting on the floor of a trailer?"

"Yes, but I was thinking about building seats in it that could be removed easy when I needed to haul firewood or deer or moose. The crawler just isn't practical for that anymore."

"That might be nice. We can surely afford it."

"How much money do we have in the bank now?"

"Just over $80,000.00"

"Wow, that much? I had no idea."

They lay on their backs until they fell asleep.

The next morning Rascal took the morning train to Beech Tree. There was only one place in town that sold tractors. The Ford garage. Rascal saw just what he wanted. He tried it out and it handled like a dream. "What about a rubber tired trailer?"

"We have some out back. How long would you like it to be?"

"I'd like to look at 'em first."

"Surely."

Rascal liked the looks of the twelve foot body. He figured he could build four or five seats and still there would be leg room. "The tires are heavy duty, so you should never have to worry about a flat tire. Oh, did I mention earlier that the drawbar on the tractor is hydraulic and lifts up and down?"

"How soon can you ship both to Whiskey Jack?"

"Probably either tomorrow morning or the afternoon."

Rascal went from there to the bank and withdrew the money and returned to the garage. "Make sure you fill the gas tank, Mr. Brown."

He still had two hours before the afternoon northbound left, so he went to the jewelry store to buy Emma a diamond ring. When he had proposed to her he was too poor to buy a ring then, but promised to do so when he could. Well, he figured now he could.

Before leaving Beech Tree he would have liked to stop and see Jarvis and Rita, but there just wasn't enough time.

****

"Did you find what you wanted?" Emma asked.

"Yes, a Ford tractor and a nice trailer which I can build some easy-to-remove seats in it."

After lunch that day, Rascal asked, "Paulette, can you and Amy take care of things here for an hour or so?"

"Sure."

"Em, let's go for a walk."

"Where?"

"Up the tracks."

"Okay."

It was a nice sunny day and the mosquitoes and blackflies were not out yet, and there was just a gentle breeze coming down the tracks, cooling the sweat on their faces. They walked happily all the way to Ledge Swamp and sat down on the grassy knoll.

"We should have brought something to drink, Rascal. I'm thirsty."

Rascal wasn't thinking about his thirst, he had something else in mind. "Do you remember, Em, that I promised you something a long time ago?"

She was silent trying to remember what it was. Then he said, "The day I asked you to marry me?"

"Yes, now I do. You said when you had enough money you would buy me a diamond ring."

He reached into his pocket and brought out a pretty ring box and gave it to his wife. Emma began crying even before she opened it. When she saw the ring tears streamed down her cheeks. "Oh Rascal, it is so beautiful. And larger than I ever dreamed it might be."

He slid it on her finger. "I love you, Em. I always have."

"Oh Rascal, I love you so much. Look how it glitters in the sun."

She hugged and kissed him and whispered in his ear, "I'm horny."

They took their time making love in the fresh air and no insects biting their backsides. "Ah Rascal, I can hear the train coming."

"You mean you want to put your clothes back on?"

They dressed and waited for the train to pass. Fred blew the whistle and waved. After the train was by, they climbed back down to the tracks and started for home. They hadn't gone very far and the train was still in sight. Emma, for whatever reason, turned and looked back up the tracks and screamed, "Bear!" She dug her fingernails into his arm. "Bear!"

Rascal turned to look. A hundred yards up the tracks was a bear running towards them. "Run, Em."

"Oh Rascal. Maybe we should live in Beech Tree!"

"Run, Em. Stay ahead of me."

They both began running. Sweat was running down their faces. Rascal turned his head to look behind him. The bear was still there and had gained some distance. They had run about a half mile and Emma said, all winded, "I don't know how much further I can run, Rascal."

The bear could have outrun them very easily, but he was a hundred feet behind them after running a half mile. "Rascal, I just can't run anymore."

"Keep walking, Em. I'll stay between you and him."

"No, I'll stay with you." They stood together in the middle of the tracks. The bear stopped also starring at them with his feet firmly planted, as if to attack.

"Rascal, he has a white patch on his throat like Bear had."

"Bear probably sired most of the bear in this whole area."

"He isn't as big as Bear," Emma said.

"I'm guessing probably a two year old recently abandoned by its mother," Rascal said. "Let's try walking backwards slowly."

"Rascal—he's walking towards us again. Step for step."

"Em, pick up your pace."

"I'll try." It wasn't easy trying to run backwards and not trip on the uneven ties.

"Rascal now he's running."

"Yeah, but he's not coming any closer. I think he's curious."

"I'm getting tired again, Rascal."

"Let's try something else," and Rascal put his arm around Emma and said, "Just walk natural."

After a hundred feet Emma asked, "Is he still following us?"

"Yes, can you run now?"

"I'll try."

"Okay, run!"

Rascal kept turning his head to look back and the bear was still running after them. "He's coming a little closer now, Em."

"You had to tell me that?"

"You keep running Em, I'm going to try something."

Rascal kept running also, but slower. There was now thirty feet between him and Emma.

The bear was closer now and if he had wanted he could easily overtake Rascal. The bear was now only about twenty feet behind him. Emma turned her head to look back and when she did she tripped and fell on the ties and rocks.

"Em!" Rascal hollered and he tripped. Emma turned to look at Rascal also sprawled on the ties. He lifted his head to look at Emma and just then she screamed. The bear had run up to Rascal and had grabbed one of his boots in his mouth.

Rascal rolled over and sat up. The bear still had his boot

in his mouth and then suddenly he let go and ran off the tracks into the woods.

Emma got to her feet and walked up to Rascal. "Are you okay, Rascal?"

"I skinned both arms, but other than that I'm alright. How about you?"

"I skinned my arms too and my head hit one of the ties, but I'm okay. How's your foot where he bit you?"

"It's funny—"

Before he could finish she said, "What's so funny?"

"The bear. He had my foot in his mouth, but I don't really think he was trying to bite me. At least it didn't feel as if he was. Look at my boot, no marks on it at all."

Rascal stood up and looked at Emma and took his handkerchief out of his pocket and wiped the dirt and some blood off her forehead. Then he cleaned the blood off her arms and then his own.

"Let's get out of here, Rascal." As they walked along they both kept looking behind them. "I'm glad we decided to leave Harvey with the girls or he might have tried to protect us and attack the bear and been hurt himself."

Emma was shaking all over and Rascal put his arms around her and held her close. "What do you suppose that was all about, Rascal?"

"I don't know. Twenty years ago Elmo and I asked the same question. We'll have some explaining to do when Paulette, Amy and the guests see these scratches and your forehead. People will think we were in a fight."

By the time they reached the lodge they were laughing. Paulette and Amy were in the kitchen and they looked at them. Their eyes and expression said it all.

"We'll explain later. For now, as far as anyone knows, we fell down. Rascal, we need to wash up and then put some merthiolate on our scratches."

Rascal sat down and took his boot off and looked it all

over and then handed it to Emma and she looked it all over and said, "Nothing."

Paulette and Amy looked questioningly at each other, without speaking a word and wondering what in heck was going on.

As the guests came in from fishing each would look at Rascal and Emma and their scratches, but no one said a word. When Paulette and Amy were alone they would speculate about what had happened.

At 10 p.m. everyone had gone to their room and Rascal shut the generator off and left one gas lantern on low in the hallway between the kitchen and the dining room. Emma knocked on the girls' door. "Come in."

Rascal and Emma came in and shut the door and sat down. "Where do we start Rascal?"

"We had walked up to Ledge Swamp and when we started back there was a bear about a hundred yards up the tracks." Together they told them the whole story.

"This one even had a white patch on his throat like Bear had."

Rascal told them about the bear biting his foot but not hurting him.

"How big was he?" Amy asked.

"I figure he was only a two year old and recently abandoned by its mother. Maybe ninety to a hundred pounds."

It was on everyone's mind. Was this Bear and he had come back. But no one said anything.

"I'm glad he came by when he did and not twenty minutes sooner." Emma said.

"Why?" Amy asked.

"Tell 'em the rest of the story, Em."

"You behave yourself."

"We were making love on the grass."

"Rascal!"

Paulette and Amy laughed and then Paulette said, "Good

for you." Emma was smiling now.

"Come on, Rascal," and they went to their own room.

Rascal and Emma laid awake long into the night talking about their experience with the bear. "Rascal, do you think it would be possible for Bear to come back as this young bear?"

"Well, animals are souls too, but I'm not that familiar with spirituality. But I don't see why it wouldn't be possible."

They eventually fell asleep and Harvey was already asleep on the floor next to the bed. Stan and Ollie were with Paulette and Amy.

****

The train stopped the next morning with the Ford tractor and trailer and Rascal drove it off the railcar and onto the platform and then down the ramp to the ground.

"How are people going to ride in this, Rascal?"

"I'm going to build four bench like seats that I can install or remove easily."

After making the four seats that he could simply bolt on or remove, he hooked the harrow to the new tractor and harrowed the garden. This worked so much better than the crawler.

During June there had been a few elder guests who wanted to visit the mill operations at the farm and Rascal installed the seats in the trailer. They all thought this was a marvelous mode of transportation so far back in the wilderness.

He had time in July to work on firewood. He still used the crawler to push the trees over in the right direction, but the tractor and trailer worked much better for hauling the wood to the lodge.

Chapter 12

On the first of August in 1948, Archer's class all received their orders to deploy and which ship they would be assigned to for six months. Archer and his roommate Ian McFarland would ship out on the SS Cutlidge, a Fletcher class destroyer built in 1939. Ian's course majors were of the engine room and propulsion and he was assigned to the engine room. Archer's course majors were more in line for bridge operations and he was assigned to the bridge.

Harry Bibley and Charles Andrews were both assigned to a carrier as machinist mates.

They were all issued work uniforms and were given their APO address. Afterwards they were split up into different departmental groups to learn what their exact duties would be.

Archer signed a pay voucher to have half of his pay sent home each month. Both he and Ian were more excited about their deployment than their other two roommates.

Looking anxiously to the day they deployed, the month of August seemed to drag on. There was too much idle time now and Archer wrote long letters home to his folks and Amy. He particularly liked her description of Rascal and Emma's encounter with the young bear. A wave of sadness went through him then as he realized he would never see again either Bear, Whiskey Jack or Anita. This was all part of growing up, but at the same time the changes could be difficult to accept sometimes.

Two days before he was to leave for Norfolk, where his ship, the SS Cutlidge was berthed, he made a collect telephone call to home. An unfamiliar voice answered. "Hello, Whiskey Jack."

"Will you accept a collect call from Archer Ambrose?" the operator asked.

"Holy cow, yes, operator. Hello, Archer? Is this really you? I'm Amy."

"Hello Amy, I really enjoy your letters. Don't stop writing. Is Mom or Dad there?"

"Just a minute, Archer, and I'll call. Emma!" she hollered, "Emma! Archer is on the telephone."

Emma came running down from upstairs. "Goodbye, Archer, nice talking with you."

Rascal walked into the lodge after Emma had been talking for ten minutes.

"My ship's name is the SS Cutlidge and the SS Kingsley is supposed to be berthed next to her."

When they all said goodbye they were reminded how much Archer was missed. "Just think, Rascal, in two days our son will be traveling on the high seas."

"He still sounds excited, doesn't he." Rascal said.

****

Two days later Archer and Ian boarded a full bus for Norfolk, the parking garage for the North American Navy, it seemed. There were two busloads of midshipmen deploying on a variety of ships tied up at Norfolk. The rest of the class would be boarding ships in three other locations on the East Coast.

Everyone stepped off the bus at the main gate and each was asked for their orders. Then they were told which numbered berth to find their ship. "Look at all of these ships, Archer," Ian said. "I don't see any carriers, though those probably are too big to tie up in here."

"Look at that water, Ian, it's brown, thick and stinks."

They were met at the top of the gangway and were stopped by the officer of the deck. "Your orders, petty officers."

Archer and Ian gave him their orders and then the OOD said, "The Captain is waiting for you on the bridge. Petty Officer

Seaman will show you the way. Welcome aboard, gentlemen."

There was already two other men in their new quarters. "Just leave your gear on the bunks. The captain wanted to see you right off."

They followed the petty officer up to the bridge. "Captain Hobbs, Sir, Midshipmen Ambrose and McFarland."

"That's all, petty officer, thank you."

"Which one of you is McFarland?"

"I am, Sir," Ian replied.

"This is Lieutenant Billings, Chief Engineer."

"Lieutenant Billings, Sir," Ian said.

"If you'll come with me I'll show you the engine room and explain your duties."

"Midshipman Archer Ambrose you come aboard with excellent references from Captain Ames at the Academy. For now I'm not concerned with what Captain Ames' opinion of you is. From this day forward I will be forming my own opinions. And I think you are aware that your immediate supervisor during these six months will be evaluating you each month. Every detail, even how well you get along with the other men. Your immediate supervisor will be Commander Thomas Riley. He is not aboard at the moment but he will be here before we leave at 1800 hours. After dinner report back here. That's all, Midshipman Ambrose."

"Yes Sir."

Ian wasn't back from the engine room. Archer stored his gear and then the other two roommates walked in, Billy Eaton and Wilson Tafford.

Dinner would be served at 1700 hours and that gave Archer two hours to himself. He was too excited to lie down, so he started walking around the ship to familiarize himself. For now he decided to stay out of the engine room, but he familiarized himself with everything topside, making a mental note of everything.

****

Shortly after finishing dinner Ian reported to the engine room to prepare for maneuvering out of Norfolk Harbor and Archer reported to the bridge. "Commander Riley, this is Midshipman Archer Ambrose."

"Sir."

"You're punctual, Mr. Ambrose. I like that in my subordinates. I understand this will be your first deployment aboard ship."

"Yes, Sir."

"Your duty shift will be from 0600 to 1000 hours and 1800 to 2200 hours. Your roommates will have the same schedule.

"As we maneuver out of the Harbor, your station will be at the telegraph. Do you know how to operate it?"

"Yes, Sir."

"Explain it to me."

"When the conning officer issues a thrust change, I make a full swing of the indicator on the telegraph and back again then to the issued order and stop."

"And who is the conning officer?"

"On all maneuvers the commanding officer or an officer assigned by the commander."

Captain Hobbs stayed in the background observing the dialogue between Cdr. Riley and his new Midshipman, Mr. Ambrose. So far he was pleased with the manner in which the midshipman was conducting himself. Everything he said was direct and decisive with an unusual amount of self-confidence for someone so new.

Archer looked at the clock in front of him, five more minutes before they left the docks. Two tug boats were securing lines to the ship and Cdr. Riley telephoned Lt. Billings, the chief engineer in the engine room. "Secure the jacking gear, Lieutenant and prepare to leave."

"Aye, Aye, Sir."

The tugs began pulling the Cutlidge away from the dock and when there was sufficient clearance, the Cdr. said, "Slow astern, midshipmen."

Archer moved the handle fully one way and then in the opposite direction and stopped on slow astern. Then the engine room answered with the same movement and the telegraph sounded its bell.

Archer could feel the ship coming to life as the two huge propellers began to slowly turn in reverse.

"Hard to starboard, helmsmen."

The bow of the ship was beginning to swing around now. "All stop," the Cdr. said. As soon as the props had stopped, the Cdr. said, "Slow ahead," and then, "Hard to port."

The ship was really vibrating now and they were moving slowly ahead on its own propulsion. The tug lines had been released.

"Okay, helmsmen, I'll take it from here until we clear the harbor."

"Yes, Sir." Archer remained at his station, taking everything in and memorizing every move and order the commander was making. He had been studying for three years for this day. Feeling the Cutlidge come to life under his feet was more exciting for him than he would ever be able to explain to his Mom and Dad.

"Mr. Ambrose."

"Yes, Sir."

"The Cutlidge was ready to set sail as soon as you and Midshipman McFarland came aboard. Why didn't we?"

"We had to wait for high tide, Sir."

They were following the channel now out to the open ocean, following red and green buoy markers. "Mr. Ambrose, are you familiar with the red and green buoys?"

"Yes Sir, red-left port and green-right starboard."

"Mr. Ambrose, we are clear of any ships now, why do we

still maintain slow ahead?"

"Because any faster, and the ships wake would wash up on shore and could cause erosion or interfere with other ships."

Several minutes later they were well clear of the shore and beyond the marked channel to the harbor. "Full ahead," and the commander relinquished the helm back to the helmsmen. "Keep her steady on this coarse until the captain has the orders.

"Mr. Ambrose, while I am talking with the captain, I want you to take a sextant reading."

"Yes, Sir."

Commander Riley knocked on the captain's door. "Come in."

"Captain, Sir."

"How is our young midshipman doing?"

"I'm impressed with him, Sir."

"Well, that's good. Let's open our orders and see where we are going.

"Well, Mr. Riley, looks like we go to the Mediterranean first. We make a counter clockwise course around it. Then we go north to Hamburg, Germany then to Oslo, Norway for more fuel. We are to use the new submarine radar detector and mark courses of the signature of Russian subs and record any and all air traffic.

"On the chart table, mark the locations of subs we find. But not to track 'em."

"What is the concern with the Russian submarines, Captain?"

"There is evidence that they may have already, or will soon have a nuclear weapon, and the DOD needs to know the locations of their subs, and if we see any of their ships identify what they are and course heading.

"That's all, Commander."

"Yes, Sir."

"Well, Mr. Ambrose, what have you?"

"Here, Sir."

"Let's see if the radar navigation agrees with you. Hum, pretty good, midshipman."

"Your scheduled duties will start at 0600 to 1000 and then 1800 to 2200 hours."

"Yes, Sir."

"The shortest distance, Mr. Ambrose, on a sphere?"

"A curved line, Sir."

"Helmsman, set course at 65⁰."

Cdr. Riley was busy looking over the charts and motioned for Archer to join him. "We are heading for the Mediterranean Sea and once through the narrows at Gibraltar we will cruise around the sea counterclockwise.

"When you are not busy, I would like you to familiarize yourself with our new submarine detector. Come, I'll show you."

They went down to the next level. "This is Lieutenant Larry Goff. Some days you'll be working here for the lieutenant. I'll leave you now and return to the bridge."

"This works much on the same principle as sonar radar, only this is a bit more sophisticated. We have learned that each vessel has its own signature mark. So when we locate a sub we'll be able to document pretty close who it is. You will have to learn these different signatures."

"We studied this at the Academy but would you have any manuals I could study?" Archer asked.

"In the bottom drawer. But they don't leave this room."

He spent the rest of his watch studying the principles of the new sonar radar.

****

During the night, an unusual wind was blowing from the north and the sea was getting rough. When Archer reported for duty at the bridge Cdr. Riley was not feeling well. And the rough sea was not helping.

After an hour his laryngitis was so bad he could no longer talk and he was sweating from a high temperature. "You'd better get yourself down to sick bay, Commander," Capt. Hobbs said. "I'll take the bridge."

"Yes, Sir."

"I'm going back to my office, let me know if the weather gets any worse." The Capt. would be able to judge for himself if the weather turned for the worse by the way the ship was rolling or pitching. But this was a test for the midshipman to see how he would react. He kept his office door open so he could hear what was going on.

"We didn't get introduced yesterday, I'm Greg Weatherly."

Archer shook hands with Greg and said, "Archer Ambrose."

"The water is getting rougher out there," Greg said.

"You're doing fine, just keep the bow quartering into the waves, just like you're doing."

Capt. Hobbs heard this. He was not impressed yet with the young midshipman, but he grinned to himself.

An hour later the wind speed had increased to 50mph and the sea was getting rougher. "This is getting hard to handle."

"You're doing just fine, Greg. Quarter into the waves a little more."

Capt. Hobbs was now beginning to be impressed. Here was a raw kid from the Academy, comfortably reassuring an experienced helmsman that he was doing just fine. Young Ambrose was acting like he had several years experience aboard ship. The Capt. stopped his paperwork and sat back listening.

A large wave hit the bow of the ship causing it to roll more than it had been. Archer knocked on the captain's door. "Yes, midshipman."

"Sir the wind is now blowing at 55mph and the water is rougher. Permission to change speed to half ahead."

"Why do you think we need to slow down?"

"We are having to quarter more into the waves now and at full ahead, the bow could ride up the crest and slam down into the next wave."

"This ship was designed to withstand the pounding from rough seas, and if this was an emergency we would continue at the present speed. But we're not in an emergency and you are correct at this speed we could have problems. It comes down to a judgment call.

"Granted."

Archer telegraphed the engine room to slow their speed to half ahead. Archer could feel less vibration in the deck as the engines slowed to half ahead.

Before another hour had passed Archer advised Greg to steer more into the waves. A huge rogue wave could topple the ship.

A half hour before the end of the watch the wind suddenly stopped and the sea returned to its usual choppy and rolling waves. Without having to be told Archer went out on the flying deck and took a sextant reading and then back inside and plotted it on the charter.

"Were we blown off course, midshipman?" the Capt. asked.

"A little, Sir, but not bad."

"Very good, plot your course to make up the difference."

"Yes, Sir." The helmsman had to only make a three degree correction.

****

Cdr. Riley was in sick bay for three days before the doctor would let him return to duty. Capt. Hobbs saw the potential of Archer and knew in his off time he was studying different systems on the ship. So when the commander was back on duty he asked him to take Archer under his wing, sort of to say, "I believe he wants to learn every system aboard this ship."

In the afternoons after his morning watch and lunch he would study the armament and tactical operation of the destroyer. The automatic cannons, anti-craft guns, the anti-submarine defense, the torpedo and depth charges systems. He would sleep after his watch ended at 2200 hours until 0500 hours. Ian was doing the same kind of studying in the engine room and they were both only getting about five hours of sleep a day. "This is like our first year at the Academy, Archer."

"Yeah, but I think this is more hands on learning and sometimes I get the feeling I don't want to stop learning. Before this trip is over, Ian, I'd like to go below with you and learn the rudiments of the engine room."

On the morning of their sixth day out from Norfolk they began the passage through Gibraltar. At the narrowest point there was only 7.7 miles separating Spain from Morocco.

"Mr. Ambrose, plot the course of fifty miles offshore all along the African Coast."

"Yes, Sir."

Archer had his camera with him and was able to take some nice pictures. Also of the ship looking forward from the flying deck and one looking aft.

Their speed had been reduced to half ahead. There were other ships in the strait plus many fishing boats.

"Mr. Ambrose."

"Yes, Commander."

"While we are making the loop around the Mediterranean Sea, your watch will be with Lieutenant Goff in the sub tracking room. This is why we are out here."

"Yes, Sir."

Once they were clear of the strait the commander telephoned the engine room and advised the lieutenant although they would have a throttle settling of full ahead he wanted the main throttle closed enough to maintain fifteen knots.

The air inland from the ocean was much warmer. The temperatures in the engine room would reach 110°F. When the men finished their watch their clothes would be drenched in their sweat.

The force draft fans were working at full capacity and the water bulkhead doors were secured open to let the heat escape.

Shortly after leaving the Strait of Gibraltar, Lt. Goff and Archer located three submarines. Two were leaving and one headed north. That one was a North American submarine and the other two were British and French. There was also a lot of air communication traffic which was recorded and would be analyzed at Naval Intelligence Headquarters.

Near the Egyptian coast, Archer located an aircraft approaching the destroyer off the starboard side. Lt. Goff radioed Cdr. Riley that an aircraft was approaching approximately ten miles off starboard. The commander immediately set off a warning and all hands reported to battle stations.

The gunners mates all knew the procedure and the lieutenant in charge was now on the observation deck ready to give commands.

When the aircraft came into view it was identified as a single prop fighter. Before closing in on a mile distance from the destroyer it turned starboard and disappeared.

For Archer and Ian, these were a few tense minutes. Twenty minutes later when there were no more potential threats the alert was canceled and everyone returned to their work station. "Do these flyovers happen often?" Archer asked.

"Along this section of the African coast they do. They just want us to know they're watching."

When they changed course near the Suez Canal there was another flyover and again the ship was called to battle stations. And Lt. Goff and Archer found signatures of two more Russian submarines and ten miles away from that sighting they located signatures of one North American submarine and one French. They were apparently watching each other.

Twenty days had passed since leaving Norfolk and both Archer and Ian were feeling like true sailors and they were both very readily accepted with the crew.

They were heading north now and the ship circled Cyprus Island and then back on its original course and then a few days later they circled Crete Island and made course for the Aegean Sea.

Here they were recording many air communications. "It would be nice to know what's being said," Lt. Goff said.

They sailed up the Aegean Sea and back again and then they did the same with the Adriatic Sea. One morning as Archer was beginning his watch, Commander Riley said, "Mr. Ambrose, plot us a course around Sicily and then to Naples, Italy.

It had now been five weeks since leaving Norfolk.

****

The fishing season was over for this year, the garden was taken care of, frog legs were canned, thirty pounds of smoked fish and the sheds were full of firewood. "How do you like the new tractor, Rascal?" Emma asked.

"It rides a good deal better than the crawler and I can actually haul more firewood with the tractor and trailer, then that old worn out wagon."

Just then the telephone rang and Emma answered it. "That was Mr. Steamer and there are nuisance beaver again at mile twelve."

"Amy, will you put out the red flag. I'll get my gear together. Do you want to go up, Em?"

"No, you go ahead, Rascal."

"Can I go?" Amy asked. "I need some exercise."

"Don't wear good clothes, Amy, and pull on some rubber boots," Emma said.

Just as Rascal was setting his pack basket and traps on the platform the train was stopping. Emma came running out with a pot to make tea in.

"We don't have any food, Rascal," Amy said.

"We'll eat beaver and tea."

The train had to switch tracks and pick up two cars at the farm and then they were on their way.

"We'll be getting off at mile twelve, Roscoe," Rascal said.

"Are you going to want a ride back?"

"Yes, if we're through."

There was a lot of water backed up this year and like usual there was a coffer dam on the uphill side of the tracks.

He showed Amy how to make a trough on the dam for the water to run through and how to place the trap. He then showed her how to open the trap jaws and set the trigger. "Always reach under the jaws to set the trigger. That way if the jaws snap closed your fingers won't get caught."

He watched as she set the trigger. "Okay, put the trap in the trough—gently so not to spring it."

With that done, she asked, "Now what?"

"We move down to the next dam. There'll be two dams between the tracks and Jack Brook."

"This is a big dam," Amy said. "How many beaver do you think are in here?"

"It has been three years since I trapped here and there usually will be twelve. We have to take even the small ones because they are a great nuisance to the S&A.

She followed him out across on the dam. "Be careful you don't fall in. If you get wet you'll have to take your clothes off and dry them by the fire."

"I'll remember that."

"You can set one right here. Just like you did the other one. I'm going over here."

Rascal wasn't long setting his trap and then he squeezed by Amy and started setting another one six feet the other side of her.

"I'm done here," she said. And Rascal wasn't long setting that one.

"Now what?"

"We go ashore."

Just as they were stepping off the dam two traps snapped closed. When Amy started to rush back out on the dam, Rascal put out his arm and said, "We have to wait for the beaver to drown. If you were to try and pull it in now, it would pull you off the dam into the water. Beaver are very strong animals and swimmers."

"How long does it take?"

"I give 'em about five minutes to make sure."

A few minutes later, "It should be okay now."

Amy began pulling, "I'm bringing something in—it's heavy, whatever it is."

Rascal pulled his in and it was a very large beaver. Amy's was even larger. They reset those and Amy's beaver was too heavy for her to carry. "While I skin these get a fire going and we'll eat. Make some tea also." While he was skinning the third trap snapped closed. Once the fire was going Amy pulled that beaver in and reset the trap. This was a much smaller beaver.

"Cut some roasting sticks, Amy, and I'll cut off some meat."

Before he had skun the second beaver and cut off the meat and castors another trap snapped closed. Amy waited and then pulled in another large beaver.

"The meat is almost cooked, Rascal."

"Okay, pour us some tea. I'm about finished with this one."

"Hum, this is so much better when it is so fresh and cooked over the fire," Amy said.

"It is good, isn't it."

They finished what was cooked and Amy put some more on to cook, while Rascal skun the next beaver. "Maybe we should have brought another pack basket as fast as these beaver are coming."

By the time they had eaten their fill of beaver and all four were skun and the meat, tails and castors cut off, the flowage had quieted.

"I think it is time we move down to the next dam."

Like in past years, this flowage was not as big. They removed three more beaver and moved back up to the middle dam. They had another beaver there.

"We'll probably have at least one beaver in one of the first two traps we set. Let's carry as many as these carcasses up to the tracks as we can carry."

"Okay, but why?"

"Well, I always used to leave them all up on the knoll by the tracks for Bear."

Amy knew what he was thinking and didn't say anything. Rascal set his pack basket down and they carried five of the carcasses to the top of the knoll. "Let's go check the coffer dam." There was one very large beaver. "Probably the mate to the first one you pulled in, Amy."

Rascal checked his watch and there was an hour and a half before the train would come through. Amy reset that trap while Rascal skun it and cut away the meat.

When Amy was through she stepped between the rails and screamed, "Rascal! Bear! There's a bear on the tracks!"

Rascal finished putting everything in the pack basket. The bear had not moved. It was about two hundred feet away. They just stood there between the rails. The bear also watching them without moving.

"What does he want, Rascal? The carcasses are on the knoll, can't he smell them?"

The bear began walking slowly towards them. "R-a-s-c-a-l he's coming closer. Oh man, now I wish I'd stayed at home. Should we run, Rascal?"

"No, if he is aggressive a bear can outrun a horse."

The bear was only a hundred feet away now. The bear stopped, and lifting his nose he began sniffing the air and then suddenly he started running towards them. "Stand still, don't move, Amy."

The bear stopped thirty feet in front of them. He had the white patch on his throat and Rascal was sure this was the same bear he and Emma had seen.

"I'm going to try something." Rascal raised his arm and made that strange laughing noise like he did with Bear. This bear sat down on his butt and raised his paw, but he did not make any noise. Then suddenly the bear ran up on top of the knoll and stood there. The train was coming. The bear stood up so he could look over the top of the grass and raised his paw again and both Rascal and Amy raised their arm. Then the bear ran off.

"When that bear started running towards us he made me pee in my pants and now it's running down my legs."

"Are you okay?"

"Just shaken up some. Hell, I'm still shaking."

The train was stopping. "This is going to be embarrassing if there are a lot of passengers."

"We'll go to the baggage car."

"It's all inside my boots now and I'm sloshing with every step."

"Thank you, Roscoe," Rascal said as he picked up his pack basket and stepped off the train.

"I'd better take these boots off out here." Amy sat down in a chair on the platform. "Will you pull these off, Rascal?"

When he had them off he emptied each boot and began laughing, "Wow, that was a lot."

"It's all that tea."

They walked inside and Paulette saw how wet her backside was and asked, "What did you, fall in?"

Emma walked in then and saw how wet Amy was and she asked, "What happened did you sit down on the dam?"

"You'd might as well tell them, Amy," Rascal said while chuckling.

"I peed myself."

"Almost filled her boots."

Now Amy was laughing. "It was that damned bear," and she told them the whole story. "When he started running up the tracks at us from only a hundred feet away, well, I just couldn't help it," she started laughing again and added, "I didn't know I was so wet, until my feet started sloshing."

Emma broke out laughing and said, "The same thing

happened to me with my first encounter with Bear."

Amy said, "This new bear raised his paw."

"Twice. He had the white patch just like the earlier bear you and I saw up there."

"It has to be the same bear," Emma said.

"I believe so," Rascal said.

All were quiet and after a few moments Paulette said, "It has to be Bear. I believe all living things—plants, animals, as well as people, are souls also. He obviously had a great amount of love for all of us here and we all sat up with him all night as his body was slowly dying. I don't think there can be any doubt but what this is Bear and he's back."

"I can accept that," Emma said.

"Me, too," Amy agreed.

"And me."

"What are we going to call him?" Emma asked.

Amy spoke up first, "How about Cub?"

They all looked at each other and everyone nodded their heads.

"This will have to be kept a secret you know."

"We know," they all said.

That night Amy wrote a long letter to Archer telling him all about Cub.

****

At breakfast the next morning Emma asked, "Are you going back up today?"

"Yes, do you want to go?"

"Not really, not until we know for sure if he just wants to play or not."

"Paulette do you want to go up?" Amy asked.

"I'm with Emma."

"I'll go up with you, Rascal. I don't know why," Amy said.

They could hear the train slowing down so they went out

on the platform to wait. "Why do you have those potato diggers with you, Rascal?" Amy asked.

"Once we have all of the beaver removed we have to open the dams to drain the water."

Emma kissed Rascal and said, "Be careful." He knew what she meant by that.

"Same place, Rascal?" Roscoe asked.

"Yes, mile twelve."

"Will you be wanting a ride back today also?"

"If we are out by the tracks."

They got off the train and the first thing Amy did was look around. "I don't see him, Rascal."

"Maybe his belly is full of beaver and he won't be around today."

There was nothing in the coffer dam traps, so they went down to the next dam. All three traps had been pulled into the water.

They pulled in the beaver and reset those traps and as Rascal skun them and cut off the meat, tails and castors Amy kept watch of the dam and for the bear. A trap snapped closed and after a few minutes she went out and pulled it in and reset the trap. "This is a small one, Rascal."

"That's good. That means we have almost all of them."

When he had finished with those they moved down to the last dam and only one trap had been pulled in, and another small one. "You might as well build a fire, Amy, and we'll have lunch here."

As they were eating roasted beaver and drinking tea Rascal said, "When I was here three years ago and eating beaver, Bear came wandering in. He sat a little to your left. I ended up giving him half of the cooked meat. That was the first time in twenty-six years that he would come in while I was eating beaver. I have often wondered if he knew then that his body was beginning to fade."

"How big would you say Cubbie is?" Amy asked.

"He has put on a lot of weight through the summer. I'd say maybe a hundred and fifty pounds."

There was no more beaver activity there so they pulled the traps and moved up to the big dam. This time two traps were pulled off the dam and they had two more small beaver.

Rascal skun them and took care of the meat and castors and said, "We might as well wait a few minutes to see what happens. But we might go back to the lower dam and pull that one apart."

When they were done and back up to the big dam, there had been no more activity there so they pulled those traps and moved everything up to the tracks. They had another small beaver in one of the coffer dam sets. While Rascal skun it, Amy removed the dam. "How much time before the train comes through?"

Rascal checked his watch, "An hour and a half. Do you want to wait here or start walking back?"

"I just as soon start walking."

Before leaving they tossed the carcasses up on the knoll.

Amy helped him to shoulder the pack basket. It wasn't anywhere near as heavy as the day before. They were down the tracks almost a quarter of a mile when Amy looked behind them. "Cubbie is running behind us, Rascal. At least I hope it's Cubbie."

"Just keep walking."

When Cubbie was only thirty feet away he stopped running and began walking at their same pace. This went on for several minutes and Rascal suddenly stopped and turned around to look at Cubbie. He stopped too.

"Ooh, I knew I should have gone to the bathroom back there in the woods. If he makes me pee myself again, I'll box his ears!" Amy said.

Cubbie was now walking slowly towards them. They just stood there. Then suddenly Cubbie turned and looked back up the tracks and then ran off the tracks and just inside the tree line. Now Rascal and Amy could hear the train coming. They stepped off the tracks to wait. Cubbie was still there.

Rascal and Amy raised their arm and Rascal said, "You stay out of sight, Cubbie." He walked off only a short distance under the shade of a spruce tree.

The train stopped and gave them a ride back. "I saw the water was gone from the beaver flowages, Rascal. Are all the beaver removed?" Roscoe asked.

"Yes, and the dams."

When they got off at the lodge, Emma and Paulette came out to greet them. Paulette walked around Amy and then said, "No wet britches this time."

"Almost and I have to run."

"I take it you saw the bear again," Emma said.

"He followed us down the tracks until the train came along."

"So, what do you think? Is that Bear come back?"

"He is certainly an offspring of his. And I'd like to believe he is. He sure acts like it. Amy started calling him Cubbie instead of Cub."

"That sounds good."

"Wouldn't it be amazing if Cubbie actually is Bear and has come back," Paulette said.

Chapter 13

It was a clear beautiful day when the Cutlidge Destroyer maneuvered into Naples, Italy. The ship was at ease and the engines were on standby readiness. The captain left the ship with the recorded communications and locations of Russian submarines to be deciphered and analyzed by the North American Naval Telecommunications Station.

After 1800 hours that day, all except for the watch officers were on shore leave. And they had to be back onboard by 0200 or suffer the consequences.

"Aren't you going ashore tonight, Mr. Ambrose?" the commander asked.

"No, I gave a package to the steward for home, but I would rather stay onboard and help with refueling, Sir."

"Okay, what's the first thing you do, Mr. Ambrose?"

"Make sure the ship is properly grounded."

"And why is that?"

"Because the ship builds up static electricity moving through the water."

"That will be your responsibility, Mr. Ambrose, to make sure there is proper ground."

"Yes, Sir."

Ian also stayed to refuel. When Capt. Hobbs returned he was surprised to see Ambrose and McFarland had stayed to refuel instead of shore leave. He made sure to document this in their evaluations and he was pleased.

At midnight refueling was complete and Ian and Archer went to bed.

The next morning truckloads of fresh fruits, vegetables, eggs and meat arrived and the steward department spent all morning loading the new stores onboard.

At 1300 hours, Capt. Hobbs gave the signal to leave. After leaving Naples, Archer went below to the engine room with Ian. He wanted to get an overview of the engine room operations.

"We'll start with the boilers, Archer. When you telegraph for full ahead, this big valve wheel opens or closes the main throttle valve. At full steam this is all the way open, and the orifices in the burner nozzles will be larger, let's say, than if you wanted a slower speed, but still require the main valve to be fully opened. When maneuvering in or out of port these burner orifices have to be changed often.

"The four boilers produce superheated steam at 950° and at 950 psi, which drive the steam turbines and reduction gearing. After the steam exhausts the engines, it is now desuperheated steam and some is bled off to power the electrical generator and to make portal water and to preheat the bunker-C fuel oil."

Ian showed Archer each system and he knew he would not have to explain anything to him again. He had learned that Archer had a fantastic mind for learning and grasping concepts of different systems.

"I have a better understanding now, Ian, about what goes on down here. Now when I give you a signal on the telegraph I'll know what you are doing."

The Chief Engineer, Lt. Billings, told the Capt. about Archer coming down to the engine room for some basic understanding of the operation. Capt. Hobbs put this into Archer's evaluation also.

For the next three days they followed the coastline of Italy and France to Spain and back to the Strait of Gibraltar.

Archer counted ten vessels sailing east and four west through the narrows which were only seven miles wide. They had to reduce their speed, as they all had to do, so not to hinder another ship with their wake.

That afternoon after they had left the strait behind and they had returned to normal cruising speed, Commander Riley was talking with Archer on the bridge, when he suddenly collapsed and fell to the deck. Lt. Goff, the communications officer, was also on the bridge. Archer didn't hesitate a second. He said, "Call sickbay." When the Lt. didn't move Archer repeated himself a little more forceful. "Call sickbay now! And tell Doctor Roberts to come to the bridge immediately—that Commander Riley has collapsed to the deck."

Capt. Hobbs overheard and came out of his office. Archer was on his knees supporting Riley's neck to keep the airway open. "What happened?"

When Lt. Goff was through talking with Dr. Roberts he said, "The commander simply collapsed and fell to the deck."

"Is he still alive, Mr. Ambrose?"

"Yes, Sir, but his pulse is very weak."

Dr. Roberts entered the bridge then and knelt down opposite Archer. "No, don't move, keep supporting his neck. Lieutenant, find a stretcher so we can take the commander to sickbay."

"What is it, Doctor?" Capt. Hobbs asked.

"He has all the tell-tale signs of a stroke and we'll have to get him to a hospital as soon as possible."

"Mr. Ambrose signal the engine room—no telephone the engine room—and tell 'em we need as much speed as possible. Then set course for Rota, Spain. The Naval Base there has a very good hospital."

"Yes, Sir."

"Lieutenant, send a radiogram to Rota Naval Base and request an emergency docking and have an ambulance there when we arrive."

"You have the bridge, Mr. Ambrose. Let's see what you can do. Rota is an easy harbor to enter and you'll not need any tugs."

"Yes, Sir."

When they were ten miles out, Archer telephoned Chief Billings in the engine room and advised him to change nozzle orifices and cut their speed. When they were five miles out Archer signaled on the telegraph for half ahead. He was in between the red and green buoys now.

"Mr. Ambrose," Lt. Goff said, "We are to tie up to pier number two; that'll be off to the left."

"Helmsman, are you okay taking us in?"

"I am, Sir, until we get to the docks."

"Just follow my commands. You're doing just fine, Greg."

Archer signaled the engine room to slow ahead. "Do you see the number two pier, Greg?"

"Yes."

"Okay, on my say so, I'll want you to go full starboard."

Archer signaled slow astern and the ship began to shutter. "Okay, now full rudder to starboard" and at the same time he signaled all stop. The ship was slowly slipping towards the pier, but there was still forward movement. He signaled again, slow astern, and this brought the bow in closer to the pier. "Full rudder to port now, Greg." All forward motion had stopped and Archer signaled all stop. The deck hands were already throwing out the ropes to men on shore who were securing them to winching posts. Then the onboard capstans were engaged and the ship was brought in tight to the pier and secured. Archer then telephoned the engine room and advised the Lt. to secure the engines but to keep the boilers in standby.

Archer looked at Greg and sweat was running down his face. "That's the first time I have ever brought her in, Sir," Greg said.

"Greg, I'm a midshipman, not a Sir."

"You sure sounded and performed like one."

"Yes, Mr. Ambrose, you did. Congratulations. An experienced executive officer could not have done better. Now, I'm going to the hospital with the commander. Mr. Ambrose, you have the bridge."

"Yes, Sir."

After Capt. Hobbs left, Greg looked at Archer and said, "You'll make one hell of a skipper someday."

"Thanks, Greg. You did okay also. In fact you did a great job."

Archer knew what the captain had said when he said he had the bridge. He went from stem to stern checking on things. He was asked several times how long they would be in Rota and whether or not there would be any shore leave. The only answer he had was, "It'll be up to Captain Hobbs."

Commander Riley was rushed right into the intensive care unit. Capt. Hobbs waited in the waiting room for a chance to speak with the doctor. An hour later Doctor Ruez came out to speak with him.

"It is fortunate that you brought Mr. Riley here when you did. Any longer and we would not be able to help him. He is conscious now but I must not allow you to speak with him. He will be with us for some time. And I don't believe he will ever be well enough to return to sea duty."

"Thank you, Doctor Ruez."

From the hospital the captain went to see Admiral Harry Baxter at headquarters.

"Come in, Captain Hobbs. How is the commander?"

"I just came from the hospital and Doctor Ruez said he will have to remain in the hospital for some time and probably will never be fit again for sea duty."

"That was some pretty fancy maneuvering, Captain, bringing your ship in so fast and without aid of tugs."

"Thank you, Admiral. But I didn't bring it in. Archer Ambrose, a young midshipman from the Academy, did."

"Impossible. How long has this Ambrose been with you Captain?"

"This is his first deployment and we left Norfolk Harbor on September first."

"I say again, impossible. How could he with no experience?"

"Midshipman Ambrose is no average midshipman. Since leaving Norfolk six weeks ago, in his spare time he has studied every system onboard. He has more knowledge about the entire ship than anyone. All he needs to be a good officer is experience. And I think I have found a way for him to get that."

"Continue, Captain, you certainly have my attention."

"It is obvious, Commander Riley will not be able to continue as commander. I intend to let Mr. Ambrose assume the executive officer's duties for the remainder of his six months at sea."

"You just can't promote an E-3 to commander, Captain Hobbs."

"No, that's correct, but I'm entitled to have any qualified sailor aboard my ship as my executive officer. And believe me, Admiral, he is more qualified than any other officer aboard the Cutlidge."

"As captain, that certainly is your prerogative. I'd like to meet this midshipman, Captain. Where does he come from?"

"From Whiskey Jack, Maine, Sir. North of Beech Tree and only accessible by train." They both started laughing then.

"Are you serious, Captain?"

"Certainly. You have heard of Whiskey Jack haven't you, Sir?"

"The name does sound familiar. Oh yes, yes, isn't that where President Cutlidge and Kingsley first met to discuss Canada and the United States merging?"

"Yes, Sir, it is."

"A young man from the deep wilderness of Maine with the ability to maneuver a destroyer without any experience! Marvelous, Captain. We don't want to lose this young man. I'm busy for the rest of today. How about I unexpectedly arrive tomorrow at 0800 hours?"

"That would be fine, Sir. I only have one consideration to make, though."

"Yes, Captain."

"What he did bringing the Cutlidge in is really remarkable, but I would prefer if not too much praise was said. I don't want it to go to his head."

"Consider it done, Captain. Tomorrow at 0800. Good day, Captain Hobbs."

****

"Captain, the crew is asking whether there will be any shore leave tonight?" Archer asked.

"Not tonight, Mr. Ambrose. And use the commander's office and type up a bulletin for me and post it. No liberty tonight. Admiral Baxter will be coming onboard at 0800 tomorrow and I want everything in perfect order. When you have it typed, assign a petty officer to post it and ask that petty officer to inform the crew Commander Riley will not be coming back aboard and to have a steward pack up all of the commander's things and then take them to the base headquarters. Then, Mr. Ambrose, you are to report back to me. Dismissed."

"Yes, Sir."

An hour later Archer knocked on the captain's door. "Come in, Mr. Ambrose, and close the door. Sit down. Do you like coffee?"

"Yes, Sir." The captain poured two cups and gave one to Archer and then sat back at his desk. Archer was wondering what this was all about.

"When Commander Riley collapsed you reacted immediately, and by instinct or your natural leadership ability you were issuing orders to Lieutenant Goff. He may have had his pride hurt some. But don't worry about it. There was no hesitation in your part and that is a good sign of an officer. I gave you an order to take the ship to Rota. And again everything you did—you did an excellent job. I could not have docked the ship any better nor faster than you did. You saw to it that everything was secured and the engines kept on standby. You checked out everything. A seasoned officer could not have done a better job.

"I am impressed, Mr. Archer."

"Thank you, Sir."

"Commander Riley had a severe stroke and will not be coming back aboard. And I need to appoint a new executive officer, and I have the privilege to appoint whomever I feel is competent. You already have more knowledge about the overall operations of this destroyer. But what you lack is experience. I'm offering the position of executive officer to you, Mr. Ambrose. I cannot promote an E-3 to commander, but I can certainly give you the opportunity for the experience. There will be no promotion nor pay increase. But you will have the authority of being my executive officer. What do you say, Mr. Ambrose?"

"What about the other officers? Won't they feel slighted or jealous? Other than that I would welcome the opportunity, Sir."

"Good, I'll have a meeting with all of my officers tonight in the officer's mess. I expect you to be there for dinner. In fact from this moment until you leave the ship you will be accredited with all the rights and privileges as any of my officers. And as soon as the steward has all of Commander Riley's belongings removed I expect you to move in. You need to be close to your place of work."

"Thank you, Sir. I will not let you down. There is one point I'd like to bring to your attention."

"Go on."

"The helmsman, Greg Weatherly. He did an exceptional job at the helm, Sir. That was the first time he had ever maneuvered the ship all the way to the pier, Sir."

After Archer left the captain's office, Hobbs wrote a letter home to his wife, telling her all about this young midshipman from somewhere called Whiskey Jack, Maine. Every once in a while he would have to stop writing because he was laughing so much. In closing he said, "I really believed he was more concerned about Seaman Weatherly getting credit than he was himself."

Everyone was busy preparing for the Admiral's visit in the morning.

When Archer walked into the officer's mess all the other officers were there and seated. Everyone stopped talking to look at the midshipman, "Up here, Mr. Ambrose."

Archer sat down and then said, "I feel a little out of place here, Captain."

In a somewhat stern voice the captain replied, "Get over it, Mr. Ambrose, from this moment these same officers will be taking directions from you. Is that understood, Mr. Ambrose?"

"Yes, Sir, it is."

"Gentlemen, before we order I have two pieces of information for you. Commander Riley had a severe stroke and will not be back aboard the Cutlidge. And I have decided on Mr. Ambrose to fill the executive officer's position. Under my direct supervision. From this moment until Mr. Ambrose leaves the Cutlidge, you will afford him the same respect and courtesy you would any executive officer. Is that understood?"

"Yes, Captain," they all said.

"I chose Mr. Ambrose because as all of you have observed, he has studied every system aboard this ship and he has demonstrated sufficiently to me that he is quite able to do the job. Does anyone have any questions or comments?" There were none.

****

The next morning everyone was in their dress uniform, even at breakfast. The Admiral arrived at 0800 hours and the ship's officers were on the dock to greet him. Even Archer Ambrose. The crew were in formation on the deck. "Very impressive, Captain Hobbs. I'd like to take a quick inspection tour of your ship, Captain. Will you and your executive officer join me."

The engine room was first and Admiral Baxter was surprised to see it so clean and the bilges were free of oil and dry.

A quick walk through the crews berthing and then the bridge. Here the Admiral, Captain and Archer were alone.

"Where do you call home, Mr. Ambrose?" the Admiral asked.

"Whiskey Jack, Maine, Sir."

"What exactly is Whiskey Jack? Is it a town?"

"It used to be a lumbering village. But in 1925 the Hitchcock Lumber Company burned the buildings and moved to Kidney Pond. The hotel was left and given to my folks and they turned it into a hunting and fishing lodge. The only access is by train."

"And what inspired you from the wilderness to seek a career in the Navy?"

"While I was at the academy in Beech Tree I read a lot about the Navy and ships and I was drawn naturally to it."

"From what Captain Hobbs has told me about you, I would have to agree that you are a natural. When the captain told me he wanted you for his executive officer I was shocked. But this is his ship and I have to rely on his confidence with you, Mr. Ambrose."

The Admiral stood then and the captain and Archer also stood. Admiral Baxter extended his hand and shook Archer's. "Don't let your captain down, Mr. Ambrose."

"I won't, Sir."

****

The Cutlidge left Rota, Spain, and continued its work up through the English Channel towards Hamburg, Germany. The fog was so thick as they steamed through the channel it was difficult to see the water at times. Archer cut their speed to slow ahead and blew the foghorn for five seconds every minute, to warn other ships in the area and smaller fishing boats. Once they were through the channel the fog was gone and they resumed their normal speed.

In Hamburg, the mail pouch was delivered to the

executive officer, Archer, and instead of handing the letters out himself, he designated a petty officer. He had letters from home and Amy.

He read Amy's letter first and when he came to the part about Cubbie and she peeing her pants, he broke out laughing for a long time. Captain Hobbs walked into his cabin and asked, "What's so funny, Mr. Ambrose?"

Archer had to tell him the whole story about Bear and now the young bear named Cubbie. "You sure have lived an interesting life, Mr. Ambrose. Someday I'd like to meet your family."

"They're good people, Captain."

****

As the Cutlidge Destroyer was entering the harbor in Hamburg, Germany, Fred Darling dropped off the mail pouch at Whiskey Jack. Amy was waiting on the platform. She picked up the pouch and newspaper and started to go back inside when Fred began blowing the steam whistle several times.

Once inside Amy set the pouch down and opened the newspaper. There on the front page in bold lettering: **Archer Ambrose of Whiskey Jack, Maine, makes Executive Officer.** Amy started screaming and crying with excitement. "Emma! Rascal! Paulette! Emma, Rascal, Paulette!" she screamed again. "Come here! Come here!"

They all came running, not knowing what to expect. "What is it Amy?" Emma asked.

"It's Archer!" she was still so excited she was still screaming and jumping around.

"Calm down, Amy. What about Archer?" Rascal asked.

"Look! Look," and she held up the newspaper so they all could see. Then she gave it to Emma.

"Oh my word!" Emma exclaimed. "Archer has been made executive officer onboard the Destroyer Cutlidge. He's in second command." She read aloud the entire article and at the end of the article the writer said, "This news was given to the North American Press for release by Admiral Harry Baxter in Rota, Spain."

They all sat down at a table and for a few moments they just looked at each other. Then Emma reread the article aloud.

"Wow, from E-3, still a student at the Naval Academy assumes the responsibilities of second in command. The executive officer."

Amy emptied the mail pouch onto the table. There were three letters for her and a package for Rascal and Emma. Everyone sat in silence and anticipation as Emma opened the package. "Hmm, a roll of film and four letters."

"Read the last one first to see if he explains more about his promotion," Rascal said.

"Yes, here it is," and she read the letter aloud.

"That explains more. He wasn't promoted but he has assumed the commander's duties and has moved into the commander's quarters. He has explained how it all came about."

That night in bed Emma snuggled up close to Rascal and began to cry. He understood and he put his arm around her and held her close.

Amy read and read her letters from Archer.

****

From Hamburg they sailed north towards Oslo, Norway. "Plot a course, Mr. Ambrose, to the mouth of Oslo Fjord. Six hours before arriving have the lieutenant contact the Oslo Port Authority and advise them our ETA. The authority requires us to use one of their pilots. I need some rest so you have the bridge, Mr. Ambrose."

"Yes, Sir."

Archer set the course and speed and he lay down in his quarters for rest. He left his door wide open so he could listen.

He was too excited to rest for long. He got up and made a sextant reading and plotted their location on the chart. They were getting close. The Lt. had already made contact with the Port Authority. There was a new seaman at the telegraph and Archer said, "Half ahead now." Then he went to wake the captain.

"Captain Hobbs, Sir, we are approaching Oslo Fjord and the pilot boat is waiting."

"I'll be out in a few minutes. Carry on, Mr. Ambrose."

"Reduce speed to slow ahead." He then radioed to the petty officer by the gangway to start lowering it and to standby for pilot.

"All stop," and five minutes later after the props had stopped, "Half astern." As the props started to turn the whole ship began to vibrate and the wake now was boiling, "Slow astern."

The pilot boat was approaching and the gangway was down. "All stop." And then, "Standby."

Pilot Bijorn entered the bridge. There was some conversation between him and the captain. "Slow ahead," he ordered. The gangway was brought up partway.

"How long will you be with us this trip, Captain?"

"Two days. We'll take on some fresh food while we are here also."

It was a beautiful trip up the fjord to Oslo and in one particular place it was narrow, but there was nothing Archer could see that warranted a pilot.

"Mr. Ambrose, find the steward and have him post in the crew's mess that short leave begins at 1800 hours and all are expected to be back onboard by 0200."

"Yes, Sir."

The ship was docked and tied off securely and Pilot Bijorn had left, and the engines were cooling down and all but two boilers were secured. Rather than buying electricity from the port authority, the captain wanted to provide their own.

"Mr. Ambrose, join me for dinner tonight ashore. I know of a nice restaurant with good food. Wear casual attire. We'll leave at 1800 hours."

This gave Archer time to walk around and make sure everything was secured. "Mr. Ambrose."

Archer turned and saw Ian. "Hi, Ian."

"Are you going ashore tonight?"

"I wasn't, but the captain insisted I join him."

"Do you enjoy being the executive officer, Archer?"

"Not so much the status, but I'm learning a lot more now. Things that aren't in books. Are you going ashore?"

"Yes, with some of the engine room crew."

"Have a good time, Ian."

Archer went back to his quarters and shaved and showered and put on casual clothes. At 1800 he and the captain left the ship and haled a taxi which took them to the Posthallen Restaurant at 10A Prinsens Gate.

"Would you gentlemen like something to drink before you order?"

"Yes, I'll have a vodka tonic," the captain said.

"I'll have a glass of chardonnay wine, please."

"Captain, what exactly are we doing in Oslo? There is no Navy base," Archer asked.

"We come to Oslo two or three times a year as a public relations visit. To let the Norwegians know we are watching over Europe and that they can trust us. We have always been treated good here. The Navy isn't always fighting some battle. Look at it as spreading some good will."

"Could you have brought the Cutlidge into the harbor?"

"Yes."

"The port authority appreciates it when we ask for a pilot."

"Tomorrow morning after you have completed the morning's reports, you and I will come ashore and visit the governing mayor and the chief of police. They will undoubtedly take us to lunch."

They both ordered the seafood platter and had another drink while they waited.

"Tell me about your folks, Mr. Ambrose."

"My dad's name is Francis, but he hates it. As a small boy his grandmother called him Rascal and it stuck. He was wounded twice in France during the first European war. Until my mom and dad started the sporting lodge, my dad was a guide and fur trapper. And he did quite well. My mom was a bookkeeper for the lumbering company that owned the village and all the land in the area, except for ten acres my folks owned. They taught me at home until I was ready for high school and I had to go out to the Beech Tree Academy.

"My folks have done very well with the sporting lodge."

"How did you ever get an appointment to Annapolis from living in the wilderness?"

"Two friends of the family," Archer hoped the captain would leave it at that. Their meals were being brought in on a cart and for now the question wasn't asked.

The seafood plate was so good, neither of them did much talking until they had finished.

"Captain Hobbs, we have a communication line connected to the ship. Would there be any way I could call my folks collect?"

"Sure you can. Just remember there's five hours difference. When was the last time you talked with them?"

"I telephoned from the Academy during the winter."

"I'll have to call my wife tonight also."

"Do you have any children?"

"A boy and a girl."

"I'll call them later tonight."

"You better wait until tomorrow after we get back from the mayor's office. Besides your work isn't through for the evening yet."

"Sir?"

"An important part of being a good commander, Mr. Ambrose, is to take care of your men. I don't mean you have to be chummy with them or go out drinking with them. When we leave here, I'll drop you off at popular watering holes, bars and nightclubs, where you'll find most of the crew. Go in and buy them a drink, ask them if there are any problems and remind them they have to be back onboard by 0200. Be friendly, but firm. Let them know you take care of your men.

"These lessons you are not going to be taught in the Academy. You can now do everything onboard the ship. You just need experience with handling men. And that is my job."

They went back to the waterfront and the street was lined with bars and pubs. "This is the crew's most popular."

At first no one recognized him when he entered. Then Ian saw him and came over. "Hey, everybody it's the commander." It was obvious that Ian had had a few beers already.

"Hello, Commander," many of them said.

Ian walked up to the bar with him and Archer ordered a glass of white wine. "And a drink of their choice for everyone."

Archer overhead one seaman say, "Hey, he ain't so bad fellas."

"Where you been?" Ian asked.

"More lessons from the captain."

He talked with the men for a while and finished his drink. "Remember fellas, 0200. If anyone is late there won't be any liberty tomorrow. Have a fun night and I'll see you tomorrow. Goodnight, Ian."

After visiting five bars, he had had enough wine and he was running low on money. It was midnight and he walked back to the ship. He was greeted at the top of the gangway by the officer of the deck. "Good evening, Sir. I didn't recognize you at first. Are you alone, Sir?"

"Yes, Petty Officer, and thank you."

A little before 0200 he heard some of the men that had come back. He got up and went out on deck. "Petty Officer, is everyone back? It's after 0200."

"No Sir, all but two. Midshipman McFarland and one of his roommates, Seaman Tafford."

"Thank you. I'll wait out here with you, Petty Officer."

An hour later the two came stumbling across the docks and up the gangway. Archer stayed back in the shadows to see how the petty officer was going to handle this.

"I presume you two must be Tafford and McFarland? You're late. Everyone else made it back on time. "

"No excuse, Petty Officer."

Archer came out of the shadows then and said, "By morning you two better have a good excuse. What did I tell you last night in the bar before I left?"

Neither of them answered. "I encouraged everyone to make sure you were back onboard by 0200 and if you were not there would not be any liberty the following night for anyone. Now go get some sleep. We'll finish this in the morning after you have sobered up."

The captain had been watching and listening from the flying deck. And he was proud of Mr. Ambrose. He went back to his quarters before Archer saw him. "Yes sir, he'll make a fine captain someday."

****

At breakfast the next morning Archer hurried through his. He had to stand up and deny shore liberty that night for his fellow officers. "May I have your attention please." Suddenly everyone was silent. "Last night two sailors violated the 0200 hours curfew and liberty for all has been canceled."

All the officers were looking at Captain Hobbs and he was smiling.

"If you'll excuse me, Captain, I have to go inform the crew."

"Men, may I have your attention for a moment, last night two crewmen violated the 0200 hours curfew and tonight's liberty is canceled. Midshipman McFarland and Seaman Tafford you'll report to my quarters as soon as you have finished breakfast. That's all."

Archer went back to the bridge to wait. Two minutes later there was a knock on the door to the bridge.

"Come in."

"You'll stand at attention." They snapped to. "There's a compliment of three hundred and forty five sailors aboard this ship. Except for those who were on watch last night, all but you two made it back before 0200 hours. You both know that any military organization has to operate with rules. These rules make us what we are. Two men have spoiled liberty for the entire crew tonight. What if the captain had received new orders and we had to leave before you were back?

"Now you go back to work and think about it. Dismissed."

Captain Hobbs met McFarland and Tafford heading back to their quarters. "Did you and the commander get things straightened out?"

"Yes, Sir, and we apologize."

"Carry on, men." The captain was smiling again. He knew from experience that it wasn't easy to discipline a friend. "But damn, he did such a good job with the officers too." And he laughed.

"Well, Mr. Ambrose, how did that go?"

"It was difficult to discipline a friend. Hell, we're roommates at the Academy."

"He'll get over it."

"Was I correct in canceling liberty for everyone?"

"What do you think?"

"If we are going to be a working unit then everyone must do their share."

"That's correct again. How did it feel to cancel liberty for all of the other officers too?"

"That didn't bother me as much. They, I think, understand uniformity."

"That and they'll surely have more respect for you. Good job, Commander."

"Yes, Sir."

"Don't forget to call your folks or I'll have to discipline you."

"No, Sir."

A refrigerated truck drove out onto the pier next to the Cutlidge and the steward's crew began unloading fish, fresh milk, eggs and some good sharp cheese.

At 1100 hours, Archer was able to talk with an English speaking operator who was helping him place his call. "Yes Ma'am, Whiskey Jack, Maine." He gave her the number and the operator said, "It will take many minutes for your call to Whiskey Jack, Maine. We'll have to go through many operators."

"That'll be okay, Ma'am."

A half hour later he could hear the telephone ringing in the lodge. "Amy, will you get that, I'm busy?"

"Hello, Whiskey Jack Lodge."

"Will you accept a collect call from Archer Ambrose?"

"You bet, yes."

"You must be Amy. I would have recognized Mom's voice or Paulette's."

"Yes, Archer, this is me. Don't hang up, Archer, I'll call your Mom and Dad."

"Emma! Emma, Rascal, Paulette! It's Archer on the telephone."

Emma and Paulette both screamed Archer's name and as Rascal was pushing back from the breakfast table he knocked the chair over.

Rascal ran upstairs to the telephone in the hallway and Emma picked up the telephone in the kitchen. Years ago they decided they needed more than one phone in the lodge.

"Oh, Archer, I can't wait to meet you," Amy said.

"You write beautiful letters, Amy. Don't stop."

Paulette came out and was sharing the phone with Amy.

"Where are you, son?" Emma asked.

"Oslo, Norway."

"Son, we read about you becoming the executive officer

aboard the Cutlidge. It was in the newspaper. Everyone knows about you now. Congratulations, you must be doing an excellent job."

Emma wanted to know all about Archer. Was he alright. Did he get lonely and then she told him about Cubbie, although she and Amy both had written to him about the new bear.

"Where to next, son?' Rascal asked.

"I won't know that until after we leave Oslo."

"When can you come home, Archer?" Amy asked.

"At the end of my six months at sea I'll have a ten day leave."

"Hello, Archer."

"Hi, Paulette, or should I say *Mrs. Colton.*"

"We're all so proud of you, son," Emma said.

"I need to say goodbye now," Archer said. "This telephone line stretches all the way across the floor of the Atlantic Ocean. I love all of you. Goodbye."

"We all love you too, son. Goodbye," Emma said.

They hung up their telephones and met in the dining room. It was quiet for a few moments and water filled eyes.

****

"Are you ready? We'd better go see the governor mayor."

"Yes, I'm ready to go."

"Lieutenant Goff you have the bridge. Call port authority and advise them we'll be ready to leave at 0600 tomorrow."

"Yes, Sir."

Captain Hobbs had insisted that they go in uniform. "The governor mayor likes uniforms; you'll understand better when you see his chief of police."

They were met at the front door by an armed guard who escorted them to Governor Mayor Flyland Nolan's office. The Chief of Police, in all his regalia, Erhart Eugenborg.

Hobbs introduced Archer, "Gentlemen, I would like to introduce my Executive Officer, Commander Archer Ambrose."

Archer shook their hands and said, "Governor Mayor Nolan and Chief Erhart Eugenborg, it is a pleasure to meet you."

"But Captain Hobbs, he is so young!"

"Yes he is, but also an excellent commander."

"Would you like to sit, Commander? Would you like something to drink?"

"Yes please, tea."

"I'll have the same, Governor Mayor," Captain Hobbs said.

They talked for an hour and then lunch was brought in for them.

Nolan and Eugenborg both still found it difficult to understand why the captain's executive officer, the second in command of a destroyer, could be so young.

When lunch was finished the captain said, "Gentlemen, we have enjoyed your company and lunch, but now it is time we went back to doing what we are trained to do."

Archer rose and said, "Thank you Governor Mayor Nolan and Chief of Police Eugenborg."

"Gentlemen."

It was a long fourteen hours before the Cutlidge was underway again without shore liberty for the entire crew. And much to Archer's surprise he did not hear any complaining about the leave being canceled.

Once the tugboat had turned back and the pilot had left the Cutlidge, Captain Hobbs opened his sealed orders. "Commander, there has been a change with our deployment. Usually we sail north of Scotland and back through the Mediterranean Sea, but we are to proceed back through the English Channel and then to Cape Verde, Dakar Senegal for fuel. Bunker-C is less expensive here than we can buy it at home. But the citizens don't always welcome North Americans so there won't be any liberty. We'll only be there long enough for fuel. Change your course commander. And full ahead until we approach the channel."

"Yes, Sir."

Chapter 14

When they sailed through the English Channel this time the sky was blue and cloudless and the white cliffs of Dover glittered like a wall of quartz rock. It was beautiful.

In Dakar, the air was stifling hot and muggy, in spite of sitting on the coast. As soon as all fuel storage holds were filled to capacity they left Dakar and the captain had Archer set course for the mouth of Rio de la Plata. "Buenos Aires lies on the south shore in Argentina and Montevideo on the north in Uruguay," the captain said.

"Intelligence has observed Russian subs being refitted and serviced in Buenos Aires and they need more information. We are to run sonar scans all along the east coast of South America and record all air communications."

"Do you ever learn what was recorded?" Archer asked.

"No, that's not our need to know. We only gather the information.

"When we reach La Plata we'll set our normal sonar scanning speed."

"Yes, Sir."

At the mouth of the Rio de la Plata they picked up sonar signatures of several submarines. Two North American subs, one English, one French and two Russian subs. In the evening after dark had enveloped the ocean, Lt. Goff and Petty Officer Bradley recorded many communications, mostly from the Russian submarines.

Lt. Goff had advised the commander and captain about this increase in communications and there was very little that they could do. Their job was to record them and naval intelligence would analyze and decipher them.

Off the northern coast of Brazil, they located Russian submarines refueling at Sao Luis. There were no suitable docks at Sao Luis so the subs had to anchor off shore and fuel was brought out in a barge.

They sailed through the Virgin Islands and then headed south towards Caracas, Venezuela. There were rich oil fields in Venezuela and a Russian sub lay just off the coast and a Russian tanker was loading.

Both Captain Hobbs and Archer were standing on the flying deck observing the Caracas Harbor with binoculars. "Your time at sea, Commander, will soon be over. From here we sail towards the Panama Canal and follow the coast north only as far as Nicaragua. Then we change course and at full throttle we start for home."

"My time aboard, Captain, has passed so fast. I wish it didn't have to end, but then as soon as I graduate from the Academy this will be my life. Out here."

"Captain's permission to speak freely?"

"Go ahead."

"From the time I came aboard until we left Oslo you called me Mr. Ambrose. Thereafter it has been Commander. Why the change?"

"I've said this before. Being a captain or commander requires more from you than ship's operation and following orders. There is a human side also. I watched as you handled the two seaman, and one being a close friend, when they failed to return to the ship before the deadline. I like how you informed the other officers and how you handled disciplining the two seamen without a barrage of anger or abuse. You were calm and precise, to the point. You conducted yourself as a gentleman, an officer and gentleman. You may only be a midshipman cadet, but you have certainly earned the right to be called commander."

"Thank you, Sir."

****

Archer set course for Guantanamo Bay. "At full throttle, Commander," Capt. Hobbs said.

"Estimated time of arrival, Commander?" Capt. Hobbs asked.

"It is now 1800 hours, we should arrive at about 1700 hours."

"Make it happen."

The ocean was calm in the Gulf of Mexico and the weather was clear and not quite as warm as they had experienced below the equator.

They arrived at Guantanamo right on schedule and that night everyone was granted shore leave. "Be back at 0100 hours as we will be leaving at 0400 hours. This is a Navy Base and if you miss the departure you will be arrested for absent without leave. Enjoy your leave," Archer said.

"Commander, tell the petty officer in charge of refueling to fill to capacity."

"Yes, Sir, but why to capacity for such a short distance?"

"The Gulf Stream and Cape Hatteras. The ocean is usually rough off the coast of South Carolina.

"After you have done that, Commander, you have the bridge. I must leave now and see the base commander and see what our orders are from here."

"Yes, Sir."

Before Ian left the ship Archer asked, "Ian, would you mail these letters for me?"

"Sure thing. Aren't you going ashore tonight?"

"No. The captain said I have the bridge tonight. Have a good time, Ian."

"I won't be late. I promise."

After dinner Archer walked around the deck. Not necessarily inspecting things, but just looking. He stopped for a few minutes and talked with the officer of the deck. "I thought you'd be ashore tonight Sir," the petty officer said.

"No, my turn to stay aboard. Captain Hobbs came back on board, Sir, while you were up forward."

"Thank you."

Archer returned to the bridge and he and the captain talked until 2200 hours and then they both lay down for a couple of hours sleep before they departed.

The next morning Captain Hobbs made the following announcement over the intercom system: "Attention please, may I have your attention. Our new orders are to proceed to Bath Iron Works in Bath, Maine. The Cutlidge will be going through some refitting which will take about eighteen months. Upon our arrival a transport bus will be waiting to take us to the Brunswick Naval Airbase, only a few miles away. Once we are at the Naval Airbase, our options will be given to us at that time. You men have served with me aboard the Cutlidge for a few years, you are all good men and I'm hoping one of our options will be to stay together.

"Would Commander Ambrose and Midshipman McFarland report to my office. Thank you. Oh, on another note. You probably have already noticed the ocean is rough now. We have just moved into the Gulf Stream. The next day and a half will be rough. So take precautions whenever you're out on deck. That's all.

"Come in and close the door. Sit down. When we arrive at Bath Iron Works you both will have five days to the end of your six months deployment. You each have done such a remarkable job. I'm giving you five furlow days along with the ten days you were told you will have at the end of your deployment.

"Ian, I will make arrangements for you aboard a Navy plane that'll take you close to your home. Of course you'll have to find your own way back to the Brunswick Naval Airbase. I will make arrangements there for you both to be flown to Annapolis. You have to be in Annapolis on the tenth, so you should make it the 9th, to be on the safe side. So that means you'll have to be in Brunswick at 0600 hours on the eighth. Is this understood?"

"Yes, Sir," they both answered.

"Good. Lieutenant Billings has already given me his evaluation of you, and he states that he has never seen anyone understand and as able an engineer as yourself. He said that during the first two maneuvers you volunteered to help, even though you were off duty. And during the last two maneuvers he let you take charge and was very satisfied with your ability.

"The reprimand by the commander is on your record. But I wouldn't worry about it."

"Thank you, Sir."

"Archer, you have so exceeded my expectations of what I assumed a midshipman on my bridge should be. You are a natural born leader. You not only know Naval Operations, but you have surely proven yourself that you know how to lead men.

"If it were up to me I would make you both officers today and request that you both serve with me on whatever ship I have.

"By the time we arrive at the Iron Works I will have your written orders ready. And as soon as the ship is cleared you'll be free to leave. Ian, you will want to take the bus along with everyone else to Brunswick and give your orders to the base commander. I will have already spoken to him.

"Dismissed and prepare for a rough day or so."

****

The air was obviously getting colder. Cape Hatteras was no disappointment, but the extremely rough water only lasted for a day. "This was a breeze compared to how rough it does get," the captain said.

"Captain, where is the closest railroad near Bath?"

The captain laughed and said, "There's a Maine Central terminal just outside of the security gate at B.I.W."

"Hmm, that'll be handy."

"Are you going to call home and tell your folks you're coming home?"

"I think I'll get on the train and surprise them."

"Someday I'd like to see Whiskey Jack."

"Well, it's a great place for a vacation. You never said where you live, Captain."

"Watertown, New York."

"What will you be doing until you deploy again?"

"I think I'll take a long vacation and spend time with my family. Then maybe some desk work until there's a ship ready."

****

The final day came when the pilot boat from Bath met the Cutlidge in the Merry Meeting Bay. Archer couldn't wait to get home and see his family. But at the same time he was regretting he had to leave. He knew in his heart that this is what he wanted to do for his life career.

The ship was eased into a dry dock. The huge gates were closed and huge pumps began pumping out the water, allowing the ship to settle onto wooden bridge work under the hull.

Archer gave the signal on the telegraph to secure the engines. And when that was done and auxiliary power connected to the ship the crew began walking off.

"Go ahead, Commander. I have a few things to finish up here. Remember this, Archer. You may be a fourth year midshipman but for five months you were Commander Ambrose."

"Yes, Sir, and thank you."

Archer walked off the ship and the entire crew was waiting near the transport buses. As he came near they all snapped to attention and saluted. Archer returned their salute.

"Commander, it was a privilege serving with you," Lt. Goff said.

As Archer walked by Ian he stopped and they shook hands. "I'll see you on the eighth at the Naval Airbase."

Archer was sorry now that he was not going with the crew. The train for Augusta was about ready to leave and he jumped on and paid the conductor for his ticket. He was still in uniform and everyone turned to look at him.

He sat down and all of a sudden he was anxious to get home, the further away from the ocean that the train was carrying him. There was a two hour wait in Augusta and two more switches he had to make before climbing aboard the train that would carry him to Beech Tree.

There was an hour wait in Beech Tree also. He was hungry, but he didn't want to miss the train.

"Where's Mr. Oliver?"

"He retired and I took his place—name is Stanley Steamer."

Stanley looked up then and recognized the uniform and said, "Oh my God, you're him ain't you? You're Commander Ambrose. You won't have to pay for your ride home. The whole town knows about you. You made all of us proud, son."

"Thank you, Mr. Steamer."

"The train is boarding now and don't worry about your ticket."

Archer picked up his duffel bag and suitcase and boarded the train. "Welcome home, Mr. Ambrose."

"Thank you, Roscoe, it's good to be home, but it'll only be for a few days."

He was tired, but he was too excited to even think about sleep now.

Twenty minutes later Fred Darling blew the half mile signal.

"Train is coming. I'll go out and see if there is any mail." Amy put on her coat and walked out to the platform. The train had stopped and there was no mail pouch. She waited. Then someone in uniform stepped onto the platform.

Amy screamed and hollered, "Archer! Archer is home!" and she ran into his arms almost knocking him down.

Emma and Rascal were still sitting at the table and heard Amy scream that Archer was home. They ran out without a jacket.

Oblivious of the cold. Archer was still hugging Amy. When he saw his Mom and Dad he began grinning like a Cheshire cat.

Emma was in tears and Rascal's eyes were watery. All three of them now were hugging him. "Can we go inside? I'm not used to this cold."

This was the first time, other than her pictures, that he had seen Amy and after reading her letters for three and a half years it felt so natural to walk beside her with his arm around her.

Rascal immediately was aware of the changes he saw in his son. He'd be twenty-one in another six weeks, but he no longer seemed like the same boy that had left home three and a half years ago.

"Are you hungry, son?"

"I sure am."

While Amy and Emma made him breakfast Rascal and Archer talked over a cup of coffee. "We received your letters you sent from Cuba only yesterday. Where did you go from there?"

"To Bath, Maine. Bath Iron Works. The ship is due for some refitting and upgrading that'll take eighteen months."

"Amy, why don't you go out with Rascal and Archer. I can finish his breakfast. I know you are in love with him."

"I am at that. Thank you, Emma." She went out and sat beside Archer. And Emma sat down with Rascal.

"How long will you be home, son?" Emma asked.

"I have to report to Brunswick Naval Airbase on March 8th. I have to be back at the Academy on the tenth. Captain Hobbs said Ian McFarland and I could fly to Annapolis in a Navy airplane."

"You certainly have seen a lot of the world in such a short time," Rascal said.

"I don't understand how or why you were promoted to commander," Emma said.

"It wasn't so much a promotion. I assumed the duties of the commander and all the rights and privileges of the captain's executive officer." He went on to explain why the captain had chosen him and how the captain had stopped calling him Mr. Ambrose and started calling him Commander. "The captain wanted me to learn the human side of being a commander. There's more to the position than Naval operations," and he went on to describe what he was saying.

"What happens or where do you go, Archer, after you graduate?" Amy asked.

"I'll be assigned to a ship somewhere. I won't know any more than that until graduation. I do know I'll have a thirty day leave after graduation.

"Where's Paulette?"

"During the winter she lives with her husband at the farm and works with Priscilla in the kitchen. She comes back out here in the middle of April to help us prepare for spring fishing."

"Tell me about Cubbie."

Emma and Amy both had written letters to him telling him all about this little bear. But it was more fun and interesting hearing them tell their stories.

"I've never been so embarrassed in all of my life," Amy said, "When we stepped into the train. There was so much pee in my boots I was sloshing when I walked and my backside was so wet if I sat down I'd leave an awful wet stain. So we rode in the baggage car standing up." They all laughed again, even Amy.

"Do you really think it is Bear, come back?"

"Either that or his latest cub with all of his genes," Rascal said. "There just couldn't be two bear like Bear."

"Maybe in the fall when I'm home I can get to see him."

They talked all morning until it was time to fix something for lunch. "I need to go to my room and hang up my dress uniform and change my clothes."

He returned in a few minutes and lunch was ready. "Oh wow, homemade fish chowder and biscuits. I haven't eaten anything this good in a long time."

"Amy made the chowder."

As they ate Archer wanted to know all about what had been happening at the lodge. "Is the fishing still as good as it was?"

"Yes, but there are large schools of semi-transparent smelts that the togue and brook trout love, so they are getting bigger.

"Deer hunting is even better now, particularly at the edges of the harvest areas. When the family gets together for Thanksgiving dinner now, no one is interested in going hunting. Presidents Cutlidge and Kingsley are getting older and I think it would be too much for them. Jarvis is still able, but he gets enough deer and moose meat from Herschel so he has no interest in hunting anymore."

"You know what I would really like to eat? Beaver and for dessert, apple pie."

"I'll bake a pie this afternoon," Emma said.

"Now I need to go for a walk. The Cutlidge had limited space where I could walk. Amy, would you like to go for a walk?"

"I'll go pull on some long underwear and I'll be right with you."

"Come on, Harvey, you need to walk also."

After they had left, Rascal said, "They act like they have known each other for a long time."

"Well, they have been writing back and forth for three and a half years. Amy's in love."

"She is? How do you know that, Em?"

"Just watch her, Rascal, when she is near him. She has been for a while now."

"Did she tell you?"

"No, she didn't have to." When he looked confused Emma said, "It's a woman's thing, Rascal."

"We'll have to walk the tracks. It's the only walkable path to the farm."

They held hands as they walked along and Harvey would

run ahead and then come charging back and then run off again. He was having a great time.

Halfway to the farm they stopped and turned to face each other. Archer put his hands on her cheeks and massaged them gently while looking into her eyes and he pulled her closer and gently kissed her. "Hum, that was good," she said. "Do it again."

He kissed her with more passion and she eagerly responded. "You are so beautiful, Amy."

They continued on, oblivious of the cold. Their hearts were pumping strong enough to keep warm.

They went to the dining room to get warm and say hello to Paulette. She came out of the kitchen with flour on her face. She immediately recognized Archer and rushed over and gave him a big hug. "When did you get home?"

"In time for breakfast this morning."

"How long will you be home?"

"I have to be at the Naval Airbase in Brunswick March 8th."

Armand opened the door and walked in. "Holy cow, it's Archer. How you doing? We all read the newspaper about you being the commander.

"We have changed things here since you been gone. No more horses. All logs brought to mill with crawlers now. Men much happier and not so many men to cut more trees.

"Good to see you, Archer. I must go back to work."

"We'd better leave too. I think it is getting colder and I'm not used to the cold yet."

"Good to see you, Archer."

****

The rest of the afternoon they all sat in the living room listening to Archer tell them about his time at sea. "Did you see any rough sea?" Rascal asked.

"Yes. Twice, the first time was only a couple of days out from Norfolk and we ran into a wind storm that was blowing

227

up huge waves and swells. And then just a few days ago as we sailed by Cape Hatteras off the South Carolina coast. But Captain Hobbs said it wasn't as rough as he has seen it."

"Did you get seasick?" Emma asked.

"No, and that is strange. I thought I probably would. I guess I was always too busy to think about it."

That evening after a supper of beaver, potatoes, dandelion greens and biscuits and apple pie and cheese for dessert they stayed up late sitting by the fireplace and talking. The temperature was dropping and suddenly the lake groaned so furiously loud the lodge shook. Rascal, Emma and Amy were so used to it they hardly noticed. "Now that's something I haven't heard for four years. The lake making ice."

"Rascal, it's late; let's go to bed." He shut off the generator first and lit a gas light in the hallway.

Archer and Amy stayed up for a while longer cuddling and talking in the fire light of the fireplace.

It was getting real late now, and Archer walked Amy to her bedroom and kissed her goodnight and then went to his own room.

The wind started to blow about midnight and by daylight it had blown the cold air out and already the temperature was above freezing.

The warm weather held for the next five days and Archer and Amy took advantage of it and went for long walks each day. The snow had settled and it was like a water filled sponge. On the sixth day the frigid artic cold returned and the wet snow now was frozen so solid a moose could have walked on it without breaking through. After breakfast they went crust walking. In places where Emma and Amy had never been.

They went crust walking again the next day and took food and coffee makings to have breakfast out on the crusted snow.

"We should go into town this afternoon and stay at the hotel and invite the Pages to have super with us. I'm sure they'd like to see Archer before he has to leave."

While Rascal was taking a shower Emma called Rita and asked her to invite Herschel and his family too.

Amy chose the prettiest dress she had and Archer wore his casual clothes he had had aboard ship.

"What about Harvey?" Rascal asked.

"Rita said we could leave him with them overnight."

****

From the train terminal Rascal took Harvey over to the Pages' and Emma, Amy and Archer went to the hotel. On the way there, Amy said, "Emma I hope you'll understand, but I would like to spend the night with Archer in our own room."

At first Emma was shocked. Then she thought how much she and Rascal had enjoyed each other and she said, "Okay."

Rascal came back and went upstairs to his room and asked Emma, "Where are Archer and Amy?"

"They have their own room tonight."

"Hum, well I guess I can't blame them none. Remember we were like that once too, Em."

"You're making me feel old now, Rascal."

Archer and Amy's room was next to his folks. Amy closed and made sure the door was locked and then she pulled Archer down on the bed. She didn't have to pull very hard. He lay down and she rolled over and lay on top of him. "You know, Amy, we don't have enough time right now."

"I know, and I don't know if I can wait for later. I've been wanting this all week."

"Me too."

"We can play," Amy said.

An hour later both Page families met them in the dining room for supper.

Archer shook hands with Jarvis and Herschel and hugged Perline, Rita and Emma Jean. She was over her crush with him.

They had wine and sampled cheeses until their roast beef dinners arrived.

Archer couldn't help but wonder at Jarvis and Rita's good health. They were each eighty nine now and didn't look or act over seventy. Herschel and Perline were forty-three. "How many years do you have on now, Herschel?" Archer asked.

"It'll be twenty-two July first this year."

"How many more years, Herschel, do you plan to work?" Rascal asked.

"I want thirty years. After that I'm not sure. I've always thought I'd like to build a house with the idea of selling it. Maybe do one a year."

Their meal finally came and Emma ordered more wine. Everyone enjoyed the roast beef and when they had finished Emma ordered more wine. Then they just sat there talking about old times.

"Times sure have changed haven't they, Rascal? Since the days of coffee and donuts at the cafeteria with Jeters and Silvio?"

"They sure have. Those were good times though."

"Those times were fun."

"When will you be home again, Archer?" Perline asked.

"After graduation we get a thirty-day leave."

Amy squeezed the inside of his leg.

"Any more of this wine, Jarvis, and we'll have to sleep here tonight."

When Jarvis and Herschel started to hand Rascal some money he said, "This is on Em and me tonight."

"Thank you."

"Yes thank you."

"Goodnight."

"Goodnight."

In the elevator Emma said, "Every time I have more than one glass of wine I have to pee. Rascal, we'd better hurry."

Amy said, "Yeah, me too."

Emma and Rascal said goodnight and closed their door. They undressed and Rascal watched as Emma removed her clothes and then crawled into bed next to him.

"You know, Rascal, every time I drink wine I get horny."

"It has been a while hasn't it."

After Amy came out of the bathroom she lay on the bed. Archer undressed and turned the light off. There was just enough light from the street lights outside to softly illuminate the room. He sat on the bed next to Amy. She was sound asleep. He laughed softly so not to wake her and then he gently removed her clothes and lay down under the covers next to her and cuddled up to her. Her warm body was feeling so nice against his own. He gently caressed her face, her hair and kissed the nape of her neck and whispered in her ear, "I love you, Amy."

****

Archer made sure he was awake early come morning and he rolled Amy onto her back. She was still asleep and he began to caress her very gently and even though still asleep she was beginning to respond. He kissed her tenderly at first and when she responded with such hunger—well, an hour later the sun was up and he said, "We must get up, Amy, so we don't miss the train."

They all had a quick breakfast and then they walked to the train terminal. Archer had had an idea during the night and when the train was almost ready to leave he said, "There are a couple of things I must do in town. You go ahead and I'll catch the afternoon train."

He waited until the train had left and then he settled down in the cafeteria with a cup of coffee and a muffin. The bank wouldn't be open yet.

He still had an hour before he could get into the bank and feeling restless he walked about town, even in the cold.

Just as the bank was being opened he was there and asked to withdraw $1000.00. His balance was $2361.10. He had one more stop to make and then he went back to the train terminal, to wait for the afternoon northbound.

Back home, Rascal asked, "Did you get everything done son?"

"Yes."

****

That evening as they were sitting in the living room and listening to the radio, Archer and Amy disappeared to the kitchen and shortly came back with a tray of smoked fish, cheese, wine and glasses. When their glasses were full Archer raised his and said, "Here's to my family."

"This wine is so good with the smoked fish," Amy said.

While Amy was taking a sip of her wine Archer removed a small velvet box from his pocket. Emma saw this and she knew what was coming. Archer put his glass of wine down and took Amy's and put it down. Then he looked deep into her eyes and said, "Amy, I love you with all my heart. Will you marry me?"

She started screaming and squealing and jumping up and down in her seat. Emma was crying and Rascal was smiling. Archer opened the ring box.

"Yes, of course I'll marry you!" He slid the ring on her finger, and she wrapped her arms around his neck and kissed him. She was crying now.

Amy sat in his lap with her arm around his neck for the rest of the evening. "When will we get married?"

"After I graduate. I'll have thirty days leave to come home. You make the arrangements for a few days after graduation."

He looked at his Mom and Dad and said, "I know September is a busy month here, but I sure would like it if you could come to the graduation."

"Of course we'll come," Rascal said.

"We'll work it out."

"How about me?" Amy asked.

"You come without question. The ceremonies will be on a Sunday, August 28th. Before then I'll make reservations for you at a hotel. Then I'll come back with you. You should plan on

232

flying down. It is quicker and less trouble."

"We'll think about it, son."

****

On March 6th sorrowful goodbyes were said. "There is no way to say how much I love you, Mom and Dad, except just to say I love you."

He turned to Amy and hugged and kissed her and said, "I love you, Amy. Take care of yourself and the folks."

"I love you, Archer, and I will."

Archer found Ian at the Brunswick Naval Airbase and together they went to see the commander. They gave him their orders and after examining them he said, "There is a flight leaving in twenty minutes. Be on it."

Chapter 15

Captain Elias Hobbs flew to his family in Watertown, New York. There was so much snow that year that people had to shovel snow away from their windows so they could see out. And like Archer, it took a few days to acclimate his body to winter weather. He had taken sixty days of leave time. Enough so he could be at his daughter's high school graduation.

And then he reported to Vice-Admiral Walter Harris at the Department of Naval Operations in the Pentagon in Sault Ste. Marie. At the end of the last war in Europe and Japan, parliament overwhelmingly passed a resolution to build a huge facility just outside of the new national capitol.

Architects had worked two years on the design before construction had started. All of the military base of operations were now under one roof, as well as the FBI and CIA. To name only a few.

"Captain, you are up for promotion but you have never had any carrier experience. You are the senior Naval captain, but without carrier experience the opening will have to go to someone else."

"I understand, Sir. I only have five more years for my retirement and I would prefer to stay aboard a destroyer."

"I thought you would say that. There is a new Gearing Class Destroyer being built at Bath Iron Works with many upgrades and improvements. It is scheduled for commissioning on October 5th. Would this be of any interest to you?"

"Yes, Sir, it surely would."

"I'm assuming you will want your old crew back?"

"Yes, Sir, with two additional men. The two midshipmen who were with me for six months. Ian McFarland, he worked for Lt. Billings in the engine room and the Lt. said in his evaluation that he had never worked with a crewman who was so adept with engine room knowledge and ability."

"I have read both evaluations, Captain. And yes they both are impressive."

Capt. Hobbs explained why he had decided on Midshipman Ambrose for his executive officer. They spent much of the afternoon talking about how Hobbs could promote Ambrose to executive officer. "I can assure you, Captain, that you will have both midshipman once they have graduated. And I think we have a resolution for Midshipman Ambrose.

"Let me take care of that, Captain. Will you be at the graduation?"

"Yes, Sir."

"Okay, after the graduation you are to report to Bath Iron Works. The new destroyer is scheduled for sea trials right after the ceremonies.

"Tell me more about Midshipman Ambrose."

"There is very little that I can add to what is not in his evaluation. Just that I have never encountered any officer who is so in tune with Naval operations and all systems and his ability to lead his crews. He is a rare person, Sir.

"There is another point of interest. Two days out from Norfolk we ran into a terrible wind storm. The helmsman was a seasoned helmsman. When he started getting nervous about the big swells and waves, Ambrose talked to him and told him just how to steer into the waves and why and he knew to cut the speed. This was his second day aboard any ship and already he knew just what to do and how to help the helmsman."

"Okay, consider it done."

"Thank you, Admiral."

****

In July, Emma received a nice letter from the Cutlidges saying they and the Kingsleys would be at Archer's graduation and asked them to sit with them during the ceremonies, and then again later at the formal banquet. "Oh my, Rascal, do you suppose I'll have a chance to wear my beautiful gown?"

"You don't suppose do you, Em, that that style, although it was very becoming on you, might be out of fashion now. I mean it has been twenty-two years."

"I suppose you're right. Amy, tomorrow you and I go to Lac St. Jean shopping. Rascal go put on your good suit of clothes and let us have a look."

"I can't fasten the pants, Em, and the sport coat is now too small across the shoulders."

"Well, I guess you go with us tomorrow, Rascal."

****

Graduation was only two weeks away now and Archer made reservations for two rooms for two nights.

Ian's family was coming down from Dartmouth, Nova Scotia, also, and he made reservations at the same hotel. "Wouldn't it be something, Archer, if we get the same ship?"

"I wouldn't count on it, Ian, but it would be nice."

"Are you getting nervous, Archer? I am."

"Not nervous, but anxious. I really liked when we were at sea."

"I lay awake at night wondering where I'll end up. I didn't before our internship. Maybe because I knew then it was only temporary."

"Stop worrying, Ian; we'll know in a couple of days."

Two weeks before graduation the class had begun practicing for the ceremonies.

****

Emma and Amy had both chosen a new fashionable knee

length dress for the ceremonies with a low neckline. Emma's was a deep blue satin and Amy's was yellow and white. And of course they had to have matching shoes.

Rascal decided on a gray three piece suit. "And, Rascal, you're not wearing your boots so get some shoes, too."

"Yes, Em."

Paulette and her husband were all set at the lodge and Emma had not scheduled any fisherman for the first three weeks of September. They went by train to Portland and boarded a DC-4 to Boston where they transferred to a Cygnus de Havilland jet direct to Annapolis, Maryland. "Wow!" Amy said, "how high are we?"

A stewardess heard Amy and said, "We are cruising at 20,000 feet."

"Wow! Emma, that's almost four miles above the ground. I don't think I want to look out the window," Amy said.

It was early evening when the taxicab brought them to Annapolis Continental Hotel. As they were registering— "Rascal, Emma and Amy."

They turned around to see Presidents Cutlidge and Kingsley and their wives. Mr. Butler and Mr. Dubois had since retired and now the presidents and family were being escorted by two much younger secret service agents. Mr. Ivan Roberts and Miss Petra Kendall.

"Are you just arriving?" President Kingsley asked.

"Yes."

"Just a moment. Mr. Willard these people are personal friends of President Cutlidge and myself. We all are here to celebrate the graduation of their son tomorrow at the Naval Academy. I think they deserve more than a simple room. I'm sure you must have another suite available."

"Yes, President Kingsley, we do, on the same floor as the two of you."

"That'll do, Mr. Willard, and put it on our bill."

Rascal asked Mr. Willard, "Did my son, Archer Ambrose,

make a deposit for the two rooms?"

"Ah, yes he did. Would you like me to give it to you?"

"Yes." When he did Rascal gave it to Amy.

"Amy, show the family your ring," Emma said. Mr. Willard heard her say family and now he was glad he had not made a fuss about returning Archer's deposit.

They all thought it was beautiful. "When is the wedding?" Pearl asked.

"Two weeks after we get back home. Will you both be able to attend?"

They both said at the same time, "We'll try."

"Kevin," Myrissa said, "Why couldn't we make the wedding and not the Thanksgiving dinner?"

"There you have it, Amy; we'll be there. Now let's go up to our suites, I need to lie down for a while."

The suite was impressive. "This is like a dream come true. Would you mind if I call you Mom and Dad?"

"Certainly not, Amy."

There was a king size bed on each end of the suite and a television set and deep piled carpeting. "Mom and Dad, would you let me give you the money Mr. Willard gave me? I'd like to help pay for part of this trip. It would really help to make me feel better."

****

They all were taken to the Academy by the presidents' limousine. At 8 a.m. there was a guided tour of the Academy conducted by third year midshipmen.

At 1100 hours everybody began gathering at the outdoor auditorium. There was seating for dignitaries behind Vice-Admiral Walter Harris and Capitan Bedford Ames and other Academy functionaries. Captain Elias Hobbs had reserved seating next to the two presidents.

"It is good to see you again, Captain," President Kingsley said.

"Presidents Kingsley and Cutlidge and first ladies. What brings you to Annapolis today?"

"The ceremonies and one midshipman in particular," President Cutlidge said.

"Who would that be, Sir?"

"I think you know him, Captain. He served aboard your ship for six months. I'd like to introduce you to his folks, Captain Hobbs. This is Emma Ambrose, her husband, Rascal, and Archer's fiancée, Amy Paquin."

"It is most certainly my pleasure to meet the parents of such an intriguing young man. Yes, most certainly. You have a remarkable son. And that says a lot for you two."

He shook Rascal's hand warmly and hugged Emma and Amy. "I didn't know Mr. Ambrose was engaged."

"We became engaged while he was home on leave."

"Congratulations to you both."

"Again I'd like to say you have an amazing son. And much of the credit is also extended to you. Our children reflect who their parents are."

"Captain, maybe you would join us at our table at the banquet," President Cutlidge asked.

"I would be delighted to join you, Sir."

"Mr. Ambrose never did say who appointed him to Annapolis."

"Knowing Archer as we do it would be our guess that he wouldn't want any special treatment from you, if you knew he had been appointed by two presidents. We all consider ourselves family. We knew Rascal and Emma before Archer was born."

The new National Anthem started and everyone stood up.

The master of ceremonies was Captain Bedford Ames and he introduced Presidents Cutlidge and Kingsley and their wives as distinguished guests and explained it was because of them that the new internship had been started.

Then he introduced Vice-Admiral Walter Harris who gave a twenty minute speech about the Academy and the graduating class of 1949. All the while the class was standing at attention on the parade ground. When the Admiral had finished, Captain Ames said, "Parade rest."

Now it was Captain Ames who was speaking. "Midshipmen of the Class of 1949, I welcome you to the North American Navy. No longer as midshipmen but as officers. Congratulations. We have made a change this year with the internship program. All but two of you will have the rank of Ensign. The other two who had the highest evaluation rating for the internship will leave today as Lieutenants. This is because of their dedication, knowledge and their ability to perform the duties of their office. This in no way shall underwrite all of you who preform your duties well. With that said I now call on Captain Elias Hobbs."

Archer and Ian heard the captain being called and wondered what was going to take place now; they didn't have long to wait.

"Thank you Captain Ames. Vice-Admiral Harris and Presidents Cutlidge and Kingsley, it is my honor to be here today.

With that said, "Officers Archer Ambrose and Ian McFarland, front and center."

Both Emma and Amy were wiping away tears. Rascal blew his nose.

"Lieutenants Ian McFarland and Archer Ambrose you both have earned the rank of lieutenant. You exceeded all expectations of an intern midshipman. You applied yourself and have proven to me, Chief Engineer Lieutenant Billings, Captain Ames and Vice-Admiral Walter Harris, that you both are deserving of this special promotion. Remember, you are officers and gentlemen in the North American Navy."

Captain Hobbs came to attention and saluted them both. They in turn also stood at attention and returned his salute.

He shook Archer's hand and said, "Quite a let down from commander, Lieutenant. But not for long." Then he shook Ian's hand and said, "Don't ever miss another curfew, Ian," and he grinned.

"Both of you are exceptional officers."

Captain Ames then handed them their diplomas and shook their hands and saluted them.

Then Admiral Harris handed them each sealed manila envelopes. "Lieutenants Ambrose and McFarland, your orders. You are to report to Bath Iron Works in Bath, Maine, on October 5th, for the launching and christening for a new Gearing Class Destroyer. Lieutenants, you both have certainly earned the rank of lieutenant that has been bestowed upon you today. Congratulations and good luck."

An hour later, all of the new officers had received their diplomas and new orders and Captain Bedford Ames said, "Officers, you are dismissed."

Archer ran towards Amy and his family. "Wow, you look so beautiful, Amy and you too, Mom." There were hugs and kisses and pats on the back.

"Captain Hobbs, I'd like to introduce you to my family."

"Already done, Lieutenant."

"Archer, President Kingsley and I knew from the start you have what it takes to be a great officer. Congratulations."

"Yes, certainly congratulations, Archer."

"I've been invited to your wedding, Lieutenant."

"I hope you will come, Sir."

"I plan on it. I want to see this Whiskey Jack for myself."

Ceremonies then were moved to the banquet hall. As they were sitting at the table waiting to be served, Archer said, "None of this would have been possible if not for you two. Thank you so much for the opportunity, President Cutlidge and President Kingsley.

"Amy, I can't get over how beautiful you are."

The banquet lasted longer than anyone had anticipated and people were getting anxious to leave. Finally President Kingsley stood and said, "Maybe if I get up to leave everyone will also." And they did.

It had been a long day and everyone was tired. Archer was surprised when he saw the suite. "Compliments of Presidents Cutlidge and Kingsley."

"Wow, will you look at this," Archer said.

****

The next morning as they were saying goodbye, President Kingsley said, "We'll see you in two weeks."

"Have a safe trip home," Pearl said.

That evening they were back in Beech Tree and the next train wouldn't be leaving until morning. So they stayed another night at the Beech Tree Hotel. This time Archer and Amy had a room by themselves.

Amy and Emma had already taken care of all of the arrangements for the wedding. Now they were doing a lot of cooking and Rascal and Archer were cleaning.

"Dad, let's go for a walk. I'd like to see Cubbie."

"Do you girls want to go with us?" Rascal asked.

"No, we're busy. You two go play with Cubbie."

They started walking along the tracks towards Ledge Swamp. "So far this is the only place we have seen him."

"You know, Dad, when I leave here this time, I have no idea where I'll be going or when I can come back. I guess what I'm trying to say is although my roots will always be here in Whiskey Jack, what I have chosen for my life's work will take me away from here. I could be happy staying here and Amy and I helping you and Mom run the lodge, but the Navy is taking me away from here."

"I understand, son. This is your home no matter where you may be in the world. And maybe someday you and Amy will want to come back."

Archer stopped and said, "There's a bear on the grassy knoll. Is that Cubbie?"

"Yes," and Rascal raised his arm and said, "Hello, Cubbie, this is my son, Archer."

"Hello, Cubbie."

"He's bigger than I had thought."

"We'll, he's been around for two years now and is probably four years old and maybe about 350 pounds."

"Does he play with you?"

"He likes to chase me when I run but he doesn't knock me down like Bear used to."

"What about Harvey?"

"Turn him loose and watch."

Archer unhooked his leash and immediately Harvey ran towards Cubbie. They chased each other round and round and back and forth for several minutes. Rascal whistled and said, "Come on, Harvey."

Harvey came over and Archer hooked his leash. "Okay, now we walk back. Cubbie will follow."

"He is following."

"Now run. This is what he really likes." They and Harvey started running and Cubbie only twenty feet behind them. After a half mile, Rascal had to stop running. They walked for a ways and stopped, and Rascal turned around and said, "Okay, Cubbie, that's enough," and he raised his arm and Cubbie stood on his hind legs and raised one paw and then he ran off towards the woods.

"Does he ever make that laughing noise or say, 'Hi'?"

"No."

"Do you think he watches over the lodge like Bear did?"

"We're not sure. The only time we see him is when we come for a walk up here."

"Do you and Mom have pictures of him?"

"Yes, your Mom took pictures once when he was chasing me."

"It's unbelievable you know, Dad. Two bear so much alike who want to play. I've been away from home for four years and coming back I understand just how unique Whiskey Jack is."

"Come on, son, it's time we were getting back."

****

Two days before the wedding, both presidents and wives, their secret service two agents and Captain Elias Hobbs and his wife, Rebecca, arrived on the morning southbound. Inside the lodge the first thing Capt. Hobbs noticed was the photos and plaques on the wall. When he saw the photo at the dinner gathering at the White House he had to ask Emma to explain. It was a wonderful story and Rebecca and Emma hit it off right away. There were photos of Mr. Butler and Mr. Dubois, and President Cutlidge explained who each man was, "...and they are still part of this Whiskey Jack family. And Captain, from now on, you and your wife Rebecca will be part of this family."

"I've heard Archer say something about a bear. So I'm assuming there is something special about this bear in the photo."

"You'd better come in the living room and sit down. This is going to be a long story. But a good one."

While Rascal and Emma were telling the story about Bear, Amy and Paulette were serving coffee. Paulette's husband Henri would be there early in the morning of the wedding day.

A half hour later, the story told Capt. Hobbs said, "That is remarkable. I would have liked to have been here to see Bear chasing you and Elmo on the tracks."

Rebecca asked, "What about mountain lions and wolves? Are they still around?"

"Not a one since Bear killed those two. I don't even see tracks when I'm trapping."

As they were eating fish chowder and biscuits, Capt. Hobbs asked, "Amy have you ever thought about living in the tropics?"

"No, not really. Why?"

"When we report to BIW and leave on the new destroyer, we will be assigned to the Pacific Ocean for a few years. We'll be stationed in Hawaii, at Pearl Harbor. Rebecca will be coming out to join me; our two kids will be in college. Maybe you might think of flying out with her."

Everyone could tell by the expression on Amy's face that she would be going. "This is a dream coming true."

The Pages, all except for Herschel, arrived on the afternoon northbound. "Herschel has a court trial today and he'll be up tomorrow."

Introductions were made all around. Then the Cutlidges and the Kingsleys retired to their rooms for a nap.

"Dad, why don't you take Captain Hobbs for a walk up near Ledge Swamp."

"I could use some exercise. How about you, Rebecca?"

"That would be nice. I'd enjoy seeing some of this country."

"Jarvis?"

"Sure, I haven't had my exercise yet today."

Going to Ledge Swamp, Jarvis half expected what they would see. He and Rita had heard the stories about Cubbie but had not seen him.

"It's difficult to believe that the only way into this wilderness is by train. How far away is the closest town?" Rebecca asked.

"Ten miles south of Whiskey Jack. Going north Lac St. Jean, much further," Rascal said.

"This is about as far as I want to go, Rascal," Jarvis said. He could have gone on, but he suspected what Rascal was up to. And right on cue, a bear appeared on top of the grassy knoll and standing up.

Rebecca saw the bear first and screamed, "Bear! There's a bear!"

The captain put his arm around his wife to protect her.

"Okay, let's turn around and walk back," Rascal said.

At first Cubbie just stood there sniffing the air. These were new scents that he had never smelled before. But they were all with the one familiar scent that he knew, so all was okay. He walked down off the knoll to the tracks and started following them.

Rebecca turned around to look and said, "He is following us, Rascal. Aren't you going to do something?"

Rascal stopped and Cubbie stopped about twenty feet away. Rascal raised his arm and Cubbie sat on his haunches and raised his paw. "Cubbie, these are friends of mine." Cubbie seemed to be nodding his head.

Rascal just had to try it. He started running first towards Cubbie and then towards the woods. "What is he doing?" Rebecca said in a high pitched voice. "That bear is going to maul him."

Jarvis said, "He'll be okay. I've watched Rascal do this many times with Bear and he was much bigger."

Rascal cut back towards the tracks and started running in the grass beside them. Cubbie was right behind him and he lowered his head and grabbed Rascal's boot in his teeth and Rascal fell. Cubbie let go of his boot and for the first time he started making the same laughing noise as Bear had done and then he ran off for the woods.

Rascal stood up and brushed the grass and dirt off, "You play with a bear? I understand now why you are called Rascal. It certainly fits," Rebecca said and then everyone began laughing. "Was he laughing, Rascal?" Rebecca asked.

"That's the same noise Bear used to make and we all thought he was laughing."

"I guess we can better understand the stories about Bear now," Captain Hobbs said.

"Yeah, but that son of a gun almost made me pee myself," Rebecca said.

"You wouldn't have been the first," Jarvis said as they were walking back.

"Aren't you afraid one of your hunters will shoot him?" the Capt. asked.

"We have a strict rule that no one is allowed to hunt

beyond mile eleven and no one is allowed to shoot any bear. There has been the occasional hunter who will hunt near Ledge Swamp and then they have to leave on the next train."

Back at the lodge, Rascal told Emma about Cubbie and how he had played with him and then Cubbie laughing, "You mean like Bear did?" Emma asked.

"Just like Bear."

After supper that evening they all sat in the living room mostly listening to Rascal and Jarvis tell stories. Captain Hobbs said, "As I understand, Jarvis, you have taken both Rascal and Emma to jail, is that right? And you now remain close friends? How unusual. What did they do?"

Emma said, "I shot a deer in closed season that was eating my lettuce."

Rascal said, "Someone complained that some friends and I were making wine and brandy."

Emma and Jarvis had just taken a sip of coffee and now they choked on it and spit up. Everyone was silent looking first at Emma and then Jarvis. They all knew there was more to the story but no one ventured to ask. They let it alone. Jarvis and Emma were perspiring.

"Agent Roberts, I presume you and Miss Kendall will take shifts securing the lodge tonight. I'll help out if you need any," Jarvis said.

"Thank you, but we'll be okay."

Jarvis and Rita went upstairs to bed. "I'm surprised a man of his age offering to help secure the two presidents," Roberts said.

"That old man," Rascal said, "has single-handedly seen more difficult situations than you two together will ever see. He's eighty-nine and I wouldn't go against him, nor would anyone who knows him. There is only one other man who is as capable as Jarvis, and you'll meet him tomorrow. His son, Herschel. Don't underestimate him. He was President Cutlidge's personal bodyguard for a week when the two came here to talk about the two countries merging together."

****

Amy's mother, father and one sister arrived the next morning. Amy's mother, an Abenaki Indian, was every part as beautiful as her daughter Amy. Her folks were quiet at first, meeting so many new people all at once. But during the day the newness wore off.

Herschel arrived on the afternoon train in uniform. "Sorry about the uniform, but I'm on call."

"Think nothing of it, Herschel. Would you like some coffee?"

"I'll get it," Emma Jean said. During the last four years she had surely developed into a very attractive young woman.

"What case did you have yesterday, son?"

"Three men from down east shot a moose last October while bird hunting and it just came to trial yesterday."

"And?"

"The jury was out for three hours and found all three guilty.

Ivan Roberts and Petra Kendall listened all day to Jarvis and Herschel telling stories of close calls and had formed a new respect for that old man.

"Jarvis, would you be willing to help out with security tonight? Kendall and I haven't been getting much sleep"

Herschel spoke up and said, "Why don't the two of you get a good night's sleep, and Dad and I will take it tonight."

Herschel relieved his Dad at one in the morning. And Jarvis was wide awake at sunup. Yes, Roberts and Kendall had formed a respect for this old man.

****

The minister from Beech Tree arrived on the morning train and would have to take the afternoon southbound back to Beech Tree.

Paulette was standing up with Amy and Captain Hobbs

had agreed to be Archer's best man.

Since they didn't have a place of their own there, was a money tree in lieu of gifts. Emma had taken three rolls of film with her new camera.

Emma Jean walked over to Archer and said, "I'm happy for you, Archer," and then she kissed him.

The reception had moved out to the platform, it was such a beautiful day. The air was cool and no bugs. Just before the southbound approached a breeze started to blow and formed a whirlwind. Amy looked at Emma and said, "It's Anita, Emma. She made it." Everyone, including Rascal and Archer, were looking at the two women and wondering what had just happened.

Emma said to Rascal, "Anita said that when Amy got married she would be here and to look for a whirlwind."

Archer and Amy took the afternoon train to Lac St. Jean for a honeymoon. Two days later Jarvis, Rita, Captain Hobbs and Rebecca remained. That evening, Captain Hobbs said, "One reason why I asked Archer to be my executive officer was the manner in which he handled the crew and the officers who had a lot more sea time than he had. After spending time here with you folks, I now understand his people skills. They came from both of you."

Before leaving, Rebecca had given Emma their address and phone number. "Tell Amy I will call her in the middle of November, and plan to fly out to Hawaii early December."

"I'm so glad she'll be traveling with you, Rebecca, and thank you for coming. We are proud of Archer and it means so much to us both that you and your husband came to his wedding so we could meet you."

****

When Archer and Amy returned to Whiskey Jack, Rascal and Emma noticed a subtle change in each of them and they were extremely happy and began talking about their future.

Chapter 16

Archer said goodbye to his Mom and Dad and his new wife. Amy would be joining him in a few months in Hawaii, and Rascal and Emma didn't know when they would see them again.

Archer and Ian rejoined the crew and the new Gearing Class Destroyer was christened the Bear. Only Archer and Captain Hobbs knew why and who had been responsible for the name.

The entire crew, to the man, from the Cutlidge had signed on to sail aboard the Bear. And when they saw that Archer and Ian both had returned, now as officers, they were all happy.

The day before, Captain Hobbs had had a meeting with all of his officers except for Archer and Ian who had not arrived yet. "Gentlemen, I have asked you here for one reason. Lieutenant Ambrose and McFarland will be here tomorrow. I'm going to ask Lieutenant Ambrose to serve as my executive officer, with the rank of lieutenant commander. He is an exceptionally gifted officer and I think you all realize this. Now, I don't want any bitter feelings among my officers. Do any of you have any objections?"

Not a word was spoken. "This promotion is unusual, but it is not unheard of, and I obtained the go ahead from Admiral Harris in Sault Ste. Marie. I thank you for your understanding."

Back at BIW, "I hope everyone has had a good meal. There are no provisions onboard until we get to Norfolk. If no one has any questions let's get the Bear out of here and see what she can do. Lieutenant Ambrose, while the pilot is taking us out through the river, chart our course to Norfolk and then after the pilot has left, set your course and speed and then come see me."

"Yes, Sir."

A few minutes later Archer knocked on the captain's door. "Come in, sit down, Lieutenant Commander."

Archer opened his mouth but he couldn't speak.

"You make one hell of an executive officer and you should at least have the rank of Lieutenant Commander. Your promotion was already approved by Vice-Admiral Walter Harris in Sault Ste. Marie months ago. I have talked it over with the other officers on board and no one had any objections. So Lieutenant Commander you better sew these shoulder braids on your dress uniform and here are your clusters. Now, before we leave Norfolk I want you to select a lieutenant as your bridge officer."

"Yes, Sir, and thank you."

"Now, Archer, I really like your folks. They both are real people. They accepted me as if they had known me for a long time."

"Well, Sir, you're part of the Whiskey Jack family now."

"Then when we're alone and not on official business, you'd better start calling me Elias. After all you're only two pay grades below me now."

"Do you know what we'll be doing?"

"No, I was told to get to Hawaii as soon as possible and we would receive our orders then."

****

The Bear was tied up in Norfolk for three days loading provisions, water and fuel oil. During those three days Archer made his choice for a bridge officer, Lieutenant Larry Goff. "Once we leave Panama, Lieutenant, I want you to train another officer as sonar and communications officer."

Off the coast of Cape Hatteras the ocean was much rougher than it was in February. They were going against the Gulf Stream.

"Mr. Weatherly."

"Yes Sir."

"Can you handle the Bear in these rough waters?" Archer asked.

"Yes, Sir, Lieutenant Commander, I had a good teacher."

"Lieutenant Goff, call down to the engine room and tell them to close the throttles some. We don't want to beat this new ship into pieces."

"Yes, Sir."

Twelve hours later and they were by the worst of it and the throttles were opened again. When Lt. Goff was not standing watch on the bridge he was instructing Petty Officer Ralph Sawyer about the communication and the advanced sonar radar operations. Archer's class had already studied these new advancements, but when he could he would sit in on the Lt's instructions.

It was a clear and calm day as the Bear entered the locks on the east end of the Panama Canal. Two locomotive engines attached lines to the bow and pulled the Bear through the locks. Then a pilot guided the ship through the canal to the locks at the western end.

"Lieutenant, set course along the Pacific Equatorial current then west along the Pacific North Equatorial current. We have the currents in our favor most of the way to Hawaii."

"Yes, Sir."

Every morning the ocean was so calm the surface looked like glass. And the color of the water was a milky blue. So different from the Atlantic. Dolphins and flying fish followed the ship and occasionally a huge sea turtle was seen just floating on the surface, basking in the sun.

Archer wrote a little every day to Amy, telling her what he was seeing, each officer and crew member. How calm the Pacific Ocean was and about the flying fish he was seeing.

Before they reached Pearl Harbor, Petty Officer Sawyer was well-trained with communications and the new radar improvements. Archer also helped to instruct the weapons officer, Lt. Fred Hardy, about the new sea to shore missiles and then he and Hardy took stock on the increased number of torpedoes and depth changes, and the new anti-aircraft batteries. Lt. Hardy made the statement one day, "We're loaded for bear."

The Bear's length had been lengthened allowing increased fuel capacity, armaments and crews if the captain needed more.

"Lieutenant Goff."

"Yes, Sir."

"You have the bridge; I'm going below to the engine room."

"Yes, Sir."

Captain Hobbs had been watching Archer very closely since leaving BIW in Maine. He was satisfied that he was right in promoting him to Lt. Commander. He was all over the ship familiarizing himself with everything. And he approved of the decisions he was making about the officers and crews. And more importantly, they all liked and respected Lieutenant Commander Ambrose.

Ian was in the port stern tube tightening the seal packing. "Hello, Commander, what brings you to the belly of the ship?"

"I just wanted to see the new improvements. Seal leaking?"

"It's new packing and needs to be tightened. Do you remember how much water is supposed to leak through for lubrication?"

"More than a gallon a minute and you have problems."

"Both tubes were leaking five gallons a minute."

"It's good that you caught them in time. If you're done, will you show me the improvements?"

"The four boilers are producing more volume of steam than the old Cutlidge. They are not bigger, only better displacement of the superheater tubes and each boiler now has three burners. We're producing steam at 1000 psi and 1000°F and much faster than the older boilers, so the steam turbines had to be bigger which increased the rpms, increasing our speed. There are more force draft air fans blowing cooler outside air below here, so the engine room stays cooler. The steam driven electrical generators are bigger, producing higher voltage and current. And on the Cutlidge we had two salt water evaporators. Here there are four. We now produce nearly 20,000 gallons of potable water each day and we do not have to carry so much extra in the hold. This is quite a ship, Commander."

Before leaving the engine room, Ian said, "Commander, I'm happy to be sailing with you again."

"Thanks, Ian. You sound more excited now about being an engineer than you did aboard the Cutlidge."

"Yes, Sir, I am."

****

Eight days after Panama, they tied up at Pearl Harbor. "Commander, I have to see Admiral Hunt at the base; you have the ship. Fuel, provisions, mail, and I do believe we'll be loading some of these sea to shore missiles. I don't know yet if there will be any shore leave. We might have to deploy soon."

"Yes, Captain."

"Hello, Captain Hobbs. Come in. Coffee?"

"Yes, thank you."

"How do you like the Gearing Class Destroyer?"

"She's quite a ship, Admiral."

"The Bear, the story behind the name of your ship, Captain, was in every newspaper in the country. I hope the ship will live up to the name.

"You made quite a daring move, Captain, first with giving a midshipman internist the authority of commander and then promoting him from lieutenant to lieutenant commander. How did your officers accept this?"

"I talked with my officers before I promoted Mr. Ambrose

254

and they all thought it was appropriate. Admiral, Lt. Commander Ambrose is an exceptional officer. He is more capable than many officers with twenty years at sea. It won't be long and he'll have his own ship, Sir."

"There is trouble rising in Korea, Captain. We have information that Kim Il-Sung, the leader in Northern Korea, with the aid of Communist China and supplied by Russia has intentions of invading South Korea and taking control of the entire Korean Peninsula. South Korea is asking for our support. Your job, Captain, is to obtain as much information as you can and a weekly helicopter will land on the Bear and take possession of the recordings and transport them to our base at Yokosuka. You are mainly to patrol north to Vladivostok. Vladivostok is Russia's main submarine base on this side of the world. Stay fifty miles offshore, and south as far as Chongjin.

"After three weeks of patrol you are to return to Yokosuka and another destroyer will be out for three weeks, while you and your crew get some well-deserved rest and liberty.

"It is imperative that you leave here as soon as you can, Captain."

"Yes, Admiral."

****

While the Bear was steaming across the Pacific towards Korea, President Scott MacGregor, a bristle-back Scotsman from Halifax, Nova Scotia, called for a special meeting with Admiral Daniels, Minister of Defense, General Rejean Martin of the Air Force, ambassadors from England, France and Australia and Vice President Stevens.

All four countries had been busy gathering information about Kim Il-Sung declaring to invade South Korea and bring all of Korea under his rule. The Chinese had agreed to support him with troops and Russia with weapons.

When the new nation of North America had gotten involved early at the onset of Europe's last war, that decision had brought a quick end to the war. And now this group of politicians were determined to stop this war before it could get started.

"We cannot do anything until the north makes it clear they are going to move on South Korea. But in the meantime we can have our preparations all set in place to stop Kim Il-Sung and his communist supporters."

Australia could send one carrier group consisting of one aircraft carrier, one battleship and three destroyers. France could send the same. England agreed to send two carrier groups with equal support for each group. North America was sending three carrier groups with equal support plus the entire Pacific submarine fleet.

Kim Il-Sung wanted to make his move immediately but China had asked him to wait until June of the following year so China would have time to assemble enough troops and supplies.

"The information we have collected indicated that North Korea will strike South Korea in June of 1950. Before he makes that move I want our fleets in position at Incheon, Nampo, Wonsan and Chongjin.

"I believe Stalin is behind this and he is only using the North Koreans and China as his pawns; that could very well be a bloody war.

"Russia is on the edge of a useable nuclear bomb. This would be a good time for Stalin to try it out. General Martin, at the same time I want a hundred B-29's loaded and ready for takeoff at our Japanese base and as a backup, if needed, and as many more as you can find places to store them.

"I want to meet like this each week so we can keep current on new information as it comes in. I don't think this should be just a police action where nothing is ever settled. I want this stopped before it even has a chance to get started."

****

On the morning of December 5th, Amy said goodbye to Rascal and Emma. "I hate so much to leave you, but I miss

Archer that much. Mom and Dad, no matter where we are I will never forget you. You mean so much to us both." Emma and Amy couldn't hold it any longer. They both were crying and Rascal had tears running down his cheeks.

Rebecca had said she would meet Amy at the Lac St. Jean terminal and from there board another train and direct route to the Naval Airbase near Sault Ste. Marie. From there they boarded a transport jet to San Francisco and then to Hawaii.

Rebecca was like an older sister to Amy. She helped her find housing close to hers and to get it furnished. Then the two explored Pearl Harbor.

At Christmas, Rebecca and Amy spent the day with other Navy wives whose husbands were also at sea. The Bear crew spent Christmas in Yokosuka. Archer did get to telephone Amy and his folks. He could tell them where he was but not what he was doing.

After the New Year, Amy suggested to Rebecca that since their husbands were not able to come back to Pearl Harbor for an undeterminable period, she said, "Why don't we go to Yokosuka for as long as they are working in that area?"

Rebecca was able to make arrangements for housing in Yokosuka before they left Pearl Harbor. Two days after arriving, the Bear just ended its three weeks of patrol and tied up at the docks. Rebecca and Amy were there to meet the ship. Captain Hobbs was excited to see his wife, as was Archer.

After five days ashore, the Bear set sail again for another three weeks.

"Commander, when you can, come to my office."

"Yes, Sir."

"Help yourself to coffee. It seems Kim Il-Sung is wanting to invade South Korea now and he has moved two divisions just across the border from South Korea. The only thing keeping him from moving on Incheon, Seoul and Chuncheon, is China. There is information coming down through the command that President MacGregor is planning something big and we are part of it. England, France and Australia are beginning to move career groups this way. And did you see all of the submarines in the harbor at Yokosuka? That tells me something big is coming."

Three weeks later when they returned back to Yokosuka the airport was almost completely taken over by parked B-29s. There were also two other airfields in Japan that were supporting a number of B-29s, and the Air Force had new jet bombers. The B-47 and the XB-51, both were long range bombers.

On April 15th in the weekly meeting, President MacGregor said, "Gentlemen, everything is in place and on May 1st I will have a message sent directly to Kim Il-Sung in North Korea and the same message sent to South Korea's President Syngman Rhee, requesting that they both meet with me on board a carrier, which will not be identified until they are on route in a North American helicopter to meet with me on May 5th, that if either of them refuse to meet with me to discuss finding means to prevent the two Koreas from going to war with each other and pulling in other countries to support them, there will be serious consequences.

"On May 1st all carrier groups will move into position as well as the Pacific submarine fleet.

"Russia doesn't want another war any more than does China."

"What about land troops, Mr. President?"

"Not unless for some reason we are drawn into the middle of this. I'm hoping with our air and sea superiority, land troops will not be necessary."

****

The Bear was patrolling fifty miles from Vladivostok and in international waters. "Captain Hobbs, Sir, there is an approaching vessel off our port beam."

"Has the radar officer been able to identify it?"

"Yes, Sir, a Russian gunboat."

"When it gets within a mile, if it hasn't broke off, put a

shot across its bow."

"Yes, Sir."

Archer radioed Master of Arms Lt. Hardy and told him what the captain had said. A few minutes later the lieutenant radioed the bridge and said, "Sir, the gunboat is now approaching one mile."

"You have your orders, Lieutenant Hardy."

Thirty seconds later a shot from the forward five inch cannon fired and the shot went perfectly in front of the gunboat and across their bow. The gunboat immediately veered sharply to port and left the area.

Archer radioed back to the lieutenant and said, "Good shooting, Lieutenant; they have turned back."

Within an hour a report of this was handed to President MacGregor. "Very well done. Send that message to Admiral Hunt in Hawaii and have it relayed to Captain Hobbs on the Bear."

"Yes, Mr. President."

This incident also rippled all the way to Moscow, Beijing and to Kim Il-Sung. Both Russia and China were having second thoughts about a confrontation with North America or its Navy. They had proven the new nation to be so strong and they were now backing up what they said. Both China and Russia were both aware by now that several carrier groups were proceeding towards the Korean Peninsula and that hundreds of B-29 bombers were massing in Japan. China was in no condition to fight a war against this new nation and although this infuriated Russia and Stalin. Both countries were telling Kim Il-Sung to pull his troops back from the southern peninsula.

But Kim Il-Sung was disillusioned and refused to back down.

On May 1st the message was sent to Kim Il-Sung and Syngman Rhee that a helicopter would arrive on May 5, 1950, at 0900 hours to transport them to one of the aircraft carriers.

The carrier groups were now all in position as were the

Pacific Fleet submarines. The Bear was positioned just outside territorial waters off Vladivostok along with the Missouri battleship, two other destroyers and two submarines. It was a waiting game now.

Amy and Rebecca didn't know any more than what was being released to the public. They both were worried. "At least we know they are still okay, Amy. I know it's difficult not to worry."

Rascal and Emma first heard the news on the radio and then the next morning when the newspaper was dropped off, the front page was all about the Bear firing on a Russian gunboat to turn it around.

****

After President MacGregor's ultimatum on May 1st, the movement towards the 38th parallel from both sides had stopped. Things were even quiet along China's border as well. It would have been obvious to both sides now of the mass of aircraft carrier groups as well as support ships.

On the morning of May 5th, two helicopters left the Coral Sea carrier and headed to pick up Kim Il-Sung and Syngman Rhee. The two men and one interpreter each were picked up and now the helicopters headed to the aircraft carrier Vancouver, which was close by.

The men were escorted inside to the conference room and the hatch was closed and locked behind them. President MacGregor and his interpreter were waiting.

There was a wall map of the peninsula and the location of the carrier groups. "Thank you for coming. This isn't going to be a social gathering with niceties. I'll get right to the point. Notice this charter. These are the locations of our carrier groups and task force. There are two hundred B-29s and long range jet bomber aircraft in Japan and twice as many at nearby airstrips that I'll call into action if the need arises. We have stopped all cargo leaving the port of Vladivostok.

"If any aircraft tries to leave your airspace, it will be shot down. No vessels will be allowed to leave any port from the entire peninsula. Not even fishing boats.

Kim Il-Sung interrupted President MacGregor and started to say, "Mr. President, if I may say—"

"No, you may not say. You are not here to say anything or argue. You are here to listen," President MacGregor said.

"You aren't living in the middle ages any longer where sons kill fathers or grandfathers or brother kills brother, so you can reign emperor. Your tyrannical form of governing your people has to stop now. There is no place for tyranny in the modern world. Where the citizens have to exist in squalid huts and newborn babies starve to death.

"China and Russia both are just using you for a bloody end so they can come in and pick up the pieces and then there'll be no more Korea. Russia has agreed to furnish you with arms, Kim Il-Sung, because he doesn't want this bloody war on his people.

"This aggression from either side, as I just said, stops today. You two need to sit down and talk with each other without outside influence or lobbyists within your own ranks. Just you two. Each of you have to give and take. I'm sure each of you have some good ideas. Compromise and come up with something that'll work for the Korean people.

"This task force is not going away until you two have come up with agreements that both sides can live with and prosper. Until you do, we stay. The first shot fired for any reason, if it is your side, Kim Il-Sung, we will come after you and level your existence. And the same goes for you, Syngman Rhee, any shot for any reason.

"You two men are not going to disrupt the world with your bickering. Do I make myself clear?"

Reluctantly they both agreed.

"Until you two work this out just between the two of you, nothing leaves the peninsula and nothing comes in. We'll be making routine flyovers and we have very advanced radar systems.

"Mind what I said. The helicopters will now return you. Remember not one shot," President MacGregor said. They could tell from the expression on his face that he had meant every word he said.

****

Two days later word was received through the chain of command that the two Korean leaders had taken President MacGregor seriously and both sides had disbanded all troop movements and aggression and were talking, just the two men, to come to some agreeable terms.

The French and English carrier groups left the area and Australia agreed to stay on for another week.

By the end of the summer in 1950, equitable terms had been found and the two leaders signed a peaceful document ending all aggression from both sides. The rest of the carrier groups left the peninsula and Archer went on a thirty day leave back to Whiskey Jack.

****

President MacGregor was being hailed a hero worldwide for stopping a war which would have cost hundreds of thousands of lives. China even agreed to help once the peace documents had been signed.

When Archer returned to duty back onboard the Bear, he was promoted to full commander. Another unique move by Captain Hobbs. But he had his reasons.

Chapter 17

Three years later Amy had their first child, a girl they named Anita. Captain Hobbs stopped in to talk with Admiral Hunt in Pearl Harbor

"What can I do for you, Captain?"

"The Bear is scheduled to leave port tomorrow morning. When I return I'd like to promote Commander Ambrose to captain."

"He hasn't had enough time at sea, Captain."

"How much time is required, Sir, when someone is as good as he is? I have never seen a more capable Naval officer. Why waste good— Sir, because of some stupid rule. To deny him now, Sir, would be a tragic waste."

"So you want two captains aboard the Bear?"

"No, Sir. At the end of this deployment I plan on submitting my retirement papers. And there is not another officer in the entire Navy that would be more capable of taking the Bear, Sir."

"I have always respected your decisions, Captain, and I agree you don't waste good— At the end of your deployment you bring Commander Ambrose in to see me and we'll make it happen."

"Thank you, Sir."

****

By now both Presidents Cutlidge and Kingsley had passed away and it was a sad time for most everyone in the new nation. Parliament had declared November 14th as the new

263

Founding Father's Day. They were being called the fathers of the new nation.

Pearl and Myrissa both passed away shortly afterwards.

When the Bear returned to Pearl Harbor, Admiral William Hunt was waiting on the pier. "Commander," Captain Hobbs said.

"Yes, Captain."

"Admiral Hunt is on the pier, I'm going down. Make sure the engine room can be left alone and the Admiral wants everyone to assemble on the pier. Come as they are."

"Lieutenant McFarland, can the engine room be left alone?"

"Yes, Sir. The boilers are still fired. It'll take a while to cool."

"Okay, everyone is to assemble on the pier. Admiral Hunt is there with Captain Hobbs."

"Yes, Sir, we'll be right up."

Archer announced on the intercom that everyone was to assemble on the pier, "Now."

Captain Hobbs was standing with Admiral Hunt and everyone else was now standing at attention. "At ease, men. First I want to commend the entire crew for your unrelenting service aboard the Bear since it was commissioned. Your sit-reps are the highest of any crew deployed on board. Congratulations, men.

"Now, Captain Hobbs has something he wants to tell you."

"I want to thank each and every one of you for your excellence. This was my last deployment. I am signing my retirement papers today. It's time I spend more time with my family.

"But before I leave I want to promote Commander Ambrose to Captain."

Admiral Hunt asked, "Is there anyone who objects to this promotion?"

At the same time and unrehearsed they all said, "No!"

"Is that the answer you wanted, Admiral?"

"It is."

"Commander Ambrose, you will come forward."

Archer saluted and said, "Thank you, Admiral, and Captain Hobbs." And then he turned around to face the crew and he said, "And thank you."

Back onboard the Bear, "You hadn't mentioned anything about retiring, Captain."

"No, I wanted to keep it a surprise."

As Captain Hobbs packed his gear, Archer was busy securing the ship. Captain Hobbs waited for Archer to return to the bridge before leaving the ship for the last time.

"It won't be the same, Captain, without you."

"You'll be okay, Archer. Hell, most of the time I have let you captain the Bear. You are the best officer I have ever sailed with. You have a gift of command, Archer.

"If you ever begin to question yourself, Archer, just remember where you came from. You are one of two people who have ever played with a 600-pound, wild bear. The namesake of this destroyer. Your ship now, Mr. Ambrose."

"What are you going to do now, Captain?"

"Well first, Rebecca and I will move back home and then maybe we'll go fishing at Whiskey Jack."

"Captain, it has been a pleasure serving under you." Archer then saluted the outgoing captain.

Hobbs picked up his gear and said, "Your ship now, Captain Ambrose. You know that sounds good. Captain Ambrose."

After the ship was finally secured, Archer checked from stem to stern and in the engine room. When he was satisfied he went home and told Amy about his promotion.

The next morning after breakfast he telephoned home and told his Mom and Dad.

"Rascal, can you believe that Archer is only twenty-five and already a captain?" Emma said.

****

There was no question in Archer's mind who he wanted for his executive officer. He promoted Lt. Larry Goff to Lt. Commander and he promoted a petty officer to lieutenant as communication's officer.

That winter, while Archer was home, Amy gave birth to a boy that they named Archer Rascal Ambrose.

A year later, Amy said, "Archer, I want to take the kids and move back with Mom and Dad at Whiskey Jack. I want them to grow up there, not on a Navy base."

Archer didn't object.

Also that year the chief engineer, Lt. Sid Billings, retired and Archer promoted Ian to lieutenant commander.

Archer wanted to transfer back on the east coast where it would be easier to get home occasionally, but he was told that the Bear and crew had such a strong reputation they were going to stay in the Pacific.

****

After another five years the Bear was scheduled for some upgrading and new advanced electronics to be installed. This could have been done in California but Admiral Webster decided to let the crew of the Bear destroyer change their base of operations to the east coast and now she was tied up at BIW in Bath, Maine. The crew were all given a thirty day leave.

****

For the next five years the Bear was back on the European route listening for Russian communications. The smooth waters of the Pacific Ocean had spoiled him. He had forgotten just how rough the north Atlantic could get. So after five years, Archer knew it was time for him to go home to Whiskey Jack.

They were scheduled to dock at Norfolk, which would give him an opportunity to go to the Naval base.

While the Bear was secured, Admiral Worthley from the Naval base walked up the gangway. The officer on deck saluted and the Admiral asked, "Is the Captain on the bridge?"

"Yes, Sir, he is."

"Come in, Admiral, what can I do for you?"

"Any coffee?"

"Sure," and Archer poured two cups.

"How old are you, Captain?"

"Thirty-seven Sir."

"Most promotions to Admiral come after the captain's career is mostly over. You are up for promotion, Captain. Just think what it would mean to be promoted to Admiral for someone so young. Just think of the good you could do and the opportunities that would open for you.

"I would like you to have some carrier time. Maybe three years, then your promotion would be a shoe-in."

"That's a marvelous opportunity, Admiral, but I have to decline. In fact, I have decided to retire."

"Why? You are so young, Captain. You would have a good chance of eventually becoming the Rear Admiral."

"I just can't, Admiral. It's time I went home. My two kids are growing up knowing me only by name, my Mom and Dad are sixty-seven and still operating a fishing and hunting lodge. I want to help them.

"The Navy has been good for me, Admiral, and I have really enjoyed my duties, but now it's time to go home. I certainly do appreciate the offer and I hope I'm doing the right thing."

"Well, Captain Ambrose, you sure have served the Navy very well. It'll be a long time before another midshipman comes along and spends his entire career as commander and captain and especially so young.

"Good luck to you, Captain."

"Thank you, Admiral."

The Conclusion to the Whiskey Jack Series

Archer was still in his captain's uniform and he was able to catch a flight aboard a Navy cargo plane to Brunswick, Maine. A taxicab to the train station, then to Beech Tree in time for the afternoon northbound.

The S&A locomotive had been replaced recently by a new diesel engine, new passenger cars and a faster speed. Fred Darling was no longer working nor was Roscoe Whelling. There were new faces all around. Even the station master was new. So far this wasn't seeming very much like home.

He knew Jarvis and Rita had both passed away ten years ago at the age of 95. Earl Hitchcock had passed also and his brother Rudy was in a nursing home. The Hitchcock Lumber Company still maintained the same name but the company had been sold to family members.

He saw no familiar faces. Everything had changed in his absence and he was beginning to wonder if he had made the right choice in retiring.

But all of the doubts faded instantly when he saw his Mom and Dad, his wife Amy and their two children, Anita and Archer, waiting for him on the platform. Tears welled up in his eyes and his vision was blurry. There was no question now. Yeah, he knew he had made the right choice.

Both Emma and Rascal were now 67, but neither of them looked that old. Amy was 38, and she was even more beautiful now than when he had first seen her. Anita was the spitting image of her Mom and she was 13 and Archer Rascal was 11. He had missed out on a lot of their childhood but he would make up for it now.

He hugged them all and said, "I'm home for good. No more traveling on the seas for me. I have retired."

****

September was always a busy month, so Rascal and Emma stayed to work through the month. When the last guest was gone, Rascal said, "Let's sit down and have some coffee. Em and I have something we want to say to you."

In between sips of coffee, Rascal asked, "Do you two plan on staying here and making this your home?"

"Yes, we would like to."

"Good. We hoped you would. Your Mom and I have given this a lot of thought. In 1925 this building, hotel, was given to us by Rudy and Earl Hitchcock. We have had a good living here. We would like to give Whiskey Jack Lodge to you two. In the warmer months we want to live in our log cabin and spend the winters here."

Emma said, "The hunting season is booked full except for the traditional last week when we have always had our Thanksgiving. We'll keep the deposits and you keep the rest. There is a large supply of food, but you'll need more. Can you afford to purchase more supplies?"

Amy answered right off. "Yes, we can. And I think now is the time to use the gift that Anita had given me." She had not said anything about this to anyone. "In the letter she left for me she said I would know when the time was right to use it. I think she knew this day would come." She looked squarely at Archer and continued, "When Anita passed away she left me a letter and her savings which at the time was $2300.00. I have had it in a savings account all this time and now it totals $5,111.94. I want to use it to get us started here, Archer."

"During the spring, summer and fall you won't have to worry about paying us," Rascal said.

After breakfast the next morning, Archer said, "Now I want to see Cubbie."

"He's friendly with the whole family, but we don't let the two grandchildren play with him."

They all went for a walk up to Ledge Swamp, and like it was meant to be, Cubbie was there as if he was anticipating their coming. They all walked up close to Cubbie and Rascal said, "Cubbie, do you remember Archer. He is our son. Raise your arm, son."

Archer did and so did Cubbie. "Okay, now you can play with him." Archer took off running in circles at first and then up along the tracks and Cubbie grabbed his foot with his teeth and tripped him. When Archer fell, Cubbie let go and ran and Archer ran after him.

Yes, this was now feeling like the home he had left behind twenty years ago.

****

The next day was picture perfect. The air was cool, but not cold. No bugs, no humidity and only a gentle breeze. Rascal and Emma went over to open the log cabin and do some cleaning and air it out.

They had worked up some dust inside and Emma said, "Rascal, let's sit out on the porch and let this dust blow out. It's such a nice day." Emma poured two cups of coffee and they went out on the porch. At first they just sat in silence, sipping coffee. Then Rascal said, "We did pretty good, didn't we, sweetheart."

"We surely have. We have had a good life. At twenty-five, our son became the youngest Navy captain ever. He's only thirty-seven now and already retired," Emma said.

"I have often wondered why Rudy gave us the hotel in the beginning and before he left the company he deeded twenty acres surrounding the lodge to us," Rascal said.

"Maybe in part he wanted someone to look after the old mill and farm and thought by giving us the hotel we'd stay."

"Well, he was right there."

They could hear Archer, Rascal and Anita playing.

"It seems nice to sit up here and once again listen to children laughing and playing," Emma said.

"I know what you mean, Em. The sounds of children playing."

Rascal said, "We have had a good life, sweetheart, but we also have worked hard for it. But I think my happiest days were before we started the lodge when the mill and village were still here. We had a good living then also, between what you made accounting and me trapping and guiding."

"But we had nothing permanent then, except this log cabin. I miss the friends we had in the village too."

"It was fun. Then coffee and donuts every morning with Silvio, Jeters, Elmo and sometimes Jarvis. I had a lot of fun trying to get away with poaching without Jarvis finding out about it. I think I miss him more than anyone else."

"He did his job and he was a gentleman at the same time," Emma said.

"I never fully understood him or his prowess in the woods, even when he came up against bigger and meaner men and more than one at a time, until Herschel became a game warden. And he's retired now. Are we that old, Em?"

"Do you feel it? I don't."

"You would have made a good warden and when Jarvis offered you the chance, I held my breath until you said no. Rita and I would talk often about Jarvis being away from home so much, and how she would worry about him. She never told Jarvis how she worried.

"I miss having other women here to talk with."

"I wonder whatever became of Jeters? He left Kidney Pond and the Hitchcock Company and we never heard from him again," Rascal said.

"Remember when Bear chased you and Elmo up the tracks? I could hear Elmo hollering long before you went through the village." They both laughed over that.

"I don't think I was ever so scared as I was that day. All

I could see in my mind was him mauling both of us."

"Why do you think Bear was like what he was?" Emma asked.

"Wanting to play when you're young and abandoned is one thing, but I'll never understand why he watched over us and protected us. There has never been a big cat track or wolf in this whole area since."

"Can you image how Hans Hessel must have felt being attacked at night when he couldn't see anything. I felt sorry for him. And I wonder whatever became of him?" Emma said.

"If I had not come up when I did, I think Bear would have done the same to him as he did to the wolf and the mountain lion."

"You know, Rascal, we only know of the wolf and mountain lion he killed to protect us. I wonder if there were any others?

"I don't know. I sure do miss him. Cubbie is fun, but he's not the same as Bear," Emma said.

"I haven't asked you for a long time about your leg and hip. How are they?"

"No change really. If I walk all day or work on firewood or something strenuous like that, it'll begin to hurt some. Then I stop."

"Do you still write to Belle?"

"I only hear from her maybe once a year. She's no longer working and she retired from the Army a few years ago.

"You know, Jarvis was thirty years older than me but he was my best friend. It's sad in a way, Em."

"What is?"

"Well, we have had such a good life here and all of our friends who helped to make life here and carve out of the wilderness a growing community, are all gone now. You and I, Em are the only old timers left."

"You keep talking like that, Rascal, you'll start me crying."

Rascal put his arm around her and kissed her and they stayed like that for quite a while in silence.

"When the village was here, Rascal, and I was working in the office for Rudy, I never dreamed our life would be what it was. I mean, we called the most memorable presidents ever to serve, family, we were invited to a White House dinner and look what they did for our son, Archer.

"You know what I miss the most, Rascal?"

"What?"

"The get-togethers we used to have when the village was here. Everyone helping out and enjoying themselves. And the men sneaking off to drink whiskey and hard cider."

"Those were good times indeed."

"How far beyond the farm do the tracks run now?"

"Five miles right now. But I've heard in a few years they'll swing south more and connect onto the Kidney Pond line."

"Have you met the new supervisor?"

"I think I heard that Paulette's husband Henri has the job. But we haven't heard from her for a long time."

"Armand surely made Hitchcock a good man."

"He was a good man."

"Look at the changes we've seen with the lumbering industry, Em. The two man cross-cut saw and axe, to motorized chainsaws now. Work horses to crawlers and rubber tired skidders, and motorized equipment to load the railcars. I just hope we never see roads in here."

"What was your most memorable moment, Rascal?"

He answered so quick it surprised her. "Oh that's easy, that special Christmas gift you gave me. What was it—forty two years ago? You had never made love like that before or since. Close though." They had a good laugh over that.

"And what is yours, sweetheart?"

She had to think hard before answering. "There's two that stand out. One, being when Bear chased you and Elmo through the village and hearing Elmo scream and hollering long after you were out of sight. But now I think that would have to take second place. I think the most memorable event was that Christmas gift I gave you. For some reason that night I was free of all my guilt and inhibitions and I was relaxed and having a little fun."

"It sure was fun, wasn't it?" Rascal said.

"I thought so. Maybe we could do it again."

"The will and desire is certainly there, but I'm lacking the where-with-all."

Emma broke out into an uproarious laughter and said, "Well, I'll give you a little wine and feed you raw deer meat."

"How much money do we have in the bank, Em?"

"Somewhere over $110,000.00. What are you thinking?"

"Oh, I don't know. Would you like to go on a vacation next summer?"

"Where to?"

"How about a south sea island?"

"That would be fun. Maybe Archer will know of a place we'd like."

"You know we'll have to do some shopping to stock up on food here until cold weather."

"We can do that. We have all the time in the world now."

They talked and reminisced all afternoon. Sometimes they felt like crying and they laughed a lot. But there were three subjects they stayed away from. The loss of their first two children, Beckie and Jasper. When Emma turned him, Silvio, Jeters and Jeff into the sheriff for making brandy, and the time Emma shot the doe deer in summer that was eating her lettuce.

The closest they came was when Emma said, "We never did get around to making the wine."

"Maybe in the spring when we have more time."

"You know, Rascal, I'm looking forward to living back in the log cabin again."

"We don't have any electricity or oil-fired heat and our

water is gravity fed."

"Well, we both agree we miss the times when the village was here."

Rascal stood up and took Emma's hand in his and she stood up. "Can you dance without any music?"

"I can manage that."

They danced as if a six piece band was playing the most beautiful music there was. "I love you, Em, and we have had a good life and I wouldn't change anything."

The End

About the Author

Mr. Probert retired from the Maine Warden Service in 1997 and began to write historical novels about the history in the areas where he patrolled as a game warden, with his own experiences as a game warden as those of the wardens in his books.

When you work at something that you enjoy, then it never becomes just a job. For Probert, it was more fun than playing baseball. But that doesn't mean that everything was easy because it certainly was not—like having to summons a friend to court or having to pull a friend's daughter's lifeless body into a boat.

Mr. Probert now has twenty-five books in print and the *Whiskey Jack* series is his favorite series, but *Ekani's Journey* is the single favorite.